THE FIFTH ESSENCE

by Rob MacGregor

He was getting deeper and deeper into something that he didn't understand, and didn't like. Isabel acted as if they were invincible, that they would never be caught. She'd told him that clandestine operations existed outside of conventional laws, and he was privileged to have an inside look, even if he would never be able to talk about anything that he saw. He could understand why. If people knew that part of their government operated like the mafia, they would be enraged.

After Simms was taken to the room, Isabel told the guards to remove the tape from her. Then she turned to Erickson. "Wait for me by the elevator."

When Isabel joined him a couple of minutes later, they stepped into the freight elevator and descended to the first floor. "What's going to happen to her?" he asked.

"Relax, Nigel. You don't have to get involved in any more unsavory activities."

He didn't like her answer or her patronizing tone. "But she'll go to the police after this is over. They both will."

" By then it won't matter. We'll be long gone. You and Wendy will get your full bonuses and you'll be reassigned. So don't worry."

He lifted the gate as the elevator stopped. "Well, I am worried. Vance recognized me from my windsurfing career, and he probably told Pierce about it. Now Pierce knows I work with you."

She paused outside the elevator. "I'm sorry to hear that, Nigel. Very sorry." She headed down the hallway toward the door, and Erickson hurried after her. "Now we'll have to take care of Pierce to save your ass."

If the wrong person uses the right means, the right means work the wrong way.

An Ancient Chinese Proverb

PROLOGUE
September 18, 1992

Death caught homicide detective Frank Davis on his day off, on his favorite reef, twenty-six feet below the surface.

The water was a glassy reflection of the lapis sky and the sun was nearly overhead as Davis steered his dive boat through Government Cut, south of Miami Beach. The air was warm and humid, just the way he liked it. Even though big men were supposed to do poorly in the heat, Davis thrived in it. He'd rather be out here diving any day than sitting in a cabin in the mountains of North Carolina, which was what most of his buddies on the force dreamed of doing when the temperatures hit the nineties.

He stretched his long legs out in front of him and gazed toward the horizon. Behind him, the Miami skyline receded as surely as his worries. Once he sank beneath the surface and descended to the coral reef, the remainder of his cares would vanish entirely. For a couple of hours, the real world of corpses and crime scenes, paperwork and department politics just dropped away. Even the circuit court judge who kept pestering him about his missing brother—as if that were Davis' only case—no longer existed.

Soon all of it would be replaced by the silent, silky world of electric-blue angel fish, grinning parrot fish, and choreographed schools of striped grunts. Great colonies of staghorn coral, sea fans, elkhorn, star coral and mounds of brain coral defined the landscape; a place where predators and prey played games of hide and seek.

For Davis, even the watchful sharks, slippery eels and

toothy barracudas were a relative relief from the pressures of his other world.

His destination was a small but pristine reef about a mile and a half southwest of the Key Biscayne lighthouse. Davis called it Secret Reef, because it wasn't marked on the charts and wasn't particularly easy to find. He'd accidentally discovered it about three years ago and it had become his favorite diving site ever since, especially when he dived alone. He never failed to surface with a catch of snapper or grouper, mahi-mahi or mackerel, and usually a lobster or two in season.

He looked over his gear as he passed Virginia Key and moved away from the eastern shore of Key Biscayne. His tank was set up in the harness, with the buoyancy compensator, octopus regulator and gauges attached. His booties and gloves, flippers and weight belt, mask and snorkel, were all laid out to one side of the tank, while his net, tickler stick, loop and spear gun were on the other.

Everything neat and orderly and ready to go. That was what he liked about diving alone. With several companions along, the boat was crowded with gear and it took forever to get started. There was always someone who couldn't find a flipper or who would put the regulator on backward or who would have trouble getting the pressure in the middle ear equalized once below the surface.

Davis' ears adjusted quickly; he could dive down forty or fifty feet without the slightest hesitation. In spite of his bulk, he could also control his breathing and easily last an hour and a quarter on a full tank. Other men his size, or divers with less experience, tended to suck air like a hungry infant with a full bottle. All too often they were ready to surface when Davis still had another half an hour of air remaining.

The water ahead suddenly shifted from blue to green, indicating the approach of the reef. The high whine of the engine deepened to a low roar and then to a quiet rumble as Davis eased up on the throttle.

He glanced back at the lighthouse on Key Biscayne and at the far point of land to the northwest, and knew that his position was correct. Right on target.

In the distance, a white Cigarette boat dashed over the waves, heading toward him.

Keep going. Nothing here for you.

When he reached the far side of the reef, he backed off a few yards, then carefully lowered the anchor. Too many clowns never paid attention to where they dropped their anchors, and destroyed coral in the process. The damage to South Florida reefs over the past couple of decades reminded him of the turmoil ashore, and he tried his best not to contribute to the deterioration.

The anchor touched bottom in a few seconds. It was a relatively shallow reef and he liked it that way. Diving without a partner always meant certain risks, and sticking to shallow waters kept them to a minimum.

He cut the engine and quickly donned his gear, deciding to dispense with the spear gun today. He had his mind set on lobster, and one bug in particular. He had dived here a few days ago, and spotted one that weighed at least four pounds before it slithered away. He knew the reef well enough that he was sure he could locate its hole again. It was just a matter of finding the big boy at home. If he was there, he wouldn't get away. *Not this time.*

Davis opened the valve on his tank and checked his gauge. Thirty-one hundred pounds of air, and he had another tank ready if he wanted to make a second dive. He reached below his gut to check his weight belt, then tested his regulator; the air was flowing nicely. Finally, he inflated his buoyancy compensator, and was about to step over the side when he heard the Cigarette boat again. He turned and saw it bearing down on him. The boat slowed a couple of hundred feet away, then edged forward.

Cocky bastard.

The man behind the wheel wore dark glasses and was young, early twenties. Two others, a man and a woman, were preparing to dive. Their tanks were already on their backs.

Why did they have to pick his spot?

He had one quick solution to dealing with a sudden crowd.

He stuck the mouthpiece of his regulator between his teeth and flopped over backwards into the warm Atlantic. With any luck, he wouldn't even see the others.

Davis deflated in b.c. and quickly dropped to the bottom. A storm yesterday afternoon had churned the silt, so the visibility was barely thirty feet. But that didn't matter much when hunting lobsters. As long as he could see ten feet in front of him, he had all the view necessary to poke around in the nooks and crannies where the lobsters hid.

He'd only been down a couple of minutes when he spotted a pair of antennas protruding from a hollow. They were waving in the current as if to signal him.

He approached the lobster head on, and thrust his hand into the hole. Sometimes he was lucky and made a catch on the first try; but not today. The instant his hand touched one of the antennas, the lobster darted back amid a cloud of silt. It definitely wasn't the big one he wanted. In fact, it might even be too small to keep.

He moved his loop into position and gently pushed his tickler stick deep into the hole. After a moment, the lobster skidded toward the mouth of the hollow and Davis snapped the loop shut over its carapace. He quickly grabbed it with his left hand. *Gotcha!* A lot of divers relied on their nets to catch lobsters, but he found the loop more efficient. He guessed the bug was within the legal size, but still decided to measure it. He was about to reach for his gauge when he turned the lobster over and saw her eggs. *Oh, shit. Good-bye.* He released the female, and watched her swim away to another hole. He was after the big bug, anyhow.

As he glided ahead, hovering over massive coral heads, he sensed motion above him and looked up. *Shark,* he thought. Then he realized it was one of the divers from the other boat. He turned away, then saw the second diver on the bottom a few feet away. The woman. Her blond hair floated out from the back of her head, rippling like seaweed in the current. She wore a pink wetsuit and a matching face mask.

What the hell? She was running her finger across her throat, signaling that she was out of air. But she was making no attempt to surface; instead she was moving toward him. He saw the bubbles rising from her regulator, indicating that she was breathing fine. *What was it, a joke?* The bottom of the ocean was no place for pranks, and he didn't appreciate them. Especially not on his reef.

He started to swim away, but the woman darted toward him, struck him on the face and pulled his mask off. He spun around, grabbed for her, but she backed away, then dropped his mask.

He saw it settling to the bottom, a blurred shape now, barely distinguishable from the coral, and started to swim down for it. But the other diver grabbed his ankle and snatched Davis's knife from its rubber casing on his leg.

These fucks were asking for it. Nothing like this had ever happened to him while diving.

His street instincts kicked in. He rolled over, shot free, and struck the man in the face with his fin. The woman loomed in front of him, and Davis angrily swung a fist at her mask. But he misjudged the distance, and his swing fell short. The woman instantly reacted by jerking the regulator out of his mouth.

The bitch knew exactly what she was doing, and suddenly he sensed the true seriousness of the situation.

Enough of this crap. He kicked hard for the surface, but the woman held fast to his regulator. *Okay, he'd pull her up with him.*

But then the man pounced on top of his tank, weighing him down. Davis struggled, sucked a mouthful of water.

Don't breathe ... don't breathe. He was on the verge of panic.

The b.c., where was the valve?

His finger fumbled over the vest, found the button that would fill his vest with air. If he twisted and kicked out of their grasp, he'd shoot to the surface ... But nothing happened.

The bastard on his back had turned off his air.

Davis struggled wildly, clawed, and gulped for air. Water rushed into his lungs, and still they held him.

As he lost consciousness, his last thought was that he wasn't going to get the big bug. Not today.

Not ever.

Chapter 1

Three weeks later

"Another fine day at the beach, Swedie," Nicholas Pierce muttered to his fifteen-year-old Saab as he opened his door and a wave of humid air washed over him. Nine a.m. in late September and the temperature was already soaring into the mid-eighties.

But he'd spent more than twenty years in South Florida, and was as acclimated as he would ever get to the sub-tropical summers.

Ahead of him, he glimpsed a wide horizon of sand and sky. He couldn't see the ocean from here, but he was confident the Atlantic was still there. He didn't take much else for granted in his life, and this morning, that was probably a good thing.

He turned into the lobby of the Edison Hotel, climbed the steps to the mezzanine and entered the Gibson Travel Agency, passing quickly through the reception area and down the corridor to his office.

As he reached for the door knob, his hand stopped inches short of it. A windsurfing board was propped up against the wall like a fishing trophy, and next to it was an assortment of other gear: a boom, a mast, a sail, some other pieces.

Maybe Walter Gibson, the owner of the travel agency, was planning some sort of exhibit? But there certainly wasn't any room for it up here, and he didn't appreciate the way it was all piled by his door.

He and Gibby had started out as partners in the travel agency, and when Pierce had become a full-time private investigator, he'd kept his office inside the agency. It wasn't the easiest place for clients to find, but the office was close to home and he liked the Ocean Drive address.

Besides, he'd never come up with a better deal. When he sold his share of the travel agency, he'd gotten a rent-free agreement for five years. A couple of years still remained.

He opened the door. The lights were off and the office was empty.

Real nice. Anyone could walk in and make themselves at home.

Then he noticed the key on his secretary's desk and the note under it. He picked it up and pulled a pair of black wire-framed glasses from his pocket.

His temples throbbed and he gritted his teeth. He already knew what was coming.

Trying to make out the scrawled note reminded him of the handwriting on a doctor's prescription.

Too boring here. I got a real job as a server. Be up later for my last check. See ya.—Trudy

He looked up as he heard the door squeak open and saw Gibby manipulate his wheelchair through the doorway.

"Morning, Nick."

"Hi, Gibby," he responded unenthusiastically.

"I know. Trudy quit."

"What did she do, give you a copy of her resignation letter?"

"No, she just served me breakfast."

"Where's she working?"

"Downstairs."

"Here, at the hotel?"

Gibby nodded. "I felt like stiffing her on the tip, but then I figured she'd pay me back with slow service."

Pierce laughed. "Don't worry about it, Gibby. I'm better off without her. You know anyone who needs a job?"

"Not at the moment. But take my advice, Nick. Don't hire another one of these kids right out of high school. They've got no discipline. I mean, a one-secretary office is not a place for a nineteen-year-old, especially since you're out of the office so much and South Beach is right across the street. Yesterday she took a two-hour lunch break … on the beach."

"Wonderful."

"A little bird told me she was topless, too. Not that I care."
He shrugged. "The restaurant will keep her busy and she'll have
more people around. You need a more mature assistant."

As usual, Gibby was ready with gossip and advice—one of
his less appealing attributes.

They were so different from each other that Pierce never
ceased to be amazed that they'd once been business partners.
They'd often been described as the sleepy-looking one and the
wide-awake one. Pierce's hooded eyes gave him a drowsy look,
while his reticence made him seem distant and self-involved. In
contrast, Gibby's bulging eyes and curly hair made him look as if
he'd just stuck his finger in an electrical socket.

"Are you planning on coming to the cocktail party this
evening?"

"I didn't know you had one planned." Gibby's cocktail parties
were travel industry affairs, boasting a mix of travel agents, tour
operators, airline publicity people and hotel reps; all trading tips
and gossip.

"Good ole Trudy. I told her all about it. The Spanish director of
tourism is the guest of honor. That's Spanish as in Spain," Gibby
quickly added, in his typical rapid-fire delivery. "He's going to
talk about the Basque Provinces. I thought you'd like to hear what
he had to say. I know that's one of your favorite destinations."

Used to be, Pierce thought. In his old life. But as far Gibby was
concerned, that 'old life' had never really ended; it had just gone
on hold while he played detective.

"Try to stop by, and bring Elise. I haven't seen her for quite a
while. What's up with you two, anyhow?"

Pierce shrugged. "We've both been really busy. There hasn't
been a whole lot of time to see each other." There was considerably
more to it than that, but he wasn't about to involve Gibby in his
issues with Elise.

"Well, I hope you can both make it."

"Yeah, me too."

Gibby started to wheel toward the door, then spun around.

"Oh, would you mind getting your windsurfing stuff out of

the hallway some time today? I can barely get out my door."

"It's not mine. I thought it was yours."

"Mine?"

"Well, I mean for a display, or something?"

"Nope. It arrived for you about half an hour ago, right after I got in. Two young guys hauled it up. They said it was for you."

"I don't know a thing about it. But I'll find out."

Gibby started to wheel away, as Pierce absently pushed the message button on his answering machine. *A windsurfer,* he thought. *Who did he know who would give him a windsurfer?* On the tape, a man named Kurt Vance introduced himself and asked Pierce to call him. No further details. Pierce jotted down the number, and wondered who he was.

Gibby was suddenly in the doorway again.

"Was that Kurt Vance's voice I just heard?"

"Yeah. You know him?"

"He's the owner of a suntan lotion factory in Fort Lauderdale. He was one of my first clients when we opened the Broward office. I forgot to tell you that he might call."

"What's his problem?"

"I think he wants you to find a missing person, an employee of his. Somebody from Miami."

"Did he say how long he'd been missing?"

"Several months, I believe."

Wonderful. A cold trail.

"Those are tough cases, Gibby."

"At least talk to him, Nick. Will you do that for me?"

"Sure. But it might not be worth his money to hire me—or anyone, at this point."

"Oh, he's got a lot of money. That's no problem. I think he just wants to find out what happened; you know, out of curiosity."

There's probably a lot more involved, Pierce thought.

"I'll give him a ring."

He ripped the top sheet from the memo pad and headed into his office, which was separated from the reception area by a glass brick partition. On the wall behind his desk, the sun hovered above the sea and in the pink sand, squiggly letters read: ON VACATION.

One of his former secretaries, a part-time art student from California, had redecorated the office one week when he was away. She'd stripped the walls of his travel posters and photos—vestiges of his past—and had turned the wall into a tropical mural. When he'd returned, she explained that she'd updated his motif.

He told her that he thought he'd hired a secretary, not an interior designer, and that he didn't appreciate her work, especially since she hadn't consulted him.

Besides, he'd told her, the sun didn't set in the Atlantic.

She'd given him a hurt look, then in a defiant voice claimed that it was a sunrise. After a moment's thought, she'd added that there was nothing creative about her job and she was through.

That was almost four months ago, and the ON VACATION mural still greeted him whenever he stepped into his office.

Pierce sank into the chair behind his desk and sighed. It had taken two months to find Trudy—and now he had to start over. This time he wouldn't wait. He found the number for the Miami Herald classified department, and was about to call when he realized who might've sent him the windsurfer.

"Oh, shit."

He swung his chair around and pulled open a file drawer, then walked his fingers through it until he found the folder marked Larry Linder. At least Trudy hadn't lost the paperwork.

The case involved a series of thefts at Linder's furniture store. Pierce had placed an investigator on the job for a week, but by the fourth day everyone had realized he was a cop. It was a costly error. Finally, after another week, Pierce had located a fence who knew about furniture coming out the back door of the store. For three hundred dollars, he'd even described the thieves, two men who worked on the shipping dock.

The problem was that Linder didn't want to believe that the pair was guilty. They were college students working summer jobs, and both were his nephews.

Pierce had planned to set up a buy from the men, but Linder had told him to wait. The furniture store magnate was uneasy about entrapping his brother's offspring, and now Pierce wouldn't be a bit surprised if Linder had decided to forget the whole thing. He was probably trying to unload the windsurfer instead of paying the remainder of the bill.

Pierce picked up the phone and punched Linder's number. Linder was a bombastic, cigar-smoking chump who had played Pierce a video of his latest, loud-mouth TV commercial on the day they'd met. It was the sort of tasteless commercial that caused people to either laugh or cringe. But Linder seemed oblivious to his own crassness. Or possibly, he reveled in it.

He'd wanted to hire Pierce because he remembered seeing him on the TV news last year, and if someone was on television, Linder figured he must be good. That's exactly the way he'd said it.

Pierce told Linder's secretary who was calling and a moment later Linder's voice shouted in his ear.

"Pierce, I'm glad you called. Listen, I've been thinking about what you told me, and if those two are the ones, well, hell! Let the cards fall whatever way they wanna fall."

"You mean you want me to set up the buy now?"

"Well, the problem is, they may be suspicious of anyone approaching them after they got spooked by your man."

Pierce was still mystified by how the employees had made his plant so quickly.

"You didn't tell anyone you hired an investigator, did you?"

"Hell, no. But you know how word can get around. Anyhow, what I want you to do is give a lie detector test to everyone. Treat 'em all the same. Then whoever's it, you tell 'em they passed the test. Get it? Then you wiretap the fuckers. We nail 'em and wrap up the whole ball of wax. To hell with my brother. If it's his kids, they pay the price. So when can you start?"

"Larry, I can't do that."

"Can't do what?"

Pierce considered lie detectors a mechanical shortcut to real investigative work, and never used them. He told Linder as much. "Besides, a lot of time they're simply wrong."

"What, you living in the Stone Age, Pierce? Everybody uses them."

"Not me."

"Then I'll find someone who does. Got that? Now, you want this case or not?"

Pierce cleared his throat. "Not on those terms."

"Jesus H Christ, a prima donna. And there I just gave you a windsurfer. What gratitude. I'll take it back if you're not going to follow through."

"That's fine. Just send me a check for $750. That's what you owe me."

Linder was quiet for a moment. "Keep the windsurfer. That's your payment."

"I don't want it."

Linder acted as if he hadn't heard him. "My wife gave it to me a couple of years ago, but I got a bad back. You're right by the ocean, so I figured you could make better use of it."

"I don't want it, Larry."

"You got it unless you want to reconsider. Think about it. I gotta go."

Pierce heard the click and he dropped the phone into the cradle.

"What an asshole."

But he couldn't say he was disappointed that he was off the case. From the first day, he'd known that Linder was the type who would get flustered and fire an investigator if things weren't going his way. To protect himself, Pierce had required more than his usual advance, just in case. Linder had griped about it but paid up.

Pierce decided to bill Linder for the seven-fifty, and tell him to pick up his sailboard. But he'd wait for a couple of days until he was sure he was off the case. He wouldn't be a bit surprised if Linder called back and demanded, in his blustery voice, when Pierce could start the surveillance on his nephews, and what was taking so long. If he said he didn't know he was still on the case, Linder would say that their little misunderstanding shouldn't interfere with business. Something like that.

He picked up a pen and quickly jotted a help-wanted ad for the classifieds. Even if a secretary did nothing but act as a receptionist, it was still worth the expense. Answering machines didn't work when it came to first-time callers. No one wanted to tell their troubles to a machine.

After placing the ad, he spent a couple of hours on paperwork that Trudy had ignored. When he was almost caught up, he called downstairs and ordered a tuna salad sandwich, asking if someone would run it upstairs.

He didn't expect to see Trudy, but that's who arrived fifteen minutes later.

"Here's your lunch, Nick. Can I get my last check from you now?"

Her frizzy red hair was bunched on top of her head with strands trailing over her shoulders. Her skin was burnt vermilion. There was no hint of guilt, apprehension, or embarrassment in her expression about the way she'd quit. She simply stared imperviously, as if it were normal to shift abruptly from secretary to waitress and deliver lunch to your former boss on the same day.

"Trudy, are you suffering from a sun stroke?"

She laughed. "That's a joke, right? You did find my note, didn't you?"

"Yeah. What happened?"

"Well, I took a long lunch hour yesterday because nothing was happening here, and I got to thinking. You see, I'd rather be around people. When I came back, I asked Mr. Gibson what I should do and he said I should wait on tables if I wanted to be around people. I didn't really like that idea at first and asked him if he needed any secretaries. He told me he'd keep me in mind when something opened up. I hope he's good on his word, because I don't want to waitress for too long."

"You got to start somewhere," Pierce said as he wrote her check. "You know, Mr. Gibson is probably not going to be too excited about hiring you since you didn't give me any notice, and you didn't stick to your work here."

She shook her head and gave him a knowing smile as he handed her the check. "I waited on him this morning. He said I was at the top of his list. Gave me a nice tip, too."

Classic Gibby, Pierce thought. He doubted that Gibby would ever hire anyone so impetuous; but he wasn't going to endanger his breakfast, either.

"Let's see, now I need seven-eighty-two for the sandwich."

Pierce gave her a five and three ones and watched to see if she would make change for him. She looked at the money, then at him. "You're not going to stiff me on the tip because I quit, are you? I mean, I delivered your lunch right to your desk."

He handed her another dollar.

"Anytime you want service up here, let me know. You hear?" She slammed the door, then opened it again. "I like your windsurfer. I never knew."

"I didn't either," he muttered, as she slammed the door for a second time.

He'd no sooner taken the sandwich from the bag when the phone rang.

Probably Linder.

"Mr. Pierce?" a woman asked.

"Yeah."

"Oh, I didn't expect you to answer your phone. This is Kurt Vance's personal secretary at TropicTan. Could you hold a minute for Mr. Vance?"

He paused intentionally, before grudgingly saying, "All right." He bit off a large piece of his sandwich, not worrying about being caught with a mouthful of food. He hated being put on hold by someone calling him. *If you're not ready to talk, don't call.* Vance was probably doing it intentionally, because Pierce hadn't called him back immediately.

"Mr. Pierce, Vance here."

He didn't respond until he'd swallowed. "Hello, I was going to call you."

"Did Wally Gibson tell you why I called?"

Vance obviously didn't know Gibby well. He hated being called Wally.

"Sort of. He said you were into suntan lotion and looking for a detective."

Vance laughed. "That's one way of putting it. But seriously, I'm calling about my former chemist, Jack Garity. He disappeared eight months ago in the Everglades."

Pierce shifted in his chair and rubbed the back of his neck. "That's a long time ago, at least in terms of an investigation."

"I know that, and I'll be frank with you. At this point, I'm concerned more about my own ass than his. The police have been giving me a hard time. They think I'm hiding something."

The chemist's body, no doubt.

"Have they charged you with anything?"

"No. They don't have any evidence, but I want to stay on top of things."

"Do they think Garity was murdered?"

"They go back and forth. His brother, Wayne, is a big-shot circuit court judge in Miami, and he won't let go of it. Now he's got this homicide detective on my back. I think he's following me, and I wouldn't be surprised if they've tapped my phones."

Vance sounded worried, but not whiney or pushy like Linder.

"What exactly would you like me to do?"

"Let's talk about it. Can you come over this afternoon? I know it's a long drive, but I'll pay you for your time, even if you don't take the case."

Pierce wasn't sure he wanted to get involved, especially if Vance was a suspect. But he'd keep his promise to Gibby. "That's fair enough. How about three-thirty?"

"See you then."

After Vance gave him directions and rang off, Pierce leaned back in his chair. One thing was certain; if he did take the case, he'd make damned sure that Vance didn't pay him in suntan lotion.

Chapter 2

"Ever since the first Spanish monks arrived in the New World and learned of the Mayan sacred calendar, it has been a source of mystery," Elise Simms explained to the forty students in her classroom. "One of the puzzles is that a two hundred and sixty-day calendar has no basis in the physical world. There is no known phenomenon that would account for such a division of time."

Her classes were usually casual, with students speaking up whenever they had a question. But today, Elise was tense and the students were quiet.

She wondered if they could tell she was apprehensive. Normally, they saw a slender, self-possessed woman with clear blue eyes, short umber hair and a quick wit. But today, they probably thought she was acting like a nervous twit.

Her gaze strayed to the back of the room, where the reason for her unease was seated.

Umberto Urella.

His intense, dark eyes were focused on her. She looked away.

"Yet, when we contemplate the Calendar Round, it becomes clear that there is something intrinsically ..." Her mind went blank for a moment. "... intrinsically right about the pattern." Did they have any idea what she was trying to convey? This was only an entry level anthropology class, which a lot of science majors took to help fulfill their humanities requirements. "The point is, we can only make sense of this pattern of recording time when we consider it as intuitively perceived."

A woman in the front row raised her hand. "Are you saying

the Mayan priests just fabricated a calendar to use for religious purposes?"

"No, fabricated is not the..."

"Can I answer that, Professor Simms?" Umberto called out. The students turned in unison.

"Certainly." Elise smiled, glad that Umberto had finally ended his silence. Earlier, she'd introduced him as a visiting Guatemalan professor who was teaching graduate seminars, and she'd told him to speak up any time he felt like it.

"The Mayans did not fabricate the Tzolkin any more than the Jews fabricated the Old Testament, or the Christians the New Testament."

"How can you compare a calendar with the Bible?" another student asked.

Umberto had brought an obscure calendar closer to home.

"You're forgetting what you already know," Elise said. "The Tzolkin is an almanac of prophecy, of revelation."

"That's right," Umberto said. "The Tzolkin was created through an attunement with nature and the cosmos. It is a blueprint of the past, present and future."

The woman in the front row raised her hand, then turned to Umberto. "Why did the Mayans mix their science and religion?"

"Your notion of science doesn't fit with the Mayan view of existence. The Mayan way does not categorize learning; it only deals with the lessons of life. Western science has created a myth that there is a realm outside of rational understanding, called belief or religion. It perpetuates this myth, and allows you to live divided lives—a scientific way and a religious way. But everything in the universe is connected, not divided. To the Mayan mind, only a child could think otherwise."

Another student raised his hand. "When you put religion and politics together, you get fanaticism. Isn't the same true with religion and science?"

Umberto smiled. "The Mayan way is only concerned with the attunement of the planet and planetary mind with the cosmos. This knowledge is not exclusive to the Mayans, and the knowledge is not archaic. It's just a matter of putting it to use, instead of ignoring it or categorizing it as silly, primitive nonsense. If that goal is what you call fanatical, then so be it."

"What kind of word is attunement?" someone called out.

"It means bringing into harmony or accord," he explained. "You could also call it atonement. I bet you've heard that one."

"I'm confused," another student said, when the laughter subsided. "We know that the Mayans were advanced in astronomy, architecture, and mathematics, that they had their own calendar and system of writing. But they were also bloodthirsty. They perpetrated sacrificial killings. How can you talk about these same people as being concerned about planetary harmony, when they were killing each other and writing about it in stone?"

Umberto was quiet for a moment, then answered indirectly. "By the time the white men appeared in the Western Hemisphere, the cultures of the native peoples had fallen into a long decline. Their period of glory was achieved much earlier. You can't take a slice of a cultural experience, and say this is what was always true of this culture. That would be like looking at Germany in the 1930s and saying that Northern European culture was characterized by the use of gas chambers to kill large numbers of people."

Elise glanced at her watch, saw that the class was nearly over.

"Good point. We've got time for one more comment or question."

A student in the second row raised his hand. "There's one thing that bothers me about this conversation. We're studying the past, but I get the feeling from Professor Urella that he views the Mayans as if they were a thriving culture, not a dead one."

Elise nodded toward Umberto.

He smiled and ended the discussion on a light note. "For most archaeologists, the only interesting Mayans are dead ones. But Mayans like myself, who are living today, have a different view on that."

A few minutes later, Elise and Umberto walked across the grassy corridor between buildings on the University of Miami campus, headed to her office. He seemed preoccupied, and she wondered if he was irritated by the comments he'd heard in class.

"I'm sorry if my students seem ignorant about Mayan culture."

"They are like students everywhere. At the University of Guatemala, I hear many of the same types of questions."

"I would think the Guatemalan students would be more open to your world than my students."

"There are some who are interested in the traditional ways, but they are outnumbered by those who see anything of Indian origin as inferior."

Umberto drew his fingers through his thick raven hair, sweeping it back over the top of his ears and collar. Elise noted that his skin was brown and toughened from time spent outdoors. His features were Mayan, but he was taller than most Mayan men and lacked the characteristically sturdy barrel-chested physique. He was handsome in his tight jeans and boots, and she noticed the stares from passing co-eds.

Elise admired Umberto, but it wasn't for his good looks. He appealed to her because he shifted easily between Western culture and traditional Mayan ways. The essential mystery of his life intrigued her, and took her mind irresistibly back to her own childhood.

Her parents had divorced when she was six, and each summer during her childhood she had stayed at the jungle ruins of Tikal with her father.

Umberto had always been there, with her tagging along after him, usually content to walk together without conversing. Eventually, she and the Mayan boy became friends. Then one summer, when she was thirteen or fourteen and longing to see him, he was suddenly no longer there, and she was told he had moved away.

Years later, her father had led her on a two-hour hike from Tikal into the jungle, saying only that he wanted to introduce her to an old shaman whom she might find interesting since he was knowledgeable in the Tzolkin. She didn't like being distracted from her work at the ruins, but was delighted that her father was again taking her on journeys as he'd done when she was here as a child.

When they arrived at the shaman's hut, she was introduced to an old man and told in whispers that the young man in the shadows was his apprentice and that she should just ignore him, as he was somewhat unbalanced.

Later, after they'd eaten and were seated around a fire in the center of the hut, the conversation turned to the Tzolkin, and she quickly realized the old man's knowledge of the Calendar Round was profound.

Again in whispers, the old man told her that his apprentice was also studying the Tzolkin, but that his interests were peculiar. He laughed, nodding toward the dark corner where the young man sat apart from the others. He explained that while the calendar's Great Cycle spanned five thousand years, the apprentice's shamanistic work was dedicated to monitoring the course of the Galactic Cycle, which was the phase beginning at the end of the current cycle, in 2012.

The old man shook his head sadly. "Watch out for him tonight. Don't listen to his nonsense if he talks to you, and don't look directly into his face."

Elise nodded, her eyes darting quickly toward the corner where the strange apprentice sat, then away again. She was curious about the man, but also concerned about the old shaman's warning.

A moment later, she was even more confused when she saw the old man cover his mouth and chuckle until tears trickled over the rete of wrinkles on his cheeks. "He is lost in the future," he muttered. "It's a very sad case."

She looked toward her father, who was staring at her, his expressionless face highlighted by the fire.

They slept in hammocks that night, and Elise positioned herself between the wall and her father so she could wake him up if she was bothered by the apprentice. She was particularly concerned that there were only three hammocks, and that the man was lying on the floor where he could easily crawl under the hammocks to her. She tossed for a couple of hours before finally falling asleep.

The next morning she was walking back to the hut from the outdoor toilet when the young man stepped out from the forest and blocked her path. She caught her breath and quickly looked for a way to get past him.

"Don't you know who I am, Elise?"

She looked into his face and was shocked as she realized the strange apprentice was her childhood friend from Tikal, Umberto, now a grown man.

Elise's reverie was interrupted as Umberto held up the notebook that she had asked him to look at.

"I know what it is."

"You do?"

Elise had found the loose-leaf notebook among her father's possessions after his death. Although she knew it dealt with the Tzolkin and was interspersed with Mayan glyphs, most of it had consisted of seemingly meaningless combinations of letters.

For months, she'd avoided looking at the notebook because it brought back the memories of her father, and her sorrow. But a couple of weeks before Umberto arrived in Florida, she had picked up the notebook once more and spent spare moments puzzling over it. She'd even left a copy of it with a cryptographer whom Pierce had recommended, and who had promised to tackle it in his spare time.

"What is it?" Elise asked.

"It's very easy, really. I'm surprised by Barba, though."

"Why?"

Barba, Spanish for beard, was the name Umberto had always called her father, whose bushy beard had reached to his chest.

"I'm surprised that he would be interested in such … such a degenerate purpose."

Elise glanced sharply at Umberto, and saw he wasn't joking.

"What are you talking about?"

"Let's wait until we get to your office."

They climbed the steps to the second floor together, but Elise couldn't hold her silence for long. As far as she was concerned, she told Umberto, there was nothing degenerate about her father's interests. Whatever he was talking about, he must be wrong.

Umberto didn't respond, and Elise continued to stew until they reached her small office, which was crammed with books, artifacts, and colorful Guatemalan crafts.

Elise sat down behind her desk, and waited impatiently for Umberto to begin. He took a seat across from her, and opened the notebook.

"I'm sorry. I didn't mean to offend you. It's just that I have always held your father in the highest esteem, and I expected that his actions would be irreproachable."

Elise stared uncompromisingly at Umberto, and when she spoke, her voice was icy.

"Get to the point, Umberto. What is it?"

He held the open notebook out like an obscure oblation.

"What he has done is revive something that the elders have always felt is best left alone. This notebook contains descriptions of an ancient divination method that was based on the Tzolkin."

Elise gazed at him blankly, giving the impression that she didn't comprehend what he'd said. But she understood his words just fine. It was the man sitting across from her whom she didn't understand.

"Umberto, so what? I mean, what's so terrible about that?"

"That's how I thought you would feel. Maybe you don't see it as I do, but I believe it is a degenerative use of the Tzolkin."

"Why do you say that?" Her thoughts were already running ahead, puzzling over what her father's intentions had been.

"Because when the Tzolkin was used for personal purposes, the people left the path. They thought only of their own selfish ways, and nothing of the gods. And you know what happened."

Umberto was referring to the collapse of the Mayan culture, when the rituals were perverted, the sacred defiled, and humans sacrificed.

"But, Umberto, it wasn't the divination that caused the degeneration. It was the people themselves. Divination isn't evil. The elders, the shamans, still use it. So do you, in a way. The Galactic Cycle is prophecy."

"Of course. But it's not personal. It's not about everyday life. 'Who am I going to love? How much money am I going to make?'" He shook his head. "Divination trivializes the sacred."

Elise realized he must have known what the notebook was about the first time he'd seen it. She told him as much.

The room was too hot, and Umberto wiped perspiration from his forehead with the back of his hand. "You're right. I was surprised, and didn't think I should say anything."

"So what made you change your mind?"

"I consulted the wind."

She laughed. "Umberto, shame on you. Using your own personal divination method. You just think your questions are more important than the ones other people ask."

He cringed and laughed, acknowledging her point. "I was told to trust you, and help you in any way I could." He cleared his throat, and Elise knew the decision hadn't been an easy one. "Look at the matrix. I'll show you how the divination is done."

Elise's hands were shaking as she opened the notebook. She didn't know whether it was from excitement or nervousness, but she was certain of one thing. Her father would want her to understand the notebook, and she thought she knew what he had had in mind.

His one great frustration in life had been that Americans only superficially recognized the Mayan culture and its attainments. They confused the end of the sacred calendar's Galactic Cycle with the end of the world, and were only vaguely aware that a new cycle would begin in the aftermath of the old, and that a subtle shift in awareness was spreading, in spite of fearful efforts to counteract the coming changes.

The Greeks were considered the civilized ancients, but Mayans, Aztecs, Olmecs and other Native American cultures were still essentially foreign and savage in their own land. Ask a high school or college student to name a mythical character, she thought, and you'd hear Zeus or Apollo. Ask about Quetzalcoatl—the Plumed Serpent—or Tezcatlipoca, the Smoking Mirror—and you could expect blank stares.

At least, that was the way it had been during most of her

father's career. Hardly anyone had known or cared, it seemed, that a mythological tradition comparable to that of the Greeks had existed at least a thousand years before the European exploration of the Americas.

Only in recent years had things started to change, thanks to the efforts of her father and of others.

Her father had spent his last years attempting to show that the Plumed Serpent was not some kind of Indian devil, but the Native American Christ figure who united the earth (the snake) and the sky (the bird)—humanity and the spiritual quest.

The divination system must have been one more attempt on his part to make the case for his hypothesis, and she was certain that he had good reason for writing it in code.

Elise turned to a page that looked rather like a checkerboard. It had thirteen vertical columns and twenty horizontal ones, for a total of two hundred and sixty, the number of days in the sacred calendar year. In each square of the matrix was a bar and dot symbol, representing a number. The counting direction was top to bottom, left to right, and consisted of twenty repeating cycles featuring the numbers one through thirteen.

To the left of the calendar, beside the horizontal columns, were placed the twenty sacred signs that represented the forces of nature, the cosmos, and the evolutionary pattern, defining a path of life that was total and inclusive. Their meanings were archetypal, and archetypes—prototypes of humanity and nature—were the basis of all divination systems. Some of the sacred signs, in fact, could be closely compared to the major arcana of the tarot deck. There was the trickster, the sorcerer, the death symbol, and the higher mind or priest.

Each number from one to thirteen was also designated a meaning. One, for example, was unity; two was polarity; three was rhythm.

That meant that each of the two hundred and sixty days in the matrix was uniquely meaningful, being the combination of a number and a sacred sign.

Elise knew all this, and also that the Mayans had developed divination systems. But she'd never seen it all applied to the present.

"Mayan priests would draw the calendar on the ground in an elaborate ceremony," Umberto explained. "Then, after a question was put before the gods, pebbles were cast into the air. The interpretations were made according to the meanings of the days on which the pebbles fell. I think your father must have used a method involving four pebbles."

"How do you know that?"

"I'll show you." He came around to her side of the desk, and leaned over. As his shoulder rubbed against hers, Elise felt a flutter in her stomach.

Umberto turned several pages of the notebook until he reached one with four words spaced across the top of the page. Each word was boxed and an arrow pointed to the right between each box. He tapped the words, written in her father's cryptic hand.

"If you look ahead, you'll see these four words over and over again. I think they represent the four pebbles."

"In what way?"

He touched the box on the left of the page. "This is the first pebble thrown. This is the second, and so on."

"Any idea what they might mean?"

He straightened up, and took a step back. "My guess is that the first pebble stands for the warrior. The second for the opponent. The third deals with the battle, and the last one is the outcome."

Elise frowned and shifted in her seat. She felt somehow vulnerable with Umberto standing behind her. "What if your question isn't about a battle?"

"Think about it. Whatever question you ask deals with someone who is at the center of it: the warrior, who is either you, or someone you're asking about. The opponent is the challenge: whatever must be overcome. The battle is the way you will react. The outcome, of course, is just that."

Elise nodded thoughtfully. "And the rest of the notebook must be the interpretations of the two hundred and sixty days."

"Exactly."

She closed the notebook and turned in her chair to face him. "I've got to break Dad's code. I want to understand all of it, see how it works, and let others see it, too."

Umberto gazed back at her without comment.

"Why do you think it's dangerous for people to know what's in store for them?" she asked.

"My concern is of people misusing it. Some of us gain a little knowledge, then use it first to impress, then to control and manipulate."

Everything with Umberto always seemed so serious, so black and white, Elise thought. "I think most Western people would see it as a game, and not take it so seriously."

She stood suddenly and as she did, felt light-headed. Umberto grasped her arm to steady her. "I guess I got up too fast."

She looked into the dark pools of his eyes and an aching desire, a revival of the past, took hold of her.

She recalled their last summer together as children in Guatemala. He'd kissed her one day when they were alone, a soft, gentle kiss, and she'd felt a warm, erotic pleasure pulsing through her, but one mixed with feelings of confusion and uncertainty. The same feelings she experienced now.

She had an urge to take him in her arms, but instead pulled her hand away and stepped back. "There, I'm all right." The telephone rang, saving her from the awkward moment.

"Excuse me."

"I should be leaving," Umberto said.

"Wait a second." She picked up the phone. "Elise Simms."

"Hi, it's me."

"Nick." She glanced at Umberto, then turned to the window. "How are you?"

"Okay. What's up?"

"I was wondering if you'd like to go to a Gibby party with me this evening."

"This evening? That's kind of short notice," she hedged.

"I just found out about it myself."

"Nick, you know I like Gibby, but I don't know what to say

to those travel agents. I don't have anything in common with them."

"You like to travel."

"But they don't talk about travel. They talk about destinations and packages, and volume. At that last party, one of them asked me how many thousands of Canadians I thought could be sent to Cartagena in three months."

"I know what you mean. But we won't stay long. We'll have a drink, get something to eat and leave. We can go to a movie."

"Listen, I've been going all day. I'm kind of tired. How about tomorrow night? We could meet for dinner at Padrino's."

A beat passed. "I thought you had a class to teach Wednesday evenings."

"I do. We could meet there at nine."

"Okay. Nine's fine, I guess. But Gibby'll be disappointed."

"He'll get over it."

Pierce laughed. "See you tomorrow."

She hung up, and smiled at Umberto. "Thanks for your help. I really appreciate it."

"You're welcome."

As they moved to the door, she felt an urge to reassure him that he'd made the right decision.

"Umberto, I'm sure that my father didn't intend to do anything to demean the Mayan people or their knowledge. And you can be sure that I won't, either."

"I believe you. But keep in mind that he must've had a good reason for coding it."

She nodded. She suddenly had an inkling of why he'd created the code, and it didn't have anything to do with a concern that divination was dangerous.

"Will I see you Saturday?" he asked.

"Of course. I wouldn't miss your presentation for the world."

He laughed. "Oh, I don't think it will be that earth-shaking."

Being with Umberto reminded Elise of the jungle and of her father, who she still missed every day, and she didn't want to let go of the feeling.

"Do you have any plans for dinner tomorrow evening?"

"Oh, Burger King, I suppose."

She wrinkled her nose, not certain whether he was serious or not. "Why don't you join Nick and me? I think it would be nice for the two of you to meet."

"I don't want to intrude on your time with Nick."

"It's not an intrusion. I'll tell him you're coming."

Umberto gazed off to one side as if he were listening to something. "Some people who don't show their emotions are more aware of them than others. Your Nick is such a man. He views the world through his emotions, but you would not know it."

Elise pursed her lips, considering his assessment and realized he was right. "You haven't even met him." Yet, somehow Umberto had just put into words what she needed to hear. Too often Pierce seemed distant, even indifferent, and it confused her because she thought he was a sensitive man. Although Pierce hadn't said anything about it, she sensed that he was apprehensive about Umberto. He probably suspected they were having an affair. This way, he'd meet Umberto and understand their relationship. Either that, or he'd be offended. *Too late now.*

"I see him through you," Umberto said softly. He touched her shoulder, then left her office.

Elise tried to recall what she'd written in her letters to Umberto about Pierce. Although she'd mentioned him, of course, she couldn't remember ever saying anything so personal.

But Umberto had Pierce pegged.

Chapter 3

Fort Lauderdale was the ideal place for a suntan lotion factory. Sunburns, hangovers, and sexually transmitted diseases were what came to mind whenever Pierce thought of this city, forty miles north of Miami. Suntan lotion, at least, could assuage one of those scourges.

A matrix of signs bracketed Sunrise Boulevard and flowed past in a blur as Pierce headed toward the beach, crossing the Intracoastal Waterway and turning south on A1A.

The ocean was on his left, and to the right was the Venice of America, an intricate web of finger canals and rivers that coursed through the east side of the city. He drove a mile or so further before turning onto a road which snaked past high-priced properties with pools and deep-water docks—the basics of Lauderdale luxury.

Finally, he crossed a canal and braked at a high iron gate that loomed across the road. He'd arrived at Tracy Isle, a private islet and miniature subdivision for the wealthy; among them Kurt Vance, founder and owner of TropicTan, Inc.

Without turning off his engine, Pierce set his emergency brake and walked over to a wall-mounted telephone, where he punched in the three-digit number Vance had given him. The phone was answered by a silky lilting feminine voice, the verbal equivalent of someone licking his ear.

As he introduced himself, he was interrupted by a quick giggle and a comment he couldn't understand. The woman apologized, asked his name again, then told him to wait. A full minute passed before she returned. "Okay, Mr. Pierce, you can come in. Keep to the left. We're all the way down at the end."

The shiny, black gate began to hum and swung slowly open.
Pierce eased ahead, passing majestic royal palms that bordered
the road, as well as several lavish estates.

The road forked, and he followed the arm to the left. Here
and there were sparges of brightly colored flowers, and the
grass was so green it looked like it was dyed.

At the end of the road he reached another gate with white
towering columns, which bracketed the entrance to a stately
Georgian mansion. Pierce knew that Vance had money, but he
hadn't expected anything quite so ostentatious. It felt like the
sort of place where time might have stopped, where you might
see servants floating across the courtyard to serve mint julep
tea to ladies in flowing white dresses.

But that, he figured, wasn't the suntan lotion manufacturer's
style. He pictured Vance as an aging playboy, with crow's feet
on his tanned face and the good life starting to spread over his
belt.

Before Pierce had the chance to get out and hit the buzzer,
the gate opened. A young woman with long bare legs directed
him around a massive old oak tree in the center of the
cobblestone courtyard to a parking space in the corner, and
opened the car door for him. She was wearing a thigh-length
t-shirt, emblazoned with the word TropicTan above an orange
sun design.

"Hello, Mr. Pierce. Welcome to TropicTan. My name's
Wendy."

Pierce felt as if he'd arrived at one of those trendy restaurants
where the waitresses and waiters all act as if they're your
friends. He climbed out, nodded, and looked around.

"Nice place."

The mansion was divided into two wings that wrapped
partially around the courtyard. Through an archway, the open
side of the courtyard faced a swimming pool where several
people lounged like exotic Easter lilies.

Beyond the pool, a couple of yachts cruised by on
shimmering blue waters, identified by his map as belonging
to the Middle River. On the ground level of the east wing was
a six-stall garage. All but one of its doors were open, revealing

a red Porsche, a Mercedes sedan, a Land Rover, and a couple of vans.

"Vance will be right with you. He asked me to keep you company for a minute."

"That was nice of him."

"I understand you're a private investigator. I always thought it would be fun to work for one."

"I've got an ad running in the paper tomorrow for a secretary. But to tell you the truth, I think you've got a better deal here."

A man dressed in white drawstring pants and a white Polo shirt appeared under the archway. He strode across the courtyard and extended a hand.

"Hello, Nick. I'm Kurt Vance."

He looked about like Pierce had pictured him—mid-forties, with blond-streaked hair falling over his forehead; a middle-aged beach boy with a few wrinkles creasing his deeply tanned face.

A comforting stereotype. If Vance had been a pasty-faced businessman, forty pounds overweight and wearing a coat and tie, Pierce would've been caught off-balance. As it was, Vance fit neatly into a framework he'd expected and that tempered his suspicions of what lay behind the man's inquiry for help. There was no logic to that, he knew. But it was how Pierce felt.

Still, one part of Pierce's preconceived image didn't hold true. Vance's physique was trim and athletic, obviously the result of regular workouts.

"Quite a place you've got here, Mr. Vance."

"Look, just call me Vance. That's what everyone does. This is both my home and my business." He pointed toward the west wing. "The offices and plant are over there. And my living quarters are on the other side."

"How did you ever manage to get a business on Tracy Isle?"

Vance grinned slyly. "It wasn't easy or cheap. I had to grease some palms—and I don't mean trees. That got me a temporary permit, but the other owners on the island can still force me to close up shop if I'm a nuisance, so I keep things low key. No big trucks. We transport our product by van to a warehouse near downtown, and only during business hours." Vance led the way toward the pool. "Come on, I'll show you around. I want you to meet my staff."

A half-dozen women in butt thongs and string tops were sunbathing around the rim of the pool. The gatekeeper had just joined the other women and slipped her t-shirt over her head, revealing another tawny, supple body with a minimal number of square inches covered by triangular patches of fabric.

No one here has ever heard of melanoma, Pierce thought.

"All hard at work, I see."

"It's part of the job, Nick. I require them to spend at least an hour by the pool each day. They all double as models for my TropicTan ads."

"What about skin cancer?"

"What about it? We've got a great line of sunscreens. In fact, Number 23 has become our second-best-selling product for the past three years." He tilted his head toward Pierce. "But you can see, no one here is too concerned about over-exposure."

Vance laughed at his own joke.

He was just what a suntan lotion mogul was supposed to be, Pierce thought.

"So what's your best selling product?"

"Our ST, of course."

"Your what?"

"Sunless tanning lotion. It's the biggest thing in sun-care products. They account for nearly thirty percent of our sales right now. That's up from two percent ten years ago."

So fake tans are the thing, Pierce thought. "But that stuff has been around for decades, hasn't it?"

"Sure, and it contains the same active ingredient—DHA, dihydorxyacetone—that goes back to the 1920s. It's made from sugar cane, which we have an abundance of here in south Florida. DHA is also used in the winemaking process, incidentally. Coppertone started using it for sunless tanning in the 1960s, but we've greatly improved the delivery system, to disperse it more evenly so you don't get streaking and that orange look."

"But your staff doesn't use it?"

"Nope. We're picky here. STs don't look like a natural tan to me, except at night under artificial light. C'mon. Let's go inside and talk."

And get out of the sun, Pierce thought.

As they headed to the business side of the mansion, Vance asked how things were down in South Beach.

Pierce never knew what to say when someone asked that question. There was no simple answer. He took the easy way out.

"It's changing all the time." *Not always for the better, either,* he thought to himself.

"I like the night club scene," Vance said. "I don't get down there as much as I'd like, though. A lot of folks around here don't appreciate Miami Beach. They have a resistance to anything in Dade County."

"South Beach is pretty safe at all hours, especially if you're with a group of friends."

"Hey, I know, Nick. You don't have to sell *me.*" He opened the door. "I love the place."

They climbed the stairs to the second floor and, halfway down the hallway, reached a reception area with a couch and several chairs. The receptionist's desk was vacant.

"Here we are." Vance motioned toward a door directly behind the desk, and they entered an office several times larger than Pierce's suite.

Vance's desk was in front of a wall-to-floor window with a view of the pool and the Middle River. On the oppose side of the room was a conference table, and beyond it a door opened to another room with a couple of tanning tables and lights—on one of which, to Pierce's amazement, was a thong-clad woman stretched out on her stomach. Vance obviously wasn't going to let rainy days or indoor duties deter anyone's tanning chores.

When she heard them, the woman rolled over, sat up, and closed the book she was reading. She stretched her arms overhead in a casual and uninhibited fashion, displaying her ample breasts.

"Hi, guys."

"Any calls, Diana?"

"Just one from the photographer confirming the shoot for Monday."

"Good. Did you tell him we'll be using two dogs?"

"Yeah. He wanted to know what the dogs have to do with suntans."

"Jesus Christ." Vance shook his head. "The most popular suntan ad of all time had a dog in it. You know, the one pulling the little girl's bikini bottom down. And this guy's second-guessing me because I want two dogs."

"What kind of dogs?" Pierce asked.

"Saint Bernards, wearing Hawaiian shirts and with little bottles of TropicTan around their necks." Then, whispering as if he were revealing a state secret, he added: "You see, there's going to be a girl lying on her towel, and behind her the dogs are going to be playing tug-of-war with her top."

"Great," Pierce said, trying to sound enthusiastic.

"Do you think it sounds tacky?"

"I'd have to see the ad."

"Exactly what I'm thinking. Describing it is one thing, but you gotta see it to be sure. So, how about a drink?"

"Just water is fine."

"Diana, two glasses of Evian." He grinned at Pierce. "That's naïve spelled backwards, you know."

"I didn't know that." *Hey, swell, Vance probably works the daily Jumble in the paper.*

"They moved over to a cozy corner with comfortable chairs. Diana poured two glasses of water over chips of ice. "You want me to hold your calls, Vance?"

"Please do." He ran a finger over her thigh, and gave Pierce a sly glance as she walked away. "We're good friends." He tipped his glass toward Pierce. "I gave up the hard stuff about five years ago, but I figured a private investigator would want something a little stronger."

Pierce took a sip from his glass.

Vance seemed annoyed that Pierce didn't fit his profession's stereotype and didn't joke about it, either. But the annoyance passed quickly. "Okay, we'll get right into Jack Garity, instead of Jack Daniels. Garity developed TropicTan products in the lab. As I told the cops, we got along well. But Jack kept to himself a lot. It was hard to figure what was on his mind. Intellectual type, you know." He shrugged. "Then he disappeared one day, on a fishing trip in the Everglades. The police and park rangers searched five days for him. They found his jeep, then his canoe floating upside down. Later they found some of his fishing gear in the water. But no body."

"How was he acting before he disappeared?"

"He seemed sort of preoccupied, like his thoughts were elsewhere."

"Where?"

"Good question. How the fuck should I know?"

"Any known involvement with the drug trade?"

You couldn't conduct an investigation of a missing person in South Florida without looking into the drug angle. Especially when the missing person was a chemist.

"Not that I know of. The cops checked out that angle thoroughly. They even came up with this wild idea about drugs in suntan lotion."

"What do you mean?"

"Oh, Jack and I had a standing joke about creating some sort of drug that we'd put in the lotion, and everyone would be floating on the sand. You know, get high while getting a tan. Or get a tan while getting high. It was just a joke, but the cops heard it and took it seriously. They even tested some of the lotion, thinking that we had some sort of special product for a select set of sunbathers."

"And?"

"Look, I've got a good business, a good life. I'll admit it. I make a lot of money. I don't need to get involved with anything illegal."

"How long had you known Garity?"

"Jack and I were old friends, but we weren't partners or anything. He was my employee. He had no capital in the business, other than a few shares of stock."

"So he was free to disappear."

"I suppose you could look at it that way. But if he wanted to leave, all he had to do was say so."

"Did you want him to leave?"

The phone rang and Vance looked across the office, waiting

until Diana answered it in the reception area.

"Something happened to Jack. His health wasn't the greatest. He'd been running himself down. But that was only part of it. He was indifferent to the job, and I like people who are supportive, you know? So I did ask him if he wanted out."

"What did he say?"

"That he was having a difficult time in his personal life. I told him to take a vacation."

"How'd he react?"

"He said he'd think about it." Vance fiddled with a gold chain around his neck. "Maybe he took my advice. I don't know. A week or so later he was gone. Vanished."

"This trouble in his personal life. You haven't mentioned a wife or girlfriend."

Vance shook his head. "He was divorced; has a grown daughter, a college student. His ex-wife's name is Carla."

"Is she still around?"

"She lives in North Miami Beach. Look, I've got a folder for Jack with names, phone numbers, photos, driver's license, social security. All of that. But there's one thing missing: the address or phone number of Isabel, his mystery lady. She was the problem in his personal life."

"Tell me about her."

"Not much to tell. I never met her. As far as I know, no one who knows Jack ever did."

"Not even his brother, the judge?"

"Ask him. If he knows her, he hasn't led the cops to her yet. They don't even have a last name."

"Let me guess. You want me to find her."

"That's right. If you find her, I think the puzzle about Jack's disappearance will be resolved."

"Maybe she disappeared with Garity," Pierce said. "Died with him in an accident, or they both ran away."

"That's a possibility, but I don't think so. You see, the night after he disappeared, we had a break-in here."

"In this place, with all the gates?"

"They came by water. They were professionals. They knew how to get past my electronic surveillance system."

"What did they take?"

"They ransacked the lab. Destroyed a lot of expensive equipment and supplies. If anything was missing, I couldn't tell. Only Jack would know."

"So you think Isabel had something to do with the break-in?"

"That's my guess."

"What were they after?"

Vance shrugged. "Again, find Isabel, and you'll find an answer. Are you interested?"

Pierce knew that Vance could've vandalized the lab himself, in order to destroy some kind of evidence. The last thing Pierce wanted was to step into the role of investigator for a guilty party.

He'd done that unintentionally once before, when he'd been hired by his former college roommate, Raymond Andrews. The multi-millionaire financier had become obsessed with a quest to obtain a pair of identical crystal skulls, and Pierce had nearly paid for Raymond's obsession with his life. He'd met Elise; but he'd lost his closest friend, Fuego, and Elise had lost her father. Andrews had gotten away with the skulls, and gone into hiding.

"I know what you're thinking," Vance said. "That I might be involved. I'm not, and I'll tell you what. Take the case on a day-to-day basis. If you find evidence that I had anything to do with Jack's death or disappearance, we end it right there."

"Actually, if I found any evidence linking to Garity's disappearance, I would be required by law to turn that information over to authorities. I'm an investigator, not your lawyer."

"I understand that. And I wouldn't hire you if I had something to hide."

That was somewhat reassuring. "I'll require a week's pay in advance. Four hundred a day, plus expenses. At the end of the week, I'll tell you what I've found and you can decide if you want me to continue."

"Fine. I'll get you two grand and you can get started." He called out to Diana and asked her to write the check.

As they waited, Pierce apologized for being insistent about money up front. "My last client gave me a windsurfer instead of a check. If I hadn't gotten anything up front …"

"You windsurf?"

"Never tried it."

Vance flipped his index finger at him. "You ought to. It's a blast. I've been windsurfing twenty years and I'm still into it. I've got eight or nine boards, and more sails than I can count. What kind of board is it?"

"I have no idea."

"Tell you what. After you get into the investigation and have something to report back, let's get together and go out. I'll show you the basics."

Pierce hesitated. "How often do you sail?"

"Whenever there's wind. I haven't been out for months, though. Florida's horrible in the summer. But the season's right around the corner. October through March are the best months. So what do you say?"

Why not, Pierce thought. That way he wouldn't have to hassle with Linder about taking back the board, and he could use the exercise. He'd given up running a few months ago, after injuring his knee and being told that it would be prone to ongoing injury if he continued running.

"Okay. It's a deal."

"Great. But I warn you, Pierce. This is an addicting sport. You can get really hooked on the wind."

"Oh, yeah. I don't think much about the wind."

"If you get into it, you will."

Diana handed Vance the check. He signed it, and passed it to Pierce along with a file folder labeled GARITY STUFF.

"C'mon outside. I want to show you my boards."

"How about showing me Garity's lab first?"

Vance smiled. "I like that. You want to get right to work. Not much to see, though."

They walked downstairs and into a large space with counters and sinks along three white tiled walls, as well as two desks with bookshelves behind them. On one of the counters was a scattering of beakers, pestles, trays and test tubes.

"This is where Jack worked. That door on the far wall leads to the vat room, where the solutions were mixed for production. The vats drain directly into the bottling line. We're fully automated."

Pierce noticed everything looked orderly and there was no sign of damage from a break-in. "Has the lab been used since Garity left?"

"Of course. I've got a business to run. I hired another chemist."

Pierce pointed to a desk. "Garity's?"

"It was."

"Did the police go through it?"

"After the burglary. It's cleaned out now."

Vance opened one of the lower drawers to show Pierce that it was empty. A pendant slipped out of the top of his shirt as he leaned over, and before Vance slipped it back inside, Pierce glimpsed a half-dollar coin that shone like gold.

Pierce jammed his hands in his pockets. "I guess there's nothing much to see then."

"Let's go take a look at my boards. I haven't cracked the door since April."

Chapter 4

From the bridge of the yacht anchored on the Middle River, Nigel Erickson gazed through a high-powered set of binoculars mounted on a tripod. With the help of the lenses, he was virtually standing next to the swimming pool where six lovely young ladies were sunbathing. One of them had removed her top; he could clearly see her full breasts and taut, pink nipples. A warm tingling seized his groin as she started to apply lotion.

Erickson was twenty-five, a few months out of graduate school at the University of South Florida. He stood barely five-eight, but was fit and muscular with bulging biceps, brawny shoulders and a hard, sculpted chest. He wore his hair in a crew cut, with the sides razor-cut to the scalp. A single diamond in the lobe of his left ear accented the look.

Isabel Martin nudged against his shoulder. Her voice was a soft hiss, her lips inches from his ear. "They're coming outside again. Get on them."

He quickly shifted the binoculars, afraid she knew what he was looking at.

Martin was quite a looker herself; blonde hair in a long single braid, blue eyes, attractive. A California girl. Well, not exactly a girl. She was probably twice his age. But she worked out regularly and looked great in her snug T-shirt and tight khaki shorts. He was intrigued by her, and he'd swear that she'd been coming onto him today. Maybe it was just the environment. The plush yacht, the girls by the pool, the way that she was leaning over him now as she gazed toward shore.

He refocused; as the view shifted from the pool to the courtyard, he could only see a small part of the open area and it took a moment to find the men. Vance was talking to the private investigator, who had arrived an hour earlier. As they crossed the courtyard, Erickson saw the visitor was carrying something now, a manila envelope or a file folder.

Erickson had been working with Martin for six weeks now and he still knew very little about what was going on. Martin had told him and Wendy Spenser that there was no need for them to know everything. They were simply to follow orders, and learn as much as they could.

Vance was supposedly shipping his suntan lotion out of the country illegally, to avoid export tax. But Erickson was starting to think the story was just a cover. Hell, who cared; it was just a game. It would be all over in ten and half months, and then his real career would begin.

As Erickson watched, Vance stopped in front of the only garage door that was closed, and pulled it open. The walls were lined with racks that held what looked like surfboards. No, sailboards. The guy was a windsurfer.

Hmm, what do you know. So he had something in common with Vance. He'd like to take a closer look at those boards himself. He pulled his head back from the binoculars, and glanced at Martin. *Does she know that I spent six summers on the Caribbean racing circuit?*

"What are they doing, Nigel?"

"They're probably talking about windsurfing."

Her breast brushed against his arm. "Keep watching."

He looked through the binoculars again. *Of course she knew about his windsurfing. She knew everything about him. It was all in the records.*

The two men walked out of the garage, and headed toward Pierce's car. They exchanged a few more words, shook hands, as the black gate opened behind them.

"Get the license number, Nigel," Martin snapped as the investigator backed his Saab toward them.

He focused on the license plate: "I-C-U-2."

"Cute, Pierce. Real cute," Martin said. "But I don't think so."

As the car pulled away and disappeared through the gate,

Wendy Spenser walked over to Vance. Erickson straightened up and slipped on a headphone set; Martin did the same. Spenser had alerted them to Pierce's appointment this morning, and now a miniature microphone was taped to the nape of her neck, well concealed under her thick auburn hair.

"How'd it go, Vance?" she asked.

Spenser had been making a play for Vance ever since she'd gotten hired. Diana, Vance's current woman-of-the-hour, still had the inside track on his attention, but Vance's attention span with women never lasted more than a few months, and Diana's time was running out. Or at least that was the way Martin told it.

"Fun and games, as usual," Vance replied. "You wanna come up later on, maybe watch a movie with me?"

"I don't know. My boyfriend gets kind of jealous."

"So we'll keep the lights on."

"What about Diana?"

"She doesn't own me. What do you say?"

"I'll think about it."

"Don't think too long."

She walked away and Vance gazed after her.

"Talk about playing it coy," Erickson said under his breath.

"She's doing it just right," Martin replied, taking off her headphones. "She's enticing him, making him work for it. He'll never suspect that he's being played."

She lifted the headphones off Erickson's head, dropping them to the floor, and stroked his rugged unshaven cheek and square jaw. "Of course, sometimes a direct approach works best."

That was all Erickson needed. He pulled her to him, kissing her roughly. His hands moved down her body and over her lower back. He gripped her firm buttocks and ground himself against her.

"Easy, boy, easy," Martin whispered. "Let's go down to the cabin."

Chapter 5

Courtrooms were like churches: hallowed, consecrated abodes of religious, ritualistic behavior; temples of decorum, where the ordained administrated the sacraments of justice.

Pierce had laughed when Elise had made the analogy after she'd served on a jury a few months ago. But now, as he sat in a courtroom watching a jury being selected, he realized certain comparisons could indeed be made.

Instead of a priest, there was a robed judge elevated behind his bench—his altar. On either side of him were the 'altar boys'— the secretary on his left and the stenographer on his right. The bailiffs were the ushers. The witness stand was part pulpit, part confessional. The spectators were seated in the pews. And the jury, who would sing the verdict, sat in for the choir.

Judge Wayne Garity had just welcomed the panel of potential jurors with a friendly smile and thanked them for their patience. He was a middle-aged man, ruggedly handsome and deeply tanned, with short-cropped dark hair laced with gray.

Father Garity. He was telling them about their duties and explaining that a public defender and a state's prosecutor would be questioning each of them for a few minutes, after which some of them would be dismissed.

"Please, don't take it personally. The decisions by the two attorneys have nothing to do with you as an individual."

Pierce, though, was having a hard time not taking the judge's snub personally. He'd called Garity's office yesterday afternoon right after he'd talked with Vance, and had been told that the judge was just leaving for the day. After he'd explained why he was calling, the message had been relayed and the judge's secretary had told Pierce to be at the judge's chambers at eight sharp this morning.

Garity was supposedly willing to talk to anyone who was seriously interested in finding out what happened to his brother. But the judge hadn't arrived until eight-thirty, and then had been too busy to chat. Pierce was told there would be a break around ten and that he should wait.

Garity called out the name of a man from the jury pool, and a burly man in a checkered shirt raised a hand. The judge chatted amiably with him for a couple of minutes, then the public defender took his turn.

"Mr. Farley, do you have any problems with our criminal justice system?"

"No sir. Well, it's slow. It just moves too slow." The man nervously shifted from foot to foot, as if the floor had suddenly turned red hot.

"I think we'd all agree with that," said the young lawyer, whose sandy hair fell over the collar of his gray suit. "And I want to personally thank each of you for being here today. I know there's a lot of waiting involved in jury duty. It's boring, isn't it?"

"Get on with it," Pierce muttered under his breath, feeling as if he were in the jury box himself waiting to be auditioned. *Waiting.* That was what jury duty was all about.

Elise had hated the waiting. She'd spent three days in the jury assembly room before she was called into a courtroom. Although from the way she described it, the waiting wasn't all that bad. Probably a grade above most of the surveillance jobs he'd handled; you could walk around, make telephone calls, and you didn't have to worry about whether or not your subject had noticed you.

As the questioning continued, Pierce recognized the red-haired man who was now under scrutiny. Earlier, while waiting in the hallway, Pierce had heard him saying that he knew how to get out of jury duty. "I'm gonna tell the judge I think all suspects should be executed," Red had boasted. "I heard that'll get you out fast." But now Red calmly answered the questions. He didn't say anything outrageous, and neither did anyone else. They all seemed uncomfortable, acting a bit like they were on trial themselves.

The defendant, a black man charged with cocaine distribution, seemed more relaxed than the potential jurors. No one was asking him anything.

As the judge called out another name, Pierce imagined what he would say if he was being questioned. Maybe something witty or biting about the trend of the current order. He'd tell them that the system was in trouble because there were too many lawyers. He'd go on to say that historically societies collapsed under the weight of too many lawyers and this one was already badly sagging.

Or maybe he would clam up like everyone else.

Two more candidates were interviewed, then the group was told to wait outside the courtroom while the lawyers picked the six who would serve on the jury.

Pierce glanced at his watch. Ten-fifteen already. He stared at Garity, tried to catch his eye, then reluctantly followed the jurors into the hallway.

A few minutes later, the bailiff signaled the group back inside. The judge's secretary, a conservatively dressed middle-aged woman, called off six names, then Garity told the others they were dismissed from jury duty and would not be required to return tomorrow.

As they filed out, Pierce stared at Garity, wondering how much longer he would have to wait. But the judge never even looked his way as he spoke quietly to his secretary. She nodded and moved away from the bench and down the aisle, as the judge began addressing the jurors.

"Mr. Pierce, would you follow me, please?"

Finally.

When they were outside the courtroom, she turned to him. "The judge apologizes. He won't be able to meet with you this morning."

"I wish you could've told me that a few hours ago."

"He thought he could fit you in, but it's just not possible. He wants to know if you could meet him at six this evening, at this address."

She handed Pierce a piece of paper with a north Miami address on it. He recognized it immediately as the home address of the judge's missing brother, Jack.

"I'll be there."

A couple of minutes later, he stepped outside into the sweltering heat, and crossed the parking lot, sliding in behind the wheel of the Saab and patting the dashboard.

"Well, Swedie, it wasn't a total loss."

Isabel Martin gazed through the darkly-tinted window of her black Lexus, parked in a courthouse lot two rows behind Nicholas Pierce's Saab. She could see his lips moving, but couldn't read them. She figured if she'd just spent four hours waiting to talk to Garity, she'd be talking to herself, too.

She couldn't blame Vance for hiring the P.I., but it wasn't going to do him any good. She was going to make sure of that. But Pierce was a new element, another annoyance in a string of annoyances since Jack Garity had slipped away.

The initial foul-up had been when his brother the judge had gotten the case re-opened. Then the first detective on the case had keeled over, all on his own, and the cops had put nosy Frank Davis in charge.

Davis had gotten too interested in the case and had stepped into dangerous territory. A terrible accident had followed. The new cop on the case, Buddy Drucker, was under control and being guided in the direction that she wanted him to go. Right toward Vance.

They'd probably never convict Vance of anything, but they could make life miserable for him, and hopefully that would give the judge sufficient satisfaction. If he continued to persist, a stronger response would be required.

The judge couldn't be allowed to get any close to Aurum, and neither could Pierce.

The Saab headed out of the lot. She followed Pierce at a safe distance across the McArthur Causeway. He was either heading to his office or home. How dumbfounded Pierce would be if he even had an inkling that the very person Vance wanted him to find was right behind him. Tailing him. Isabel laughed.

Thanks to Wendy Spenser, she'd confirmed that Pierce's visit to Vance was directly related to Garity—and to herself. It wasn't a good situation, but Isabel was on top of it.

Spenser was surprisingly good, and she knew quite a bit more about the project than Erickson. She knew the export fraud story was a cover, that the real case had something to do with a missing man, and that Isabel was somehow involved. Isabel had told her to say nothing about it to Erickson; it was part of the training, she'd explained.

Isabel turned her thoughts to her new recruits. Ever since Aurum had come under the auspices of the Department of Energy's intelligence office in the mid-nineties, it had been deemed a training ground for such assets. At the same time, its own special brand of clandestine activities had continued, buried away from public accountability.

Martin studied the files on every new employee in federal intelligence, and handpicked her recruits from those who were headed for analyst positions. Supposedly, a year's experience in clandestine operations would give them a larger perspective and enhance their careers. In almost all cases, the one selected felt honored. Especially when they were told about the bonus they would earn at the end of their year's training.

Although these analysts-to-be generally didn't like dirtying their hands in fieldwork, they were eager to do their best and move on once their training ended. But before they left, Isabel always made certain they were sufficiently compromised so that they could never talk about Aurum without endangering their careers.

The last two recruits, Randall Forrester and Heath Bingham, had departed several weeks ago. They had learned a lot about Aurum, but they wouldn't talk. They'd both become accessories to murder, and knew that killing a cop could get them life … or even death.

Sure, they might be able to convince a jury that Isabel was the mastermind, and that they'd unwittingly become involved. But they also knew there was a good chance they'd never even get that far. They'd seen the sort of consequences that Isabel could inflict on those who crossed her.

Still, she wasn't taking any chances. Forrester and Bingham were being monitored. If they tried anything, she would know.

She had picked Nigel Erickson for one particular reason. Martin knew all about Vance's fanatical pursuit of windsurfing, and Erickson was an expert in that field; otherwise, she wouldn't have given him a second thought. He was too much of a playboy, who probably daydreamed about wine, women and wind—rather like Vance himself. That, she hoped, would work to her advantage.

Wendy Spenser, on the other hand, should work out fine. She fit the description of Vance's fantasy woman, and even reminded Isabel of herself back in the early days of her career, when she was a training recruit herself, working with Manfred Finestone, the man who created Aurum.

Isabel had learned the true mission of Aurum, fallen in love with Manfred—Mani, as his close friends called him—and become obsessed with the program's mission.

She never left. Twenty years later, she was now Aurum's chief field officer. She reported quarterly in writing to a bureaucrat at the Department of Energy, who was biding his time and waiting for retirement. Her reports focused exclusively on the training effort and he didn't look any further.

Besides, her budget was a pittance, especially since the salaries and bonuses of her assistants came from general training funds. It was the perfect refuge for a project that would never survive the light of day.

"Mr. Pierce, my name is Anita, and I saw your ad. I've always thought that working for a private investigator would be so exciting. Just the other night, in fact, I saw this re-run of a really popular detective show. I can't think of the name now, but ..."

"Right," Pierce muttered as she prattled on. When she finished her spiel, he jotted down her name and number.

The ad had run in the Herald this morning, and the hungry and eager were already calling. He wasn't looking forward to taking applications and conducting interviews, especially with Anita and her ilk, but he needed a secretary.

After a couple more seconds of silence, the recorder beeped

and a second applicant nervously introduced herself as Maria Perez. She spoke in a Spanish-accented voice, was twenty-two, and had worked as a receptionist at a computer company for a year. She lived in Little Havana and was bilingual. She ended by saying she hated answering machines, and hoped she could talk to him in person.

"What's your phone number, Maria?" he barked at the machine as she disconnected. He could hit call back, but it wasn't a good sign that she didn't tell him the number he could call. So maybe he wouldn't.

He heard a beep, and the same woman's voice again. She apologized, and left her phone number. He jotted it down and circled her name. Maybe he could get by with one interview this time.

He heard another beep from someone who'd hung up. Probably Anita calling back with further adventures of TV private eyes. When no more calls played, he hit the rewind button then reached for the phone to call Maria.

A rap at the door interrupted him.

Probably Gibby with another complaint about the windsurfer.
"Come in."

An attractive, well-dressed woman stood in the doorway.
"Mr. Pierce?"

"That's right. What can I do for you?"

She moved into the office, showing the lithe, graceful movements of an aerobics instructor. A faint but distinct scent of perfume surrounded her. She was a brunette with shoulder-length hair and an oval face. At first glance he thought she was about thirty, but as she moved closer, he realized she might be older. She wore make-up, with lipstick accenting her full lips, and a dress that was business-like yet casual.

Pierce took her for a potential client, and guessed what her story would be. She was married to a wealthy man who was a few years her senior, suspected that he had a mistress, and she wanted Pierce to prove it.

He looked for a wedding ring, expecting to see a sizable chunk of ice. But the only ring she wore was on her right hand, and looked like an opal.

"My name is Janet Howarth. I'm here about a job."

For a moment, he thought she was joking. She was so different from his recent secretaries. More sophisticated, more self-assured, and probably more intelligent. He noticed her diamond earrings, one per ear. The art student's ears had been virtual pincushions studded with silver and gold.

He motioned toward his office, and she moved ahead of him.

"So how did you find me? There's no address listed in the ad."

Janet laughed as she eased into a chair, keeping her spine straight and her shoulders back. "That was easy. A reverse directory gave me your address. I also called the Better Business Bureau and found out you're in good standing with them. No clients have filed any complaints against you. At least, not in the past five years."

"Glad to know I'm legit." He sat down in his chair. Already, he was impressed.

"In fact, the woman I spoke to even knew who you were, because of publicity on a case you handled last year."

The Crystal Skull case.

"So, tell me about yourself," Pierce said, steering the conversation away from his past.

"Sure. I just moved to Miami about a month ago. I had a messy divorce, and wanted to get out of St. Paul. Anyhow, I've got an apartment in Coral Gables. It's about fifteen minutes from here. Let's see; I've worked for two other private investigative agencies, five years at the last one. I can handle all the routine tasks, and I've also done some basic investigative work. You know, background checks, that sort of thing."

Pierce felt like asking her when she wanted to start. But he needed a secretary, not a partner.

"Your qualifications sound great. But I'm not really looking for an investigator. When I need investigative help, I work with other P.I.s on a case-by-case basis."

"Don't get me wrong, Mr. Pierce. I know what job I'm applying for. I just want you to know the full range of my capabilities."

"I see." He told her what he could pay her.

"That's not enough."

"I thought you might feel that way."

"I'll be frank, Mr. Pierce. If you pay minimum wages, you're going to get what you pay for. Minimum work, minimum quality. I thought you might be looking for something better." She stood to leave. "It was nice meeting you."

He was about to lose the best secretary that had ever walked through his door. "Hold on. Maybe we can work something out. Would you consider working thirty hours a week to start, if I went up another five dollars an hour? Maybe we could increase the hours later on."

She sat back down. "Thirty hours is perfect, and I bet I'll get more accomplished in them than your last assistant did in forty."

Try eighty, he thought. "That's great. The job's yours."

She paused a moment, then smiled. "All right. But ..."

"But what?"

"I'd like you to commit yourself on one point."

Jesus. Whose interview was this? "What's that?"

"I want to do more than just paper work and answering phones. I'd like to be actively involved in some of your cases right away, and I'd like you to sponsor me for a Florida investigator's license."

"You're planning on leaving already?"

She laughed. "I'll stay at least a year."

Enthusiastic and looking to the future. How could he turn her down? Hell, he'd save money by not having to hire other investigators.

"All right. Welcome aboard. As you can see, it's not a large ship, but the ocean view is almost the same as the one from the luxury liners." He pointed to the window.

"I see another building."

"Come here." He guided her to the window, pointed to the right. "You gotta lean close to the glass. You'll see the beach and the Atlantic." As she arched her long, graceful neck, he drank in the smell of her perfume. It was going to be interesting working with her.

"An ocean view with an asterisk," she said, turning toward him.

Their noses were inches apart. He could get lost in those green eyes.

"That's one way of putting it." He took a step back. "So, how soon can you start?"

"Oh, I don't know. Tomorrow?"

"Fine with me."

She looked up at the sunset painting on the wall, a question mark forming in the arch of her eyebrow. He told her how the mural had gotten there.

"I guess you've had some problems," she said with a smile.

"That's an understatement." The phone rang and he reached across his desk for the receiver, but Janet beat him to it. Their eyes met again as his fingertips grazed the back of her hand. The moment seemed to expand into minutes, hours, infinity.

The phone rang again. He withdrew his hand. "Just take a message."

"Mr. Pierce's office ... He's busy right now. Can I help you with anything?" A pen materialized from her purse and she wrote down a name on a notepad. "Your number, please?" She tapped the pen on the desk. "You mind giving it to me again? He may have lost it."

Pierce stood up and peered over her shoulder as she wrote ELISE SIMMS on the pad. "Tell her I'll call her right back."

Janet relayed the message, then jotted something down, and hung up. "She said to tell you that a Professor Urella is joining you at dinner this evening."

"Oh, yeah?" He reached for the phone, and dialed her number. He wanted an explanation. She hadn't said anything yesterday about Urella joining them, and he didn't like the idea. Not a bit.

"She said she was just leaving her office," Janet said, "and not to bother calling. She'll see you tonight."

Elise's phone rang several times before he hung up. "That was a fast break. Listen, whenever she calls from now on, just put her through."

"Your wife?"

"No, just a friend. A good friend." Oddly, he felt hesitant to tell Janet about Elise. *Ridiculous.* He was acting like a high school kid who'd just met a new girl and didn't want her to know about his girlfriend. "Let me give you an application form." He reached into a drawer, and found the file containing the forms.

"You want me to fill it out now?"

He waved a hand. "Take it with you. Bring it back in the morning. Let's meet here, say around ten?" They moved out into the reception area. "Normally, I'd like you to be here by nine at the latest, but I usually won't be in myself until later."

"Sounds just like the last place I worked. See you tomorrow."

Incredible, he thought, as she disappeared through the door. She no doubt understood that a P.I. actually worked primarily outside the office, a fact his last couple of secretaries had apparently failed to grasp.

He would check her credentials, of course. But he already suspected everything would pan out. Add in the fact that she was not only capable, but stunning, and he felt as if he'd just won the lotto. Or something.

Chapter 6

A bank of menacing thunderheads clustered in the western sky as Pierce cruised through an old, tree-lined neighborhood near the Intracoastal Waterway in North Miami. The houses were a mix of one- and two-story structures, most with stucco finishes and tile roofs.

He found the address Judge Garity had given him, and parked in the driveway under a huge spreading banyan. The single-story house stood out from the others on the block only because it was shrouded by bougainvillea in full crimson blossom.

Pierce walked up to the front door, knocked, waited, but no one answered. Although he was a few minutes late, Garity was even later.

He moved around the side of the house. The backyard, bordered by a tall, neatly trimmed ficus hedge, was dominated by a massive mango tree. The yard looked well-tended as if someone was taking care of the place.

"Who're you?" a voice said from behind him.

He turned to see a woman holding a broom over her shoulder and eyeing him suspiciously. She appeared to be in her sixties, wearing a shapeless housedress and a mop of unruly, dyed-black hair. Her eyebrows were penciled into steep arches, giving her a quizzical expression as though she were perpetually at the edge of asking a question.

"I'm meeting Judge Garity here." He made a point of emphasizing 'judge' so the woman knew he had the law on his side.

"He doesn't live here."

Normally, he might say it was none of her business. But perhaps the neighbor lady might prove helpful. He explained who he was and what he was doing here.

The woman shook her head. "Oh my God, another detective. I live next door. I keep a watch on the place."

Pierce nodded, eyeing the broom. "I guess you don't see many people around here any more."

"Are you kidding? I swear more people come around this house now that Jack's gone than when he lived here."

"Really? What kind of people?"

She lowered the broom, but still held it in a defensive manner, as if she were playing goalie for a broom hockey team. "Mostly cops. Do you know that every month or two they send a new detective out here to look at the house and go around bothering all of us with the same questions?"

"I didn't know. Who else comes around here, besides cops?"

"Well, there's your judge, and a man in a sports car."

"What's he look like?"

"Never got a chance to see him up close. He came twice that I know of. Both times late at night."

"What does he do?"

"He's got a key, goes inside. Who knows what he does."

"Maybe he's a police detective." Or maybe it was Kurt Vance.

"That's what I thought, but when I asked Lt. Davis about it, he wanted me to call him right away if I saw him again. I did, too. Weirdest thing."

"What happened?"

"They transferred me three times until some woman came on the phone and asked a bunch of questions about how I knew Davis, then told me he was no longer on the case, but that someone else would be coming out here to talk to me."

"Another detective?"

"That's right. Bunker. Not a very friendly fellow. No manners. I asked him what happened to Davis, and he told me he was dead. Just said it flat out like that." She glanced up at lightening flickering in the distance. "Gonna rain. Better see how the cats are doing. Some of them don't like the thunder, you know."

Pierce watched her waddle off, walked back to his car, glancing momentarily at the caliginous sky, as a drum-roll of thunder rumbled. "Looks like you're going to get a bath, Swedie," he said, leaning against the driver's door. He glanced at his watch. Ten to seven. He was supposed to meet Elise at nine.

He heard a swishing sound, and glanced across the street to see a young woman in white shorts sweeping her sidewalk and peering in his direction. *The Broom Brigade.* He'd have a chat with her later.

He felt a raindrop, then another. A strobic flash lit the sky, followed instantly by another thunderclap. The sweeper disappeared into her house and Pierce slid back inside Swedie.

In seconds, the rainfall went from a patter to a downpour. Jack Garity's house was a blur through the rain-streaked windshield.

He heard the purr of an engine and saw a white Mercedes pull into the driveway, with Garity at the wheel.

Garity tapped his horn, then rushed to the front door. Pierce raced after him. Garity, dressed in a trench coat and hat, nodded as he fumbled with a set of keys. "You been waiting long, Nick?"

Nick. Like they were old buddies.

Pierce wiped the rain from his hair as they stepped inside. "A few minutes. Just long enough to meet the neighbor lady."

Garity took off his coat and hat and a drop of rain ran down his face, tracing its craggy lines. "Glenda Greenfelder." He jabbed his thumb over his shoulder toward her house.

"That's her."

His gray eyes assessed Pierce. "She's a real snoop. Unfortunately, she doesn't seem to know any more about Jack than any of the other neighbors."

"Too bad." He would ask around anyhow.

"So you've been hired by Kurt Vance. Interesting."

"Why's that?" Pierce asked.

"It sounds as if he's finally taking an interest in the case."

"Out of self-preservation. He says the cops are watching him. He wants to clear his name."

"News to me. About the cops, that is."

From where he stood in the living room, Pierce could see the dining area and part of the kitchen. Everything was spotless, orderly; utterly ordinary.

The judge walked over to an oak buffet, and nodded toward two framed photographs on a middle shelf. One was of a catamaran with two men leaning far over the side, balancing the vessel as it plied through the sea. The other showed two grinning shirtless men on either side of a five-foot sailfish. Pierce recognized one as a younger version of the judge, sporting a muscular frame. The other man was taller and younger, probably in his late twenties, bearded with longish hair.

"That's Jack, of course, with me. That was more than ten years ago. I caught that one, a trophy sailfish. It's on the wall in my den."

"Nice. Tell me about Jack."

Garity was quiet a moment. "I've checked you out, of course. Otherwise, you wouldn't be here. I'm not sure what Vance's motives are, but I do welcome any assistance in finding my brother. What do you want to know about him? Fire away."

"What do you think happened?"

"Initially, I thought he might have suffered a heart attack, and that the body had become caught in mangrove roots, or the gators got it."

"But you changed your mind."

The judge puffed out his chest and rose up slightly on the balls of his feet. Even away from his courthouse, bench and robe, he lost none of the bearing of his position.

"I think he was murdered, and his body was disposed of somewhere else."

"What makes you think so?"

Garity explained that when his brother went to the Everglades alone, he usually stuck to the spots where he could fish from shore. Instead, on this trip he'd taken his two-man, fifteen-foot canoe out onto Hell's Bay Trail, a maze of switchbacks through a mangrove jungle. It was difficult canoeing for two people, let alone one.

"That made me suspicious. And when they found two paddles, I knew Jack wasn't alone."

"Maybe he took a spare."

He shook his head. "Not Jack. He never took along extra supplies. He traveled as lightly as possible. He was a fanatic about it. Someone was with him, and I doubt that they would both accidentally drown and disappear."

"Do the police agree with you that there was a second person?"

"It hasn't been firmly established. Not yet."

"Did Jack tell you about his plans that day?"

"No, but he talked to Vance, and apparently didn't mention anyone joining him."

Pierce tapped his notebook with his pen. "Do you think Vance has something to hide?"

"That's a good question, and a tricky one for you."

"Right. I'm not investigating Vance, but if the evidence points to him, I'm not going to hide it."

"That would be ironic."

"Yeah and I probably wouldn't get paid."

Garity laughed. "More irony."

Pierce rubbed his jaw. "How was Jack acting before he disappeared? Did you notice anything unusual about his behavior?"

Garity sank down into an upholstered chair. "I'm convinced Jack was involved in something that he was keeping from me, and he was in over his head. I could tell something was bothering him. It was affecting his health. He wasn't the same anymore."

"Can you be more specific? How was he different?"

"We were good friends. We fished whenever we could get away. But in the last couple of years, he'd become reclusive, and he seemed almost anemic. He'd divorced his wife and spent most of his time by himself at home or in his lab."

"Divorces can do that sort of thing." Pierce spoke from experience. When he and Tina had separated, he'd stopped seeing most of their old friends.

"No, there was more to it. Every time I saw him, I felt this barrier. I had the feeling he was holding something back from me. It was almost as if he'd gone through some sort of religious conversion and couldn't talk about it. I asked him once if there was anything he wanted to tell me, but he just shrugged and said he was having a little difficulty with a woman he was seeing."

"Isabel?"

Garity looked up, and Pierce tried to read his expression. *Confusion. That was all he saw.* "That's right. What do you know about her?"

"Not much. Tell me about her."

"Nothing to tell. Jack didn't want to talk about her."

"Do you think she was the other person in the canoe?"

"Maybe. I'm disappointed that the police have found nothing on her. It's as if she never existed."

"Speaking of the police, the lady next door said one of the investigators died. Is that true?"

"Actually, two of them are dead."

"Oh, yeah?"

"Morales, the first detective assigned to the case, died of cardiac arrest about four months ago. He had a history of heart problems. Frank Davis took over, and he died three weeks ago in a scuba diving accident."

"How'd it happen?"

"He was out diving alone and made a big mistake. He jumped overboard without opening the air value on his tank or inflating his buoyancy compensator. He sank right to the bottom; he must have panicked."

Lightening momentarily lit up the room. Pierce moved over to the window and looked out at the rain. Despite the oddities— the extra paddle and the missing girlfriend—in all likelihood Jack Garity was dead and his death, like those of the detectives, was accidental. His brother suspected murder, and was using his political power to keep a detective on the case.

"Mrs. Greenfelder said that a Detective Bunker is on the case now."

"Drucker. Buddy Drucker has been on it for two weeks. I've only talked to him once briefly. If he's focusing his investigation on Vance, he didn't tell me."

"Who reported your brother missing?"

"Vance. He called me when Jack didn't show up for work." Garity's gray eyes studied Pierce. "Are you going to talk to Jack's ex-wife, Carla?"

"I'm planning on it."

"Ask her about Vance. Before the divorce, Jack thought that she and Vance were having an affair."

Great. The whole thing was getting murkier by the minute. "I'll ask Vance about it, too."

"You might also look at the police file. It's probably a mess, with all the changes in detectives, but it might be worthwhile."

Garity was starting to sound as if he were running Pierce's investigation, and that made him uneasy. "The police don't usually hand over the files of an active case to just anyone who walks in the door, even if he's got a P.I. license."

"I'll call the sheriff tomorrow morning and see that it's made available to you. He's a friend, and sympathetic."

The file would be helpful, but Pierce was wary about the judge's motives.

He walked over to a glass cabinet and examined the trinkets Jack Garity had left behind. Among them were a cup with his name on it, several sterling silver candle holders, a collection of carved stone turtles, and a few more photographs.

He opened the cabinet door and picked up a snapshot; a young Wayne Garity in uniform holding a rifle.

"I was a second lieutenant," Garity said as he came up behind him.

"Did you see any combat?"

"I didn't only see it, I was part of it. Two tours."

So he knows how to kill.

Pierce put the photo back on the shelf. "Can I take a look around?"

"Of course."

Pierce inspected every room. The house gave him a sense of what Jack Garity was about, but he was also looking for anything that was out of place or didn't fit.

When he commented on how neat everything was, the judge said that his brother's life was like that. "Everything had its place. Jack never acted out of confusion."

They stepped into Garity's study, a room in the rear of the house. French doors opened from it onto a wooden deck, with a Jacuzzi in one corner. Sheets of rain swept across the deck and backyard and pounded against the window.

"Mind if I look in his desk drawers?"

"Go ahead."

"Did the police remove anything?"

"They took his computer. That was it. They gave the place a thorough search, but didn't come up with anything else."

Pierce sat down in Garity's desk chair, and opened the top desk drawer. It contained the usual office supplies—writing paper, envelopes, pens and pencils, stamps. Two additional drawers on either side were deeper, like file drawers. The left one was stacked with technical journals and newsletters related to industrial chemistry. The other drawer was empty, except for a couple of news magazines fanned across the bottom.

Pierce looked around the room. "No files?"

"There's a file cabinet in the closet. It's mostly income tax returns and other household files. I think every detective on the case has looked them over."

Pierce stepped over to the closet, and picked through the files for a few minutes. They were neatly labeled and alphabetically organized. Garity hovered over him as if he were watching to make sure Pierce didn't mess anything up.

Finally, he closed the file drawer and turned off the closet light.

"So, what's your impression, Nick?"

"My impression is that this place doesn't look like the home of a man who was depressed and who might want to run away from his life."

"I didn't say Jack was depressed. I said he kept to himself." Garity rose up on the balls of his feet again as he spoke. It was something that Pierce had seen other short men do, especially those in positions of authority.

He moved over to a bookcase built into one of the walls of the study. A couple of the shelves were dedicated to chemistry manuals and texts. On another, he saw several biographies of scientists—Einstein, Edison, Tesla, De Vinci. There were also a few more eclectic titles: *The Presence of the Past,* by Rupert Sheldrake; another called *Margins of Reality* and subtitled, *The Role of Consciousness in the Physical World.*

Pierce was about to pull that one off the shelf when he noticed a couple of markers sticking out of a book called, *The True Chemistry of Humankind.* The volume looked old, so old that the name of the author was worn away. He carefully picked it up. The binding was loose; it had been well read.

As he paged through it, he saw that the text was sprinkled with terms like 'seed-water', 'spirit-fire', and 'thought-earth'. There was a whole section called 'The Circulation of Light', and frequent references throughout to the 'true chemistry'. On several pages, paragraphs were underlined, and there were occasional comments penned in the margin.

One paragraph was boxed in red ink. He read it over twice.

I was no longer breathing. Yet, somehow I was alive. It seemed that my normal respiration had been replaced with an inner breathing, of a nature that was totally foreign to me. It was as if another being was keeping me alive. I was in a state of rapture. I knew ecstasy.

It sounded like a description of auto-erotic asphyxiation, masturbating while a rope or some other binding cut off one's oxygen supply—a practice that sometimes resulted in accidental death. He doubted that was what *The True Chemistry of Humankind* was about, but he wanted to read more. Especially because of the margin note against the marked paragraph, which read: *YES! YES!*

He pointed to the words. "Do you think that's your brother's handwriting?"

Garity's eyes ran across the page. "I know it is. That's his capital Y. He makes a little hook at the bottom."

"You ever seen this book?"

Garity briefly paged through it, his brow furrowed. "No, but Jack never talked much about his professional life to me."

"You mind if I borrow it?"

"I suppose it's okay. The cops took the computer. You can borrow a book."

Pierce didn't know what the book had to do with Jack Garity's career, but he figured it might have something to do with his state of mind at the time of his disappearance.

He glanced out the window. "I think the rain's letting up."

"I should be going," Garity said. "I'd appreciate it if you would keep me apprised of your investigation."

"I'm sure we'll be talking. Thanks for your help."

Dealing with Garity would require a delicate balance. He wanted the judge's help, but he also wanted to keep him at arm's length.

They stepped outside into the humid evening and Garity locked the door. "Good luck, Nick."

Pierce slid behind the wheel and set the book on the passenger seat as Garity backed his Mercedes out of the driveway.

He glanced at his watch. *Five to eight. Still time to talk to a few neighbors.*

Pierce waited until Garity was gone, then quickly crossed the street.

The first couple of people he talked to had little new insight to offer into either Garity's disappearance or his day-to-day life. They were helpful, but didn't know much, and he could tell their answers were a repetition of what they'd already said two or three times.

That was the problem with this investigation. Overkill.

He stopped at the house where he'd seen the woman in shorts sweeping, hoping for something better. She was in her mid-twenties, as slender and attractive as a star on an afternoon soap. He focused on her brown eyes as he told her who he was. She stared at him a moment, then slowly shook her head.

"Don't you guys ever give up? Garity's been dead since January. Is this what our tax dollars pay for, harassing neighbors about a dead man?"

"Sorry, but I'm not a police detective." He reached into his shirt pocket, removed a card, held it out. "As I said, I'm a private investigator."

"Good for you." She didn't even glance at the card. "Don't bother me again." She stepped back and slammed the door.

He heard the lock snap in place as he dropped card back in his shirt pocket. *Real friendly sort.* He decided to stop by Mrs. Greenfelder's house before he left. The way things were going, she might be the only helpful one on the block.

When Pierce knocked, the door opened a few inches. "You bringing the Persian?"

"The what, ma'am?"

She turned abruptly and he heard her say: "Get back now. You can't go out."

She looked up at Pierce again. "Well, are you Delilah's father or not?"

"Delilah? No."

"Then who are you?"

Pierce handed her his card. "Mrs. Greenfelder, I'm the private investigator you were talking to at the Garity place."

"Oh, I thought I recognized you. How'd you know my name?"

"Judge Garity told me."

"He did, did he. Well, if you want to talk, come in, but be quick about it."

Pierce stepped inside, his nose immediately twitching at the pungent odor. Lounging on the top of a piano to his right were two cats. There was another on the couch and two others under his feet.

He reached down to the nearest one. "Lots of cats."

"Right now, there're eleven or twelve, and I'm expecting Delilah any time. This is the Kitty Hotel. That's what I call my service."

Pierce noticed a couple more cats, several scratching posts, various stuffed toys, and in one corner a three-level, carpeted jungle gym.

She squinted at his card. "So what do you want now, Mr. Pierce?"

"I've just got a couple of questions. Did Mr. Garity have many visitors?"

"I already told you, didn't I? There've been more now that he's dead."

"What about when he was alive?"

"Not many. He used to go out a lot. Late at night. See, I'm an insomniac. I usually don't fall asleep until about four. I'd hear his car door slam around two or three some mornings."

Pierce rested his elbow on the top of the piano. "Was he leaving or coming home?"

She shrugged. "Sometimes one way, sometimes the other."

"Any idea where he spent his time that late?"

"I never asked. I didn't really know the man. He'd wave or say hello once in a while. That was it."

"Did he have a girlfriend?"

A black cat leaped up on the piano, hunched its back and rubbed against Pierce's shoulder. He absently petted it, and as he did, a Siamese also vaulted onto the piano top. Both cats hissed and bounded nimbly across the piano keys, performing a hurried, dissonant arpeggio before scampering away.

"Hey, you two! Stop it!" Mrs. Greenfelder shook her head. "Every time we have a thunderstorm, they get so nutty. Now what were you saying?"

"A girlfriend. Do you remember seeing one in the last months before he vanished?"

"Well, there was Carla. But I wouldn't call her a girlfriend."

"His ex-wife."

"She used to come over and visit quite a bit before she left him. Now I only see her a couple of times a year, when she leaves Percy, Bysshe and Shelley here. Three beautiful Himalayans."

"Did she stop by Garity's house much after she left him?"

She shook her head. "No reason to, I suppose. She'd had enough of him."

As Pierce figured he'd run out of questions, the older woman added that she'd last seen Carla some months ago. "I thought she was coming here, but she went into his house."

"Mr. Garity's been gone nine months. Was it much before that?"

Her eyebrows arched even higher in their penciled curves. "It was right before he disappeared."

He made an effort to sound casual. "Are you sure?"

"I remember thinking that maybe she and Mr. G were going to get back together, because she spent the night. Then a few day later, all the police started coming around."

"Did you tell that to the detectives?"

"I told Lt. Davis. Too bad about him. Such a nice man."

"Have you told Drucker, the new one?"

She shook her head. "He's allergic to cats. He only stayed a couple of minutes. Kept twitching his nose and his eye got all watery. He pushed one of the cats off the piano. I didn't like him much. You seem to like cats, though."

"Oh, sure. I like them fine." *One or two at a time, though, not a houseful.*

She nodded. "The world, you know, is divided between those of us who like cats and those who don't. We're the better ones, of course."

He let out a short laugh. "At least the cats think so. One more question. Any thoughts on what happened to Garity?"

She shrugged. "Me? I don't know. He was probably killed by a drug dealer, or he was running away from one. Or maybe he just died from drugs and they never found his body."

"Why do you think it was drug-related?"

"Most of the crimes down here are. I'm sure you know that." She leaned over and picked up a plump cat that must have weighed twenty pounds. "You know who this is?"

Pierce looked at the cat, which was staring at him. It was black, with one white paw and a coin dangling from its collar. "'fraid we've never met."

"Why, this is Two-Bits. See the gold quarter on his neck? That's his lucky charm."

"Nice." He'd already taken a step back, ready to leave, when he suddenly realized he'd seen another coin like that just recently.

"It's Mr. Garity's cat. I sort of adopted him."

Vance had a similar coin on a chain. A coincidence?

His thoughts were interrupted by a knock.

"Oh, this must be the Persian. What was her name again?"

"Delilah," Pierce said.

She held out Garity's cat. "Hold him, will you? He always tries to escape when I open the door."

Pierce carefully took the cat, keeping its claws from digging into his chest. He reached for the coin to take a closer look, but Two-Bits struggled as the door opened, jerked its head around and clawed his shoulder. The coin fell into his hand.

A blond woman surrounded by an aura of perfume stepped into the house. Pierce moved aside, ducking to avoid her umbrella. As he did, a pug-faced Persian scowled at him through its travel cage, then hissed at Two-Bits.

As the door closed, he set the cat down and Two-Bits scampered away. Thanking Mrs. Greenfelder, he nodded to the woman, and quickly exited the cat house, taking a deep, refreshing breath of warm, humid air.

He rubbed his scratched shoulder and as he did so, realized that he'd forgotten to return the coin.

He was about to knock, but thought better of it. He dropped it into his pocket and headed for his car. Now he had an excuse to come back. She'd probably be grateful and talkative.

He glanced at his watch and cursed under his breath. *Ten to nine.* He would never make it to Padrino's on time.

Late again.

Chapter 7

By the time Pierce arrived at Padrino's, another thunderstorm had erupted and torrential rains were sweeping across the parking lot. He pulled into a space less than fifty feet from the entrance, but knew that he'd still be soaked by the time he reached the door.

He peered through the rain-splattered windows and spotted Elise's VW Cabriolet a couple of spaces away. He could sit out here until the rain let up, but Elise had probably been waiting at least fifteen minutes already.

He found a plastic bag in the back seat, and wrapped it around the book he'd taken from Garity's house. Holding it over his head, he rushed across the parking lot.

He burst through the door, and futilely attempted to shake the rain from his clothes, wiping his face as best he could and running a hand through his wet hair. As usual, Padrino's was packed. Nearby several patrons were laughing and talking amiably as the cashier rang up their check. No one had noticed his explosive entrance. No one except Elise, who was leaning against a wall a few feet from the cash register. Her arms were crossed and she'd been staring glumly ahead until she spotted him.

Pierce smiled and blinked as a raindrop rolled down his forehead and into his eye. "It's really pouring."

Elise handed him a couple of napkins. "Punishment for your tardiness," she said.

"Is that the only greeting I get?"

"Hey, I've been here for eighteen minutes now."

"Sorry. I got tied up. A new case."

"Forget it. What's the book?"

"Let's get a table, and I'll tell you about it."

The hostess approached. "How many?"

Pierce held up two fingers.

"No, three," Elise corrected.

He glanced sharply at her. "That's right, Umberto."

"I thought you might like to meet him. " They followed the hostess across the room. "I think you two might like each other. Or at least you'll know who I'm talking about." The words rushed out of her mouth as if she were trying to explain away the awkward situation she'd created.

"I already have something in common with him. We're both late. Where is he?"

"I'm sure he'll be along any time now."

Pierce set the book on the floor as they sat down. Suddenly, he wasn't in the mood to talk about his case. He stared at the menu, which was doubling as a shield between them.

"Nick, hello. Talk to me, will you? What's wrong?"

He raised his gaze and shrugged. "Nothing."

"Are you jealous of Umberto?"

He lowered the menu. "Should I be?"

Her hand snaked across the table toward him. "Of course not. I mean, Christ, Nick, if there was anything going on between Umberto and me, I certainly wouldn't bring him to dinner with you."

He forced a smile. It was the first encouraging thing he'd heard from her about the mysterious relationship. "I guess not."

"Don't be angry, okay? You'll like him."

"I'm not angry. I just don't know what to think." After a year, he was used to her peace-making overtures, as well as her quick-tempered salvos. Outburst and reconciliation happened in such rapid succession that it was difficult to keep up with her.

They ordered a carafe of wine, and Elise suggested they give Umberto another ten minutes before ordering dinner. Pierce glanced toward the entrance, and said that was fine with him.

There was nothing particularly special about the ambiance of the place. The decorations were mundane. No one wore traditional costumes. No one serenaded them. It was simply a

Cuban restaurant with large portions of tasty food for low prices;
and he couldn't complain about that.

"By the way, who answered your phone this afternoon?"
Elise asked.

"I've got a new secretary."

"Another one."

"Trudy quit." He told her what happened. Elise shook her
head in disbelief as she heard how Trudy had delivered his lunch
and collected her last check.

"But I got lucky. The ad just came out, and Janet was the first
one to apply. I didn't have to look any further. If anything, she's
over-qualified. She even has experience working for investigators."

"Is she good-looking, too?"

"Sort of. I mean, yeah, she is."

"Did you check her references?"

"I'm going to, but I don't think she's lying."

"If she's so experienced, why doesn't she work for a big agency
with good pay?"

"Because she wants to become an investigator herself. I'm
going to sponsor her for a license."

Elise' smile faded, her mouth turned down. "Does that mean
she's going to be your partner?"

"I didn't say that. I'm just going to sponsor her. Like Harold
Dixon sponsored me. You remember, I told you about him."

Dixon had worked as a P.I. on Miami Beach for forty years.
They'd met when Dixon had stopped by the travel agency to talk
about possible places to retire outside the U.S. Within a couple of
months, Pierce had begun working part-time for Harold. Two
years later, he'd become a licensed P.I., and Dixon had retired to
Costa Rica.

"Sounds like things progressed pretty far with you two in a
very short time."

"Hey, I'm just glad to have someone in the office who knows
the difference between a plaintiff and a defendant. Let's talk
about something else. Have you talked to Bill Sabo lately about
your father's notebook?"

"As a matter of fact, I have. I'm going to see him tomorrow to
discuss it in more detail."

Pierce had met Sabo a couple of years earlier at a seminar he'd given on cryptography. At the time, Pierce had been baffled by a series of coded messages a young woman had received on three consecutive weeks. She'd wanted him to find out who was sending them and what the messages said. It had taken Sabo about ten minutes to unravel the first two, and another ten minutes for the third. They were cryptograms, like those that were published on the comics page of newspapers.

The first one said: *She was going out with a painter, but she gave him the brush off.* The second was similar: *She admired a skydiver, but he wouldn't fall for her.* It was the last one that held the key. *I was her teacher, but she's taught me so much. Francine, my love, you are a puzzle to me, a mystery deeper than the farthest reaches of the universe. What secret message is hidden here? Only one: Happy Birthday. Yours, Sam.*

The message had been sent to her anonymously by her boyfriend, who lived with her, and who had insisted that she seek help when she'd been unable to figure them out. Pierce was somewhat annoyed by the frivolous boyfriend, who answered the phone when he called. But Pierce had agreed to hold off two days and to deliver the transcribed message on Francine's birthday.

"Hello, Nick. You still here? I swear you can leave the planet between sips of wine."

"Sorry. So has Bill gotten anywhere with the notebook?"

"He says he hasn't had much time to work on it, but I've got a lead that may help speed things along." She explained what Umberto had told her, and his thoughts about the notebook.

"So Umberto doesn't believe in divination for the masses, only for advanced beings like himself," Pierce said when she finished.

She was trying not to laugh. Then her back stiffened. "Here he is now. He just walked in the door. Please, be civil."

Pierce turned as Umberto approached the table, wearing jeans, cowboy boots and a black shirt. He greeted Elise, then extended his hand to Pierce. "How are you, Nick?" Umberto nodded, and took the chair across from him. "I hope I didn't keep you waiting."

"No, not at all," Elise said. "Nick just arrived."

Pierce cleared his throat to keep from laughing. Then he noticed that Umberto looked perfectly dry. "I'm still wet. How come you're not?"

Umberto shrugged. "It stopped raining."

"Glass of wine?" Elise asked.

Umberto declined, saying water was fine for him. "To make up for the rain I missed," he added in his accented English, smiling at Pierce.

Pierce signaled the waitress. *"Estamos listo."*

"You're ready to order?" she answered.

The waitress exchanged friendly banter in Spanish with Umberto and Elise, but replied to Pierce in English when he ordered.

"I hate it when they do that," Pierce said when she walked away.

"She thought she was doing you a favor," Umberto said. "You've got an accent. It sounds like you're speaking English."

"Thanks a lot. Your English sounds like you're speaking Spanish."

Umberto laughed. "So we're in the same ship. When I speak English, the Latinos answer me in Spanish."

"Boat. We're in the same boat."

Spanish had always been hit and miss for Pierce. After his family moved to Miami, he'd enrolled in a Spanish class at North Miami High and found himself surrounded by Cubans who already spoke the language fluently. He'd felt like a first grader among seniors. His Spanish finally improved during a summer spent in Mexico, and by the time he'd graduated from high school and attended Columbia University, he'd become fluent in the language—in spite of his accent.

Elise, on the other hand, was truly bilingual. She'd grown up in Guatemala, attending school in the capital. She was an *aplatanada*, literally a 'banana-fied person', someone who shifted smoothly between Anglo and Hispanic cultures.

"I was just telling Nick about our meeting this afternoon,

and how much I appreciate your help."

Pierce expected to hear Umberto boast that it was really nothing, a sort of Mayan crossword puzzle that insiders did before breakfast. Instead, when he spoke, his tone was serious. "I gave Elise the form. Now she must find the contents. I know nothing of Barba's strange writing."

"I couldn't figure it out, either," Pierce said.

When neither men said anything further, Elise broke the uneasy silence. "Nick has a new case he's working on. Can you tell us about it, Nick?"

"Not really much to tell yet. I've been hired to look for a missing person."

"Who's missing?"

Pierce usually didn't talk about his cases with anyone other than Elise, but in deference to her attempt to keep the conversation flowing, he described his evening at Garity's house and his interviews with the neighbors. "They weren't much help. They've already been interviewed by three detectives, so no one was too pleased to see me."

"Why so many detectives?" she asked.

"The first two died."

"That's strange. What happened?"

"Accidents."

Elise frowned. She had a face that emotion loved; nothing was ever hidden there for long. He knew she was going to say something about the deaths.

"I don't like it, Nick. It sounds suspicious."

"People die all the time."

Elise turned to Umberto. "Don't you think it's dangerous for him to be involved in a case like that, where two investigators have already died?"

Umberto stared at Pierce in a way that made him feel as if the man were looking through him. "He uses danger to draw energy to him. The threat of death makes him feel more alive."

Pierce laughed. *This guy talks like a fortune cookie.* But he could tell that it wasn't the answer that Elise had expected.

"Well, I just want him to stay alive," she murmured.

What Umberto had said sounded vaguely profound, but it

was also something that could apply to anyone who dealt in life-or-death matters. "I wouldn't say that my job is exactly a thrill a minute."

"That's why you crave danger," Umberto answered.

More jungle psychology. "I guess you've got me all figured out, Umberto."

"He didn't say that, Nick," Elise replied sharply.

"No offense meant," Pierce responded.

"I only told you what I see, Nick," Umberto said. "I mean no offense to you, either."

"Well, I'm glad nobody's offending anyone," Elise said as their dinners arrived, shaking her head. During the meal, she made another attempt to explain Umberto's comments. "Nick, Umberto has a way of sometimes seeing things that aren't readily apparent."

Pierce popped a chunk of buttery plantain in his mouth. "That's nice."

"Umberto, can you tell Nick something about his case that he should know?"

The Guatemalan looked irritated by the question. "I am not a gypsy fortune teller. My work is serious, and it takes all my energy. I have little left over."

"I know that you're teaching at the university," Pierce said. "Is that the work you're talking about?"

"Umberto is writing a book about the Tzolkin."

"Do you know about the Mayan sacred calendar?" Umberto asked.

"It's impossible not to know about it, with Elise around." He wondered if Umberto could possibly be even more preoccupied with the calendar than Elise was. He'd once suggested that she diversify her professional interests to give her more flexibility in case she ever lost her job, but she'd taken umbrage and told him that he didn't know what he was talking about; you either specialized or got out of the field. High school science teachers were generalists; archaeologist were specialists within a specialty.

"My book is called *The Galactic Cycle: Beyond 2012*," Umberto said. "It's about what happens to the world after the current five-thousand-year cycle ends."

"So, you're going to spill the beans?"

Umberto looked down at the black beans on his plate, taking it literally. Elise touched his arm. "Nick is just making a joke."

"I don't think life would be much fun if we knew in advance what was going to happen," Pierce explained.

"That's a very good point. The world would be a dull place if we knew exactly what was going to happen. What I'm doing is presenting a blueprint. Many of the details of course are not set, and the times are imprecise. But I see a pattern, and that's what I want to reveal in my book."

"Even a blueprint sounds sort of fixed."

"I'm sure there will be many surprises and unanticipated shifts. My work is not perfect. I am not God."

"That's a revelation in itself," Pierce muttered.

"Nick!" Elise snapped.

"He makes light of the mystical, but he's interested in it," Umberto said. "I can tell."

"Whenever people get overly serious about mysticism, they build a church or temple around it and act like they have all the answers," Pierce remarked. "Then the codified religion with its rules and rituals becomes more important than its original mystical roots. That's a direct quote from Dr. Elise Simms."

"Not so loud," Elise hissed.

"Sorry. It must be something in the beans."

Umberto set his fork down next to his plate, and seemed to stare broodingly into his black beans. "This man who disappeared. What was he involved in that he kept hidden from everyone?"

Pierce shrugged. "I don't know."

Umberto looked up, his eyes narrowing. "There is something, and when you realize what it is, you'll be on the right track."

"That's good to know." Pierce picked at the chicken on his plate. Maybe Umberto was right, but what case *didn't* have something hidden to uncover?

Elise was about to say something more when Umberto suddenly struck the edge of his plate with his fork. "Someone thinks this hidden thing is very valuable. This person wants it very badly."

"I thought you didn't do this sort of thing," Pierce said.

Umberto stared blankly at him, then smiled. You're going to need all the help you can get with your investigation. Something is wrong about the way you are thinking about it."

Thanks for the encouragement. But what the hell. He'd play along. "The missing man had a girlfriend name Isabel. Is she important?"

Umberto cast his eyes down again. "Yes, and she is closer than you think."

Word games. "Tell me this. Was Jack Garity's death an accident?"

"Is he dead?" Umberto asked without looking up.

"Good question."

Umberto mixed his rice and beans together. "The man may still be alive. But he may not be for much longer."

Pierce pulled the napkin off his lap and wiped his mouth. As he did, his foot touched the book on the floor. He picked it up. "Do you think this book has anything to do with the case?"

He held it out for him, but Umberto made no effort to take it. "Who wrote it?"

Pierce hadn't looked at it since his first quick perusal, and realized he didn't know the answer. He opened to the title page.

"Lydia Mullen."

Elise held out her hand for the book, and he passed it to her.

"She is connected with the hidden thing," Umberto said confidently.

Pierce didn't know whether to be amazed or annoyed by Umberto's knowing, self-assured manner.

Elise paged through the book. "This is interesting," she commented. "It says that Mullen is a professor of chemistry at the University of Miami. But I've never heard of her."

"Look at the publication date," Pierce said.

"Oh, 1954."

"The time is unimportant," Umberto said.

Pierce couldn't let the comment pass unchallenged. "It is when you're looking for someone. It's damn important."

Elise didn't even bother to frown at Pierce's caviling remark. She concentrated on a page of the book. "You know what this is, don't you?"

"Not really."

"It's a text on alchemy."

Elise turned off the MacArthur Causeway and threaded her way through the dimly lit streets of South Beach on her way to Pierce's place, passing rows of aging Art Deco buildings. Even though he'd moved to a quiet neighborhood and had a great view of the bay, she still didn't like much of South Beach at night, especially when she was alone. There was always the sense that something was about to erupt here. Something bad. There were too many people, too many problems. The intensity registered under her skin and gave her the creeps. *Deco-decadence.*

But it wasn't fear that had kept her away from Pierce's house recently. She'd visited the place once, but had stayed only a few minutes.

The place symbolized his wish for independence, and she resented that. For several months, he'd all but moved into her house in Coconut Grove. He'd even been planning to get rid of his apartment; but then one night they'd discussed marriage, and Pierce had said he wasn't ready. *Just like that.* His memories of his failed marriage were still too strong, he said.

"Then maybe you shouldn't move in," she'd snapped.

"Maybe you're right," he'd answered, and had left.

She'd called and apologized the next day, but a month later he'd rented the South Beach house, leasing it for a year. He'd been living there for several weeks now, and she still felt hurt.

She turned into the narrow, tree-shrouded driveway, stifling an urge to just back up and go home. She could call him later, and say she'd changed her mind. But if she and Pierce were going to stay together, she had to accept the house, at least as a temporary situation; a transition.

Besides, there was another matter on her mind. In spite of Pierce's jovial remarks at dinner, she knew he was still feeling at odds with her over Umberto, and she wanted to deal with the problem right now.

Pierce was waiting outside his door for her. She wasn't surprised that he'd gotten here first, considering how he drove. Sixty through town was his style. This irreverent, impulsive side of him fascinated her; it contrasted so sharply with his more usual manner, which was generally very reticent. But it also made her wonder if she really knew him that well.

"I'm here," she said.

"You sure you want to come inside?"

"What do you mean by that?" she asked defensively.

"You've been avoiding the place like I've got demons hiding under the bed or something."

She touched his arm. "I've been busy this month. We both have."

"Don't you like the neighborhood?"

"I didn't say that."

"But you were thinking it. You know, the Grove has its share of crooks, too. They're just more successful."

"Real funny." Pierce liked to rib her about her living in Coconut Grove because it was considered a trendy neighborhood. "Truce, okay?"

He grinned in response and his hands slipped over the flare of her hips, as if to re-learn them. She felt the warmth of his palms through the fabric of her clothing.

"I guess I can let you in."

She ran her hands over his chest, hooked her fingers in his belt, and rolled up onto the balls of her feet to kiss him. She felt him growing hard against her and stepped back. "That guy says you'd better let me in."

He laughed, and they moved inside.

"Sambuca over ice?" he asked, already heading to the kitchen.

"You remembered."

"You're the only person I know who likes the stuff."

"Except you," she called after him.

She flopped down on the sofa, and saw the Mullen book sitting on his desk in the corner of the living room. He'd obviously already been inside, and had gone back out to meet her. She looked around now and noticed streaks of paint on the wall. *Pierce sampling the colors,* she thought. *Pierce the fix-up guy.*

The house was about fifty years old and had been renovated a few years earlier, but the best thing about it was its waterfront location. Many of the older homes like this one had been torn down and replaced with high-rise condos, but this one had been spared. It wasn't the greatest place, but it was far better than the previous apartment where he'd been living. That place had been awful. Cramped rooms, pipes that rattled, neighbors who you could hear through the walls, and roaches that invaded regularly.

"Here you go." He handed her a drink as he sat down next to her. "I'm glad you came over."

"I like your paint job." She pointed to the streaks on the walls.

"Oh, that. I'm going to paint this weekend."

She sipped her drink. "Don't go with the hunter green. The room's small enough as it is. That'll shrink it more."

"Thanks for the advice. You want to help with the painting, too?"

"Can't. I've got a conference at the university this weekend."

"What's the conference?"

"Meso-American astro-archaeology."

"Sounds very cosmic."

"Actually, it's a bunch of stuffy archaeologists and staid astronomers sharing their fieldwork fieldwork experiences and presenting papers."

"Is Umberto going to be there?"

She'd known he was going to ask that question. "Yeah, he will. He'll be presenting a paper."

"Is that why you're going? Because of him?"

"Nick, it's my field too." She hoped she sounded convincing. She hated conferences and rarely went to them unless she was directly involved. This one was an exception because of Umberto, but she couldn't tell Pierce that without making him feel even more jealous than he already was.

She sipped her drink. "Mm, a nice aperitif."

"An aperitif is a drink before dinner."

She smiled slyly and leaned toward him. "It can be before anything you want."

He slid an arm around her shoulder.

"What did you think about Umberto's comments on your case?"

"The pressure on her arm eased. "Do we have to talk about him?"

"Not if you don't want to." *He resented Umberto as much as she resented the house.* She leaned over and kissed him. "I guess you don't like him."

He pulled back from her. "I like Umberto just fine. He's a little arrogant though. I mean, for a guy with the initials U.U., he seems sort of me-me. But at least he did admit he wasn't God."

Elise squeezed the back of his neck. "Come on. Be serious. Do you think he said anything that 'll help with the case?"

"Was he getting that stuff from his beans?"

"What?"

"I swear, every time he came up with anything, he was staring at his beans."

She laughed. "He was just concentrating."

"We'll see how well he does. He did make some interesting observations." He sipped his drink. "What do *you* think of him? That's what I want to know."

"Well, he's engaging, intelligent, mysterious. I like him, but I don't love him. I love you."

"If he's all of those things, what am I?"

"Handsome, honest, fair-minded. A great lover. Mm ... reckless, a tad cynical ..."

"Okay. Stop there. You ran out of good qualities awful fast."

She wrapped her arms around his neck. "Oh, there're a lot more. But I've got something else on my mind." She pulled him close and one of her hands loosened his belt.

"Does this mean you're going to stay the night?" He stroked her through her blouse.

"You couldn't chase me out."

Chapter 8

Gibby and his wheelchair blocked Pierce's path to his office. "Nick, good morning," he said in a formal voice. "I hate to bother you, but about the windsurfer ..."

"Don't worry, Gib. It's going in a few minutes. I just got a roof rack this morning. It cost me a hundred and fifty bucks, if you can believe that. At least it's Swedish like the car."

"A Swedish roof rack?"

"That's what they said at the windsurfing shop. One of the maintenance guys from the hotel is going to help me haul everything downstairs."

"Hello, Nick." Janet Howarth had appeared like a mirage. She wore a red dress with a string of pearls.

"Morning, Janet." He introduced her to Gibby, who was tongue-tied for possibly the first time since Pierce had known him. He was staring at her high heels as if they were Cinderella's slippers.

"Nice to meet you." He pushed back into his office. "Talk to you later, Nick."

Pierce unlocked his office door, and ceremoniously handed Janet a key. "Now you are officially part of the ever-so-humble Pierce Agency."

"Glad to be here." She handed him her application. "While you look it over, I'll check your messages. The light's blinking on the machine."

He moved past her into his office and sat down with the application.

She was thirty-five, divorced. No dependents. All of her answers were neatly typed. He'd never hired anyone prior to taking the person's application before, but then Janet Howarth was no ordinary applicant. She was spectacularly well-qualified and her application revealed nothing that triggered any warning lights. Three referees were listed, all with addresses and phone numbers in Minneapolis or St. Paul.

"Hi, Nick. It's Wayne Garity." He looked up from the application as he heard the judge's recorded voice. "I just wanted to let you know that I had a chat this morning with Carla, Jack's ex, and she's more than willing to cooperate. In fact, she'll be home this afternoon. It would be a good time to catch her, because she's leaving town tomorrow and will be gone for a few days. Just let her know you're coming. Here's her number."

"That's the only one," Janet said as Garity hung up. Before Pierce could reply, the phone rang, and she snapped it up. "Pierce Agency. How can I help you?" She sounded as if she'd worked for him for years. "One moment, please. I'll see if Mr. Pierce is available." She press the hold button. "It's Kurt Vance."

"I'll take it in my office."

"I was going to call you," Pierce told Vance.

"I beat you to it. How's it going?"

"Okay." He briefed Vance on his visit to Garity's house.

"So you met the judge. I'm glad he's being helpful. What's he got against me, anyhow?"

"Nothing that I can tell. I'm going to look at the police file this morning, and see if I can talk to Detective Drucker."

"That's good. Tomorrow's Saturday, and there's supposed to be a light breeze out of the southeast. Perfect conditions for a first windsurfing lesson. What do you say about tomorrow afternoon? That'll give you another day on the case, and then we can talk things over."

Pierce didn't feel much like taking a lesson in anything right now, but at least he could double it up with business. "Okay, where?"

"I'll save you some time. I'll meet you on Key Biscayne. You know the causeway just over the Rickenbacker, where everybody goes? It's a good place to learn."

"Sure, I know it. I live down here, remember?"

"And you're in windsurfing heaven. Hell, I'd love to live

within a few minutes of Virginia Key, especially when those nor'easters blow in. Let's make it two o'clock. I'll be driving my gold Range Rover, and why don't you pick up a video on beginning windsurfing. It'll help you out."

Janet was picking her way through one of his file drawers as he hung up. "I'm just trying to get a sense of your filing system. I hope you don't mind? I'm not looking into any files."

Pierce laughed. "Look all you want. You'll be working with the files every day. If you think you can come up with a better way organizing them, let me know. I'm going to make some coffee."

She brushed her dark hair over her shoulder, revealing a tanned neck. "I'll make it."

Pierce shrugged. "Be my guest. My last secretary didn't drink coffee, so she figured she shouldn't have to make it, either."

"Well, I drink it. Besides, it's no big deal to make. Just show me where you keep everything."

As they waited for the coffee to brew, Pierce told Janet about the Garity case.

"So do you think that he's still alive?" she asked, as she filled two cups.

"I don't know much of anything yet. If I could find Isabel, the girlfriend, I'd be a lot better off."

Janet sat on the edge of her desk, one knee crossed over the other. "Any leads yet?"

"Only an off-beat one and it may have nothing to do with the girlfriend or with his disappearance. But I'd like you to check it out for me."

"Be glad to."

"Lydia Mullen."

She wrote down the name.

"You think it's an alias for Isabel?"

"I really doubt that. Mullen's a little old for our boy Garity. She was a professor at the University of Miami in the early fifties. See if you can track her down? Garity seemed to have some interest in her work. It's just a hunch."

"What kind of work was she involved in?"

He told her about the book, explaining that it was as treatise on alchemy. Reaching into his pocket, he flipped the cat's gold quarter in the air, caught it, then held it up between his thumb and index fingers. "You know, transforming base metals to gold?"

"Where did you get that from?"

Pierce grinned. "From Garity's cat. It hung from his collar."

"Really. Is it gold?"

"Well, it's gold colored. Maybe gold plated. I haven't taken it to a jeweler yet."

"I could do that for you."

He waved a hand. "I want to show it to his wife this afternoon. She may have something to say about it. Now—I've got to move that windsurfer out of the hall before Gibby has a fit."

"Do you windsurf?"

"Not yet. But soon."

Just then, the hotel maintenance man stuck his head into the office and said he was ready.

"Good timing. I was just about to look for you." He turned to Janet. "You got that number for Carla Garity?"

She ripped off the top square of paper from the pink memo pad on her desk and handed it to him.

"Thanks. First I'm heading downtown to Metro-Dade PD. Sorry to leave you by yourself on your first day. You can clean out your desk, of course, and I'd appreciate it I you put a new announcement on the recorder. Nothing snappy; just straight-forward and business-like."

"Got it. No problem. I'll field calls and get acquainted with the place. Hopefully, I'll have an answer for you on Lydia Mullen before I leave."

"You think so? That would be terrific. I'll call you this afternoon." Pierce glanced back as he was about to close the door behind himself. "By the way, if there are any more calls about the job, just tell them the position's been filled."

Elise drove around Bill Sabo's neighborhood in Kendall for ten minutes before finding Bougainvillea Lane. She glanced at her watch as she parked in front of his two-story house; a couple of minutes to eleven. As usual, it paid to leave early, no matter what Pierce thought.

She rang the doorbell and waited. When no one answered, she wondered if Sabo might've forgotten their meeting. Then the door swung open and Sabo was standing there in a bathrobe.

"Elise, you caught me in the shower."

"I'm sorry."

"Come in. I'll be right with you." He led her to his study and she took a seat in a chair next to his desk. The clock on the wall said eight minutes to eleven, and she remembered her watch was set five minutes fast. She felt like an idiot.

When Sabo joined her, she apologized again.

"Oh, forget it. I'm glad to see you." He sat down behind his desk.

Sabo was in his late forties, balding at the crown of his head. He sported a trim goatee and horned-rimmed glasses, with an open-collar shirt and dress slacks. Socks, but no shoes. He reminded her of Dr. Seuss, minus the bow tie.

They chatted for a couple of minutes about the university and the new fall session. When the conversation waned, Elise briefly told Sabo about Umberto and his impression of her late father's cryptic notebook.

Then she showed Sabo a sheet of paper on which she'd copied the four shorthand words. Next to each she'd written the meanings Umberto had suggested. From top to bottom, they read: WARRIOR, OPPONENT, BATTLE, AND OUTCOME.

Sabo studied the sheet for a few seconds, then laid it on his desk and scribbled something to the right of each key word. "Hopefully, his deduction will work right into what my students and I have figured out. You see, I made it a class project."

"Your students translated the notebook?" she asked.

Sabo held up a hand. "In a way, yes. But don't worry, they didn't read it. I'll show you what I mean."

Elise looked over his shoulder and saw he'd written from top to bottom: KOT, AVOT, K'OSHOSH, VAH. She said the four words to herself. "What is it?" she asked.

"It's my transcription of the code."

She shook her head. "I don't understand."

"Do the words mean anything to you?"

"Not off-hand. What are they?"

"I was hoping you knew. Here, take a look." He opened a briefcase and took out a file of type-written pages. "This is the transcribed version of the notebook. You see, there's a consistency in the placement of vowels and consonants that resembles language, not code. Maybe your father spoke a native idiom?"

Elise stared at the first page. When she'd seen just the four words, she hadn't recognized them. But now with a page of writing, she realized immediately what it was. ", Bill, you've done it! It's Tzotzil, a Mayan dialect. God, this is great. How did you do it?"

"I'll show you." He picked up the original notebook, turned to the last page, and tapped his finger against two words. "I guessed that this was your father's name, and the key to the code. You see, if you shift forward one letter in the alphabet for each letter in these two words, then INGM RHLLR becomes John Simms. Not much of a challenge there. The problem is that nothing else spelled anything that made sense."

"Fascinating."

"At first I thought the notebook was written in double code, and that I'd transcribed it from one code to another using the name as the key. But when I couldn't break the second code, it led me to believe that it was in fact a language. Since your father spent so much time in Central America, I assumed it was an Indian language. Do you speak the dialect?"

"No, but I can get the notebook translated. Umberto speaks Tzotzil fluently."

"That's wonderful."

She stared at the page, looking forward urgently to showing Umberto the transcribed text. "How did your students get involved?"

"After I'd broken the code, I made copies for everyone and gave them one night to break it. Four of the twenty-two were successful. All the others got another assignment, a more mundane one, to transcribe and type five pages each using the code. By the next class, I had the whole notebook ready for you.

They're all very interested in finding out what it's all about, by the way."

"Give them my thanks and tell them that as soon as I know more, I'll let you know."

Sabo stroked his goatee. "Tell me one thing, Elise. Why in the world would your father go to such lengths to first translate his text into Tzotzil, then codify it?"

"I think I know. He wanted to protect his work from the wrong people. You see, toward the end of his life, he became concerned about his work being stolen from him. He had a bad experience with a partner."

In fact, his career was virtually ruined when his attempt to promote knowledge of the ancient American legends through a commercial venture with Raymond Andrews was misused. Replicas of artifacts, which were sold with a booklet of legends, were promoted as having mystical qualities that would heal or protect their owners. They were sold primarily in Europe and Asia for outrageous sums. In the aftermath of the scandal, her father had been forced to retire, but Andrews had somehow escaped untarnished.

"I don't know anything about divination systems," Sabo said. "But I'd be interested in seeing how it works when you've got it translated. Maybe you can make a presentation to my class."

"I'd be happy to do it. Divination is sort of a paranormal cryptography, after all."

"It should make for an interesting class. What are you planning to do with it?"

Elise thought a moment. "I don't know. Maybe that's the first question I'll ask the oracle. 'What should be done with you'?"

What a job, Erickson thought, as he cruised along Sunrise Boulevard in Fort Lauderdale, en route to a windsurfing shop.

Windsurfing, for chrissake. His passion, his avocation; and now, part of his job.

During his college days, he'd spent four years on the Caribbean summer race circuit, and in his senior year he'd won an event in the Dominican Republic and finished in the top five overall. And that had been with only one sponsor and a fraction of the gear that most of his competitors had available to them.

After he'd graduated, he'd considered going into racing full-time, but had eventually changed his mind. He'd gone on to the police academy instead and had worked for the Dare County Sheriff's Office in Cape Hatteras, where he'd windsurfed in his spare time. After two years, he'd quit his cop job to go back to racing, but after a year he'd grown tired of the traveling and waiting.

That more than anything. It seemed he was always waiting: waiting for the next race, then waiting for the wind to kick up.

At his parents' urging and expense, he'd gone back to college for a master's degree in criminal justice studies, and had then landed the job with the intelligence branch of the Department of Energy. And that had led him here.

He turned into a parking lot of Windsurfing Madness on Sunrise. He'd never figured that his windsurfing experience would ever help him in a real career, especially one related to law enforcement. But here he was at work and ready to buy all the gear he needed, and then sail.

Incredible. Just to spy on a fellow windsurfer. *What a hoot.*

He thought of several of the rookies he'd gotten to know in Washington, before he'd been asked to transfer to Miami for a year of training in clandestine operations. They wouldn't believe it if he told them what he was doing or how much he was getting paid to do it. And that he was banging the boss lady.

But of course, he couldn't talk about any of it. The only person he felt he could confide in was Wendy, and he'd arranged to meet her in an hour, at a coffee shop down the street.

It hadn't been easy to arrange the meeting, either. Martin kept close tabs on him, and kept him going twelve hours a day, requiring reports at the office every evening.

Erickson was a bit surprised by how easily their relationship had developed. She was great. Not a bit inhibited, and she'd shown him a thing or two, but it was like sport for her; nothing serious. Not like his relationships with a couple of other women his own age, who had both wanted exclusive relationships.

But she was still his boss, and she still wasn't telling him the real story about what they were doing. He was hoping Wendy Spenser would fill him in.

Erickson walked into the shop, and smiled as he saw the array of boards and sails. At his suggestion, Martin had allocated five grand for this trip. Hell, he should've asked for six … but five was fine. He'd pick up a long board, preferably a Fanatic Mega Cat just like the one he'd seen on Vance's garage wall; that would give him an opening for a conversation. He'd also need a slalom/wave board for the windier days. Maybe a Seatrend Bump'n'Jump, or a BIC Electric Rock, or a Rap.

He'd also need three or four sails, a couple of masts and booms, and a few accessories.

Spenser might have the inside track on Vance's heart, but Erickson knew how to reach his soul.

When Erickson arrived at the coffee shop, Spenser was seated in a booth eating an antipasto salad. He slid in across from her.

"So, I was wondering if you were going to stand me up," she said.

"I had to finish my shopping spree and load the van with the gear."

"How's your goose jibe?" she asked.

Erickson grinned. "Say what?"

"Goose jibe?"

"Duck jibe. You duck under the boom. You don't get goosed by it."

She tossed her head and her thick blond hair rippled off her shoulders. "I wouldn't know. I heard Vance talking on the phone to one of his windsurfing buddies."

"Sounds like he's anxious to get out there."

"I swear it's all Vance talks about, and I don't know what he's talking about half the time. He listens to long-range weather forecasts everyday on a weather radio."

"He's hungry for wind."

"Maybe you should be working for him, not me."

Erickson gave her a long assessing look. Blue eyes, high cheekbones, full lips. He'd been looking forward to working with her from the moment he'd met her, but other than a couple of meetings at the office, he'd hardly seen her in the past month. "I think he's more interested in someone like you than me. Are you and Vance, you know ...?"

"What? Are we what?" She glared at him.

He smiled. "C'mon, you know what I mean. Are you two doing a number together?"

"How about zero? How's that for a number?"

"It's more of a place-holder. You telling me that you're shutting him out?"

"I'm telling you I'm not doing anything I don't want to do. What about you and Isabel?"

Erickson looked surprised.

Spenser leaned across the table. "She told me."

"What did she say?"

"That you grabbed her on the boat," Spenser replied.

"That wasn't exactly the way it happened. And why would she tell you anything?"

"She confides in me. I think she likes to try to shock me."

"What else did she say?"

Spenser leaned back and picked at her salad. "That's why you wanted to see me, isn't it? You wanted to know what it's all about."

"I like to see you, too."

"You don't have to flatter me."

"No, I mean it. I like you. If things were different, who knows ..."

"Right. Well, things are the way they are."

"So, what's the deal with Vance?" Erickson asked. "Why are we on the guy's case?"

"I'm not supposed to talk. She'd have my ass if she knew I was here."

He leaned over the table, picked a jalapeno pepper from her salad, and bit into it. "I'll tell you something about her, then you tell me what you know."

"Only if your gossip is worthwhile," Spenser said. "What is it?"

"I think she's coming down with a virus or something. I spent the night with her, and she got sick. You know, she threw up."

"Maybe that was your influence. Tell me something worthwhile."

"Real funny. Okay. It's got something to do with gold coins."

"Oh, yeah. How did you find that out?"

Erickson hesitated. "That's all I'm going to say. Now tell me about Jack Garity. Who is he, and why is she so interested in him?"

"All I know is that Garity's got something. Maybe it's gold coins. I don't know, but she wants it."

"So Garity's alive?"

"She thinks so."

"I get it," Erickson said. "She's hoping that Pierce can smoke him out."

"Could be."

Hell, he thought. *Spenser didn't know much more than he did.*

"What are you going to do this afternoon?" she asked.

"I'm supposed to go watch Garity's ex-wife again."

"What's she like?"

"She shops a lot, and plays tennis. How about you?"

"I'm going to get a little closer to Vance."

"Sounds like a good deal for him," Erickson muttered.

Chapter 9

Pierce approached the counter at Metro-Dade, and smiled as he spotted a woman intensely pecking away at a computer terminal. *"Psst. Flaca, como andas?"*

Deputy Carmen Horton raised her eyes from the video screen and a grin slowly spread across her face. *"Con dos pies,* Pierce. Be right with you."

He called her *flaca*—skinny—because Horton was long-legged and slender; and she liked the nickname. He'd met her here at the records office a couple of years ago when he'd stepped in and acted as translator for an old Cuban man who needed the report on a burglary for his insurance company. Horton had thanked Pierce in perfect Cuban Spanish, and then mimicked his accent. He'd been surprised and embarrassed. Not only had he not realized the black woman was Cuban, he'd even ignored her when she'd told him she could understand the old man.

Since then, he and Carmen Delgado Horton had sprinkled their conversations with Spanglish, Miami's own peculiar dialect, and she'd been a helpful contact. She got him public records on cases promptly, and she usually filled him in on any details she knew about the case or the investigating officer.

"Thought you'd be by today," she said.

"A premonition?"

"No, an order from the sheriff. I hear you got a new case."

So the judge had kept his word. "Jack Garity. Missing person. Do I get the file?"

"After you run through a one-man gauntlet."

"Who, you?"

"Huh, no such luck." She glanced around to make sure no

one was listening. "You've got to deal with Sgt. Detective Buddy Drucker. *Pobrecito.*"

"What's the story on Drucker?"

Her dark eyes flashed as she leaned over the counter and spoke in a low voice. "For starters, he's had three brutality complaints filed against him in the last year and a half."

"That doesn't sound like a new record or anything."

"No, but Drucker's a detective, not a patrolman. You take that into account and it's kind of peculiar. And it just so happens that the complaints were filed by two blacks and a Latino."

"Does that mean I'm safe around him?"

"Don't count on it. I hear he doesn't like P.I.'s much either, and he's pissed that you're getting the file."

"Figures. Any idea why he was put on this case?"

"Sure. He's being punished. Nobody wanted that one. It's jinxed."

"I heard about the mortality rate of the investigators. Accidents, though, right?"

She shrugged. "They're still dead."

"Good point. Do you know if Drucker has orders to let me make a copy of the file?"

"I don't know about copying it. But you're supposed to be able to look at it. He's in his office. I saw him walk by a few minutes ago."

"Show me the way."

She unlatched a gate, lifted a section of the counter and let him through. They moved along a hallway until they reached a large room divided into cubicles. Drucker was seated in his cubbyhole with his back to them.

Pierce knocked on an imaginary door at the cubicle entrance, and Horton elbowed him in the ribs. "Detective Drucker, someone here to see you."

Drucker was leaning over his desk, writing on a legal pad. When he ignored them, Horton crossed her arms and threw Pierce a look that said, *Told you so.*

Finally, Drucker slowly turned in his chair, eyed Pierce a moment, then focused on Horton. "Don't you know, Corporal Horton, that the proper procedure is for citizens to report to the dispatcher who then announces that a visitor is waiting?"

"Sorry. It's just that Mr. Pierce came to records, instead of to the dispatcher."

"Doesn't matter. Don't do it again." His low, gravelly voice made the order sound like a threat.

He pointed to a chair. "Sit down, Pierce."

Horton walked away—probably quietly cursing the detective with every step, Pierce thought, as he settled into a chair.

"I swear, it's getting so this place is as bad as the street, full of misfits and mutants."

Wow, Horton wasn't kidding.

Drucker's sandy hair was mussed, and he slouched in his chair in a way that emphasized his pot belly. There was a half-eaten sandwich on his desk and a yellow spot on his shirt where he'd recently tried to remove a mustard stain.

"I've been on this police force for eighteen years, Pierce." His penetrating brown eyes narrowed. "How long've you been a private investigator?"

"Almost eight years." Pierce didn't mention that five of those years had been part-time.

Drucker picked up his sandwich, took a bite, and spoke as he chewed. "I suppose Horton told you that I was some kind of bad-ass."

"Something like that."

Drucker laughed to himself, then stuffed the rest of the sandwich in his mouth. When he'd swallowed it, he brushed the crumbs from his shirt, and looked up at Pierce. "Relax, will ya? You're looking at me like I'm a goddamn attack dog, for chrissake. I've got a little problem with my temper sometimes, but this city is a zoo, a fucking madhouse some nights, and the bastards deserve what they get."

Drucker wiped his hands on his pants, then clasped his hands behind his head and leaned back in his chair. He gazed at the ceiling, probably re-living some late-night confrontation, then lowered his gaze, skewering Pierce.

"I've never laid a hand on a law-abiding citizen. Except maybe one guy with a video camera, who came nosing into a drug bust. He could've gotten himself blown away. I smashed that little Handicam right over his head."

"Is that why you got assigned to the Garity case?" Pierce asked, trying to turn the subject to the matter at hand.

"Something like that. So what do you want, Pierce?"

"I'm here about the file."

"Good for you." Drucker shook his head in disgust. "Lots of man-hours wasted on that case, and it's all politics. That's the only reason the fucking case is still open."

"Whose politics?" He had a good idea what Drucker meant, but wanted to hear him say it.

"Jesus," he groused, leaning back in his chair again. "Your boss, the judge, is one of the sheriff's cronies. And the sheriff happens to be up for re-election this fall."

"The judge isn't my boss."

"What do you mean? Garity hired you, didn't he?"

"No, Kurt Vance did."

Drucker looked startled, then angry. "I'll be damned. And the judge knows that?"

"Sure he does."

"Sonuvabitch." Drucker leaned forward as if he were about to launch himself over his desk at Pierce. He grabbed the handset of his phone and punched two numbers. "Captain, did you know this Pierce, the P.I. dude, is working for Vance?" A couple of beats passed. "Yeah, the Garity case, what else am I doing?" He tapped his fingertips on the desktop. "Yeah, Vance. Mr. Suntan in Lauderdale."

A muscle in Drucker's reddened cheek twitched as the captain said something to him. His fingers curled into a fist. "All right. All right." He hung up, spun his chair around, and grabbed a file box from the floor. "Shit, I don't believe this. Might as well let the crooks run their own investigations."

"You think Vance has something to do with Garity's disappearance?"

"He's only my prime suspect. But you won't get anything on him." He pulled out two file folders, then shoved the box across the desk. "There, take that. If it was up to me, I'd start investigating you as a goddamn accomplice."

"Accomplice to what? Two days ago, I'd never heard of

Vance *or* Garity. Now you think I'm involved in the guy's disappearance?"

"I didn't say that," Drucker growled. "You're a diversion. He hired you to make it look like he's interested in solving the case."

"Wait a minute. If you're so sure that Vance was involved in a criminal act, why don't you arrest him?"

"Circumstantial evidence. That's what they call it."

"Like what?"

"Don't you wish." He glanced at his watch. "You've got one hour."

Pierce looked around the crowded cubicle. "Where can I work?"

"Not in here, that's for damn sure. C'mon."

Pierce followed Drucker to a corner office that was empty except for a table, several chairs, and three dirty ashtrays. "Where can I make copies?"

"You can't. If you want to do that, you better go consult with the judge again. Maybe he can make a ruling on it and give you a court order." Drucker laughed. "Wouldn't that be a helluva deal? Wouldn't surprise me, either."

Pierce moved around the table and sat down.

Drucker jabbed his index finger at him. "Now I know why your name is familiar. You're the P.I. who got involved with the rich guy, what was his name, Andrews, who blew up the boat in the bay and took off. They never caught him, did they?"

Pierce pulled out the first file and opened it. "No, they didn't."

"Hey, you were working for him, weren't you? Yeah, that was it. I'll be damned. A dick who works for crooks."

"Bullshit. If you show me what you got on Vance, and it's convincing, I'll drop the case right now."

"Good try, Pierce. But I'm not as dumb as you think." He slammed the door as he left.

Pierce felt relieved to be rid of the detective. But now he was more concerned than ever about Vance.

Inside the box were a couple of dozen file folders. He took out the first one, pushed away an ashtray, and opened it onto the table.

On top of the file was a five-by-seven photo of Jack Garity. His hair was thinning at the temples, his face looked gaunt, he wasn't smiling. Pierce noticed a spot on the bridge of his nose that suggested the man wore glasses and had taken them off for the picture. *Probably far-sighted,* Pierce thought. Far-sighted people like himself, usually didn't wear glasses for photos.

An envelope was clipped to the back of the photo and inside it were several wallet-sized photos. Pierce slipped one into his shirt pocket.

Below the photos was the missing persons report, filed in January. It described Jack Garity as forty-six years old, five-foot-nine, one hundred and sixty pounds, brown hair and blue eyes. It briefly described the circumstances of his disappearance. Stapled to it was a day-by-day follow-up log, detailing the search. On separate sheets were reports on the discovery of Garity's Jeep Cherokee, then his Grumman canoe, its seat cushions and paddles.

Pierce turned to the background summary and read a concise history of the man, his education, career, and personal life. He slipped his notebook out of his pocket, and jotted down a few notes. Next, he perused transcripts of interviews with Garity's ex-wife and Wayne Garity.

Another file folder listed Jack Garity's numbers—social security, driver's license, credit cards: the codes that unlocked the daily patterns of a life.

From those codes, the investigators had assembled a detailed financial profile. Garity earned $45,500 last year from j, Inc. and had left $5,200 in his interest-bearing checking account. The last checks he'd written were typical end of the month payments, and only one of his credit cards wasn't paid up. The records showed he had $56,000 invested in Certificates of Deposit and treasury bonds. As of last week, none of those investments had been touched.

The rest of the financial report included a list of Garity's magazine subscriptions, and the organizations to which he'd belonged or contributed money. Nothing stuck out except the fact that Garity had kept up on the latest developments in his field.

In yet another file was a copy of Garity's divorce papers. Carla Garity had initiated the proceedings, claiming irreconcilable difference. He'd kept the house, and paid her $700 a month for five years. He'd also set up a trust fund of $20,000 for the college education of his daughter Dawn, who was now nineteen and attended the University of Florida.

Next came transcripts of interviews with several neighbors. All were carried out on the same day, about five days after the disappearance. None of the neighbors knew him well. Three of the neighbors said they thought he had a girlfriend, but their descriptions of her sounded like three different women.

Real helpful. Pierce guessed that the detective who had interviewed the neighbors had thought he was completing a routine task, and hadn't really expected to uncover anything unusual. The investigator was probably convinced that Garity had drowned and become gator bait.

That was close to the conclusion of the initial investigation that found no evidence of either foul play or an attempt by Garity to disappear. All indications were that he'd died in an accident—a heart attack or a drowning—on his solo fishing trip.

The police must have assumed that since his brother had never met the girlfriend, she was a minor figure in the missing man's life, and hadn't come forward because she didn't want to get involved. Or maybe they'd broken up, and she didn't even know that Garity was dead.

He turned the page and found an addendum written in red ink. The unidentified missing girlfriend, the second canoe paddle, and the unlikelihood of a solo canoe trip along Hell's Bay trail were listed as reasons that the case would remain open. Also included were notes of new comments by Wayne Garity that supported the two-person theory.

He read over several files of log notes made by the investigators and noticed that Wayne Garity and Carla Garity had been interviewed by all three detectives. The neighbors had been re-interviewed once or twice, but hadn't added anything new. Frank Davis, the second detective on the case, had done the most thorough work.

Pierce quickly paged through Davis's interviews, then went

back to the beginning again and took detailed notes. About ten minutes later, the door opened and Drucker stepped into the conference room.

"That's it, Pierce."

He glanced at his watch, saw that only forty-four minutes had passed. "You said an hour."

"Tough, ain't it? But I need the files right now." He dropped his card on the table. "In case you come up with anything that you should report. I'd hate to have to arrest you for withholding information related to a crime. You got that?"

Drucker scooped up the files, dropped them back into the box. As he did, a loose scrap of paper fluttered to the floor.

Pierce bent over and picked it up. It was from a notepad with Detective Davis' name printed at the top. The only thing written on the paper was a name that was underlined twice.

It read: *LYDIA MULLEN?*

As Pierce arrived, the lunch rush was just getting underway at Jimmy's Diner. A few cops sat at the counter and several other people were waiting to be seated.

The diner was open for breakfast and lunch, and existed on the business of police personnel, employees from the bail bond offices, and the courthouse crew.

Pierce had eaten here once, and had no intention of doing so again. He just wanted to use the pay phone.

The telephone booth, which was in the corner by the cashier, was occupied, so he leaned against the wall to wait—out of the way of customers, but directly in the view of the man in the booth.

As he waited to call Carla Garity, he wondered how Davis had found out about Mullen, and what he had learned before his scuba accident.

Somehow, Mullen was tied in with Garity's disappearance. But right now, the only thing he had to go on was her book, *The True Chemistry of Humankind.* The book made little sense to him, but he was more curious than ever about its author.

Ironically, he'd only tasked Janet with tracking down Mullen as a test of her skills—supposed busy work to keep her occupied on her first day.

The man on the phone hung up abandoned the booth, and Pierce sidled past him. He reached into his pocket for a quarter and pulled out the gold coin from Two Bits' collar. He found another quarter, and momentarily compared the two. As far as he could tell, they were identical in size and weight. They were both Washington-type quarters, and the markings on the gold one looked authentic. But the cat's coin was thirty-five years older, a 1952, and it was worn as if it had been in circulation. That seemed unlikely, though. Even if a gold-plated quarter had gotten into circulation, it wouldn't float around for long; someone would no doubt remove it for a keepsake.

He dropped his regular quarters into the slot and dialed Carla's number. A woman answered on the second ring. He introduced himself and told her why he was calling. She quickly agreed to see him at two o'clock.

The judge was working wonders today, and Pierce finally forgave him for making him wait four hours in court.

The smell of food had changed his mind about not eating here, and he walked over to the counter to order a turkey sandwich on rye and a cup of coffee to go. Five minutes later, he was on his way. But he'd only driven a few blocks when a car pulled out in front of him and he slammed on his brakes. Coffee spilled over the sandwich and onto his pants.

"Ah, shit." He brushed at his wet pants and more coffee spilled. "Damn it."

He eased the aging Saab to the curb, grabbed a rag from under the seat and did his best to clean up the mess. Luckily, his khaki slacks were almost the color of coffee. When the stain dried, it would barely be noticeable.

This near-downtown neighborhood wasn't the greatest, but he decided to eat the remaining half of his sandwich and finish what remained of his coffee before driving another block.

He noticed a brightly-painted yellow brick wall across the street. In the center of it at street level was a door with a sign above it that read: ALBERT'S PAWNSHOP—JEWELRY AND GOLD BOUGHT AND SOLD. There was something familiar about the place, although Pierce was certain he'd never been here. But now, he realized he had reason for a visit. He'd go see what Albert had to say about the quarter from Two-Bit's cellar.

He chased the sandwich with the rest of the coffee, then got out. "Don't go anywhere without me, Swedie. That's an order." He looked up at the windsurfer strapped to the roof rack. "That goes for you, too."

Iron bars covered the windows of the pawnshop. There were probably more bars on the roof and over the air conditioner vents to keep intruders from dropping in after hours. All too often, ceiling vents were the mode of entry in this neighborhood. A few years ago, the owner of a business in the same area had become a controversial hero when he'd set up an electrical trap and grilled a thief who was breaking in through the roof of his clothing shop.

The interior of the place was dim, gloomy. All of the goods were behind a counter that spanned the length of the store, and a wire mesh security screen provided another layer of protection.

Pierce gazed down at a glass case containing dozens of gold necklaces, but not a single gold coin.

"If you want to pawn that old windsurfing board you got out there on your car, you're in the wrong place," the man behind the counter said. He was burly and bearded and stared at Pierce through thick glasses with dark frames.

"That's not why I'm here."

As soon as Pierce looked closely at the man, he recognized him. Albert had been one of the few shop owners on the street who'd disagreed with the predominant sentiment on the avenue that the thief-grilling shop owner had the right to set a potentially lethal trap. Pierce remembered Albert because he'd been the sole white business owner in the predominantly black neighborhood, an immigrant from South Africa.

Because of this odd twist, Albert and the black clothing store owner had been featured on CNN, after the Herald published a story about the two men. In the article, Albert had said it was nothing unusual for a white South African to be surrounded by blacks, and that he was comfortable in the neighborhood.

Pierce pulled the gold coin from his pocket. "You ever seen one of these?" He handed the quarter to Albert, who examined it as he turned it over in his fingers

"Sure, I've seen them. Some are electro-plated, others like this one are solid. I can give you thirty bucks for it."

"How was it made?"

"Probably from a wax mold. Looks like a real quarter, doesn't it?"

"But there's nothing mysterious about it?"

"Mysterious? Not really. I've seen this kind of thing from time to time. Keepsakes, jewelry, what have you."

Pierce took back the coin.

"You don't want to pawn it?"

"No, it belongs to a cat."

"Well, it's worth a lot of cat food."

Pierce laughed. "That's one way of looking at it."

He considered telling Albert that he'd seen him on CNN, but then he'd probably have to listen to him rehash the whole story, and he had to be on his way or he'd be late to Carla Garity's. Instead, he thanked him and slipped the coin into his pocket.

"Hey, what's that windsurfing sport like?" Albert asked.

"Don't know. Never tried it."

Pierce stopped by the door as something else about the coin occurred to him. "Oh, by the way, why do you think the coin looks so worn?"

Albert shrugged. "Maybe someone had it on a key chain as a good luck charm, and it rubbed against other coins. Or the mold wasn't very good."

"Yeah, that must be it."

The other possibility was that the coin was a regular quarter that had been changed somehow. Not cast from a mold, but transmuted, whatever that meant.

As in alchemy. He didn't believe it, but Garity was apparently interested in alchemy, a fact he couldn't ignore.

Great. He'd been hired to look for Garity's missing girlfriend and suddenly he was faced with the possibility of being lured into the labyrinth of an ancient, enigmatic science. *Or was it a religion?* He didn't know much about it.

But he did know one thing: finding the missing girlfriend would be easier than discovering the fabled Philosopher's Stone.

Chapter 10

The guard in the air-conditioned, smoked-glass booth slid open his window as Pierce pulled up to the entrance of Summertree. "I'm here to see Carla Garity," he called, and gave his name. "She's expecting me." He glanced at the clock on his dash. The stop at the pawnshop had taken a little more time than he'd expected, but he was only a few minutes late.

The man nodded and dialed Carla's number. Ripples of heat seeped into the Saab and it was a relief when the guard hung up his phone and gave Pierce directions to Carla's building.

The gate rose, and Pierce drove into the North Miami Beach condominium complex. Gated communities with guard stations had become virtually de rigeur for high-end new developments. They represented country club prestige and at least a symbolic sense of security. To Pierce, they were contemporary fortresses, and this one should be more aptly named Fort Summertree.

Carla Garity was waiting for him outside her door. Attractive, early forties, ash blonde hair pulled back into a bun, penetrating green eyes. She wore a tennis outfit that emphasized well-proportioned hips and legs. "You're not very prompt, Mr. Pierce. You're lucky I'm still here."

"Sorry. Traffic was bad on I-95."

As she led him inside, he noticed two tennis rackets leaning against a wall, on either side of a rubber tree. He followed her across a floor of ceramic tile, through the dining room and into a spacious living room. The condo was a forest of house plants, and the windows facing the rear of the house revealed a well-tended garden.

"Okay, guys, off the sofa."

A pair of Himalayan cats leaped from the white couch onto the matching plush carpeting, eyeing him warily, but apparently decided he was okay and flopped down on their sides.

"Nice cats."

Carla dropped down on one knee and petted one of the cats as it arched its back. "This is Percy and that's Shelley."

He recalled that Mrs. Greenfelder had mentioned three Himalayans. "Percy Bysshe Shelley. Did you name them after the English poet?"

"In fact, I have a third one from the same litter name Bysshe. He's off in another room."

Carla's eyes slid down to the stained crotch of Pierce's pants as if she suspected him of jerking off before he'd arrived, possibly accounting for his tardiness.

"It's coffee. An accident." He sat down on a straight-back chair with a red velvet cushion, and Carla sat on the edge of the couch.

"So what can I do for you, Mr. Pierce?"

Uncertain where to begin, he asked: "I understand you teach high school English?"

A beat passed. "I teach English."

"That's what I said."

"What I hear in the halls is high school English, and it's not what I teach."

Jesus. She was serious. "I guess you do teach English."

"Wayne told me that you're looking for Jack. The police have interviewed me three times now."

"I know. I saw the police report. It said you have a daughter."

"She's attending the University of Florida in Gainesville."

Pierce heard a nervous edge to her voice, and tried to put her at ease. "You seem too young for a college-aged daughter."

"Too young to *have* ..." she corrected.

"What?"

"Too young for a college-aged daughter doesn't make a damn bit of sense, Nick."

Pierce laughed. "Sorry."

"What is it you want to know about Jack?" She glanced at her watch. "I'm playing tennis in twenty minutes, so please, let's get on with it."

Then let's skip the grammar lessons, teach. "Do you think your ex-husband was murdered, Mrs. Garity?"

"Call me Carla, Nick." She crossed her arms, and leaned back in her chair. "Look, it's tempting to call it murder, since the body was never recovered. I believe that's the reason why Wayne hasn't let it go. I sympathize with him, but there's very little evidence to indicate anything other than what the original investigation concluded: an accidental death."

"Maybe he's still alive."

"No. Jack wasn't the type to just wander off without notifying anyone, and especially without liquidating his assets."

"I'm not sure *anyone* is that type, but sometimes when people get themselves into a fix, they act in unexpected ways."

Carla rose from her chair, walked across the room, and slid open a cabinet door. For a moment Pierce thought she was going to pour herself a drink. Instead, she picked up a tube of tennis balls.

"Jack was a loner." She returned to her chair, absently fiddling with the cap on the tube. "I never knew what he was thinking. But I have a hard time believing that he would get involved with any low-life characters. He wasn't the sort."

"What sort was he?"

She removed the cap from the tube and examined one of the balls. "He was very dedicated to his work. He had a great curiosity about his profession. It was his whole life."

Pierce sat forward. "What was your relationship with him at the time of his disappearance?"

"We'd been divorced three and a half years. There wasn't much of any relationship. Dawn, our daughter, was our only link."

"I've heard different."

"Differently," she corrected automatically, as if she was talking with one of her students. "What do you mean by that?"

"I heard you were seeing him occasionally right up until his disappearance."

She gave a short, clipped laugh. "I suppose you heard that from Glenda Greenfelder."

He didn't answer.

"I'm afraid that Glenda get things confused." She nodded toward the cats on the floor. "One day I picked up Percy, Bysshe and Shelley, and she was sure she'd only had them two or three days. They'd been with her for two weeks."

In the lull of the conversation, Pierce thought he heard a squeak coming from outside the room, the sound of a rubber sole against ceramic tile. One of the cats was staring in the direction of the noise. He wasn't imagining it; someone else really was here.

"Actually, Glenda was right in a way," Carla continued as she returned the ball to the tube. "Jack and I started seeing each other again once in a while, about a year and a half after our divorce. But I hadn't seen him for at least three months when he vanished."

"Why were you seeing him?" His eyes slid toward the doorway.

"I know it probably seems strange that a divorced couple would spend time together. But I guess I felt sorry for Jack."

Pierce nodded. It didn't seem so odd to him. He was well aware of the temptation to return to a former spouse, when both parties were lonely and accessible to each other. His relationship with Tina had extended beyond their marriage, an endless merry-go-round of breaking up and patching up. Just the thought of it now made him uncomfortable.

"See, I'm not the easiest person to live with, Nick. I have a critical streak."

Yeah, about a mile wide. Pierce threaded his fingers together, and looked back at her without giving away his thoughts. He was about to ask to use the bathroom as a pretext to look for the other person, but decided to wait. He had something else he wanted to try first.

"Maybe Mrs. Greenfelder mistook you for someone else. Maybe she thought you were Isabel."

"Who?"

"Isabel was the name of Jack's girlfriend."

"I don't know anything about Jack's girlfriends." She stood up. "Is there anything else, Nick? I have to go meet my tennis partner in a few minutes."

"What about Lydia Mullen?"

It was a long shot, but worth a try.

"I don't know her, either."

Pierce thought he'd caught a momentary glimpse of recognition in her eyes. He was about to ask if the name was familiar to her, when he heard the squeaking sound again.

"Mom?"

A young woman in a white tennis outfit stood in the entrance to the room. "I think you should tell him. It might be important."

"Dawn, go back to your room," Carla said tersely. "I told you to stay out of this."

"No, Mom. You know they're going to find out sooner or later."

Carla's blue eyes flickered in anger, but there was a look of uncertainty on her face. "Come in here and sit down. Nick, this is my daughter, Dawn. For her own good, I didn't want to open this can of worms, but it seems that she's insisting on it."

Dawn was attractive, a younger version of her mother, but vulnerable where her mother was formal and icy. She was more slender, and her lips were fuller, a fact that softened her appearance. Her flaxen hair was longer than her mother's, and tied in a ponytail with a pink ribbon.

"I see you're not in Gainesville," Pierce said.

"Dawn and I are going to our cabin in North Carolina for a few days," Carla explained. "We're leaving for Asheville in the morning."

"What did you want to tell me, Dawn?"

Dawn glanced at Carla, who stared coldly back at her. Then the words rushed out. "My father was very much involved with Lydia Mullen's life. She was his ... his pet project."

Pierce sat forward. "Go on."

"I found out about her last summer when I was down here. Dad and I were going out to dinner, and I arrived at the house early while he was still at work. I'd kept my key, even though I lived with my mother. So I let myself in."

She paused a moment, collecting her thoughts, then explained that although she hadn't intended to pry, she couldn't help taking a look when she found a notebook open on his desk.

"Dad always seemed preoccupied. At first, I just thought he was still upset about the divorce. But then I started thinking it was something else. I asked him if he was involved with anyone. He just laughed it off, but when I read the notebook, I realized he was infatuated with this Lydia person. It was all about her. Notes on things like the route she took to the university in the morning, where she ate lunch, who she talked to."

"Wasn't she sort of old for him?"

"Let me finish. I opened a desk drawer and found copies of papers or speeches Mullen had written, and there was a file with newspaper clippings about her as well. I remember one headline said, 'Controversial Prof Under Fire'; something like that. All the articles were from the early nineteen fifties. There were other files, too, labeled M-1 through M-26. I really didn't have a chance to look closely at them, though, because Dad came home."

"Did you ask him about her?"

"When he saw me come out of his study, he walked right over to his desk. He saw the open notebook and slammed it shut. I thought he was really mad, but when he turned around, he smiled and said he was working on a biography of a chemist. He tried to make light of it, but I could tell that it was important to him. That it was the thing which was what he was so obsessed with."

Pierce eyed Carla, who was pacing, clearly anxious to leave.

He turned back to Dawn. "What did he find so interesting about Mullen?"

"He didn't want to talk about her."

"Your uncle didn't tell me anything about Jack writing a book."

"Uncle Wayne didn't know about it. No one did. It was just an accident that I found out."

"Did you see him after that dinner?"

"A couple of times, but we never talked about his project. I stopped by on New Year's Eve and we had a glass of wine together. He was kind of quiet and preoccupied, but like I said, that wasn't unusual. I left about ten-thirty to meet some friends; New Year's Eve, you know."

Glenda Greenfelder might've seen Dawn and mistaken her for Carla, Pierce thought. From a distance, the two women looked similar. "And that was the last time you saw him?"

She nodded. "I came by on the third to say good-bye before I went back to Gainesville, but he wasn't here."

"The day he disappeared."

"That's right. I waited about half an hour, then I left. I called him that night from my dorm, but I didn't get any answer."

"Did that bother you?"

"I didn't think much of it. He'd said something about a fishing trip."

"What did he say about it?" Pierce asked.

"Nothing. Just that he was going." She looked on the verge of tears.

Carla moved to sit next to Dawn and touched her shoulder.

"Did he tell *you* anything about his project?" Pierce asked Carla.

She shook her head. "Not a word."

"But Dawn told you about it, right?"

"Yes, but not until a couple of months after Jack vanished."

"Dawn, why didn't you say anything to the police?"

"I think that's enough, Nick," Carla said. "You can see Dawn is upset."

"No, it's okay, Mom. I want to clear this up. I didn't think it had anything to do with his disappearance. Everyone was saying it was an accident, that he'd probably had a heart attack and fallen out of the boat."

"But you've changed your mind now?"

"When I was waiting for him that day, I went into the house to look for that notebook and those files again; I was curious. But they were gone."

"So the police never saw them?"

She shook her head.

"How did you find out about Mullen?" Carla asked.

He told her about the book he'd found in Garity's study, and then how he'd seen the name on a piece of paper in a police file on the case.

"I called Detective Davis and told him about Mullen," Dawn

said. "He was going to come to Gainesville to interview me, but he didn't live long enough to make the trip."

Carla picked up the tennis rackets. "Time to go. We've got a court reserved."

Pierce stood up. "Thanks for your time." He wondered what else Dawn knew, and if he would have a chance to talk to her alone. "Oh, one other thing." He reached into his pocket and took out the gold coin. "Do either of you recognize this quarter?"

"Yes, it looks like the one Two-Bits wore on his collar," Dawn exclaimed. "Daddy said it was his good luck piece."

"Do you know where he got it from?"

"He said that someone he knew made them. It's real gold." Dawn pulled on a gold chain around her neck, and held up a fifty-cent piece that was attached to it. "Here's another one. He gave it to me last Christmas."

Pierce took the coin in his hand, saw that it was dated 1950. "How many of those did he have?"

"He said he had eight of them, four half-dollars and four quarters. But one of the half dollars was cut in half, and he only had half of it. He showed it to me to prove that it was solid gold."

Carla opened the door for Pierce, and stepped back. "He never gave me one, or said anything about them. Good afternoon, Nick."

Dawn, he thought, was forthright, honest, and concerned. Carla was another matter. He'd bet a dozen old coins that she was hiding something, and keeping Dawn in line as best she could.

Pierce had just sat down to eat take-out chow mien for dinner, when the phone rang. Maybe it was Elise. He'd left a message on her recorder a few minutes ago.

"Mr. Pierce? This is Nora Williams. I'm a supervising operator for Southern Bell. I have an emergency call for you from a Dr. Howarth."

"Dr. Howarth?" The name was familiar, yet he didn't know why. Then he remembered that Janet's last name was Howarth. He imagined a husband appearing out of nowhere and telling him that Janet wasn't going to work for him. "Go ahead, put him through."

"It's a her. Dr. Janet Howarth."

"Hello, Nick."

"Dr. Howarth?"

She laughed. "Sorry. You didn't give me your home number, and it's unlisted. So I had to improvise."

"Very clever." He'd forgotten all about calling her. She was either trying to impress him, or she'd changed her mind about the job.

"You're not still at the office, are you?"

"No, I'm home. I just wanted to fill you in on what happened when I called the university about Mullen."

He straightened up. "I'm all ears."

"Well, I got hold of a secretary in the chemistry department, and as I expected, she didn't know who I was talking about. I figured Mullen had either died or retired years ago. Anyhow, when I told her that Mullen was a faculty member back in the fifties, she said I'd have to write to the university's personnel department for any information about her."

As Pierce listened, he poured himself a glass of ice tea. "I've got the feeling you didn't stop there."

She laughed. "You got it. I told her I didn't have time for that, and asked if there was anyone on the staff who was there that far back. It was a long shot, but it paid off."

"Really?"

"After a minute or so, an older woman came on the line and identified herself as the executive secretary to the head of the department. She asked in a stern voice how she could help me. But I could tell she was really saying, "How can I get rid of you?" I knew I needed a good simple reason why I was looking for Mullen, so I told her that I was a legal assistant to the executor of a will, and that Lydia Mullen was listed as one of the beneficiaries."

"And it worked?"

"Well, she wanted to call me back, so I had to expand the story. I told her I needed to know immediately if Mullen was alive. I explained that if we could prove that she was deceased, the secondary beneficiary would receive more than a million dollars, and I quickly added that the University of Miami was that recipient."

Pierce didn't like using deception to obtain information, but he knew that sometimes there was no choice, if you wanted answers.

"I know I overdid it, but I've got experience dealing with bureaucrats. You threaten a money source and they'll move."

Savvy lady. "So what happened?"

"The secretary excused herself and the department chair himself got on the phone; a Dr. Kaufmanus. It turns out he was a student at the university in the early fifties. He's got this gravelly voice like he's a hundred years old. Anyhow, I recorded the conversation. You want to hear it?"

Pierce took a bite of his chow mein. "Sure. Put it on." *And this was her first day.* As the tape clicked on, he wondered what she planned to do for an encore.

"Lydia Mullen. Why, I haven't heard that name for years. She was French, you know; came to the States as a young woman, right after the war."

"Do you know where I can find her?"

His laughter was deep and hoarse-sounding, and ended with a sputtering cough. "Excuse me. No, I'm afraid not. The whereabouts of Lydia Mullen is an intriguing mystery. In fact, I'm surprised that she'd still be listed in a will. It must be a mistake."

"Why is that?"

"When I was a graduate student here, the Lydia Mullen mystery was a hot topic of discussion. One day, the professor simply didn't show up for classes, and she was never seen again. It was all over the papers at the time. There was a big police investigation, but they came up with nothing, not a single lead as I recall."

"Do you remember the month and the year?"

"Let's see … I received my Ph.D. in fifty-seven. So that would have been fifty-five. The fall."

"Do you remember anything about the circumstances of her disappearance?" Janet asked. "I need as much information as possible."

"Well, I recall she was an eccentric lady for those times. An odd duck." Kaufmanus coughed, and excused himself again.

"She was trying to revive alchemy as a legitimate field of study within chemistry. She even claimed she was an adept. One day, she took four quarters and four half dollars from her students and turned them into gold right in front of their eyes."

"Really?"

He sputtered again. "Well, so it seemed. She melted them into a molten mass and mixed in a yellow liquid that she said had taken her several years to create. A couple of hours later, the hot metal was poured into molds made from the original coins."

"Were the coins really gold?"

"Oh, yes. But she'd been left alone in the room part of the time, so there were allegations of fraud, naturally. It was also all very unscientific since she wouldn't reveal every step of the process. Her colleagues thought it was hocus-pocus, of course, and that she was mentally unstable. When she disappeared a short time later, it seemed to lend some credence to the latter idea."

"Very interesting," Pierce said, as the recording ended and Janet returned to the line. "So Garity wasn't the only one who's disappeared.

"I know, and what about the gold coins? Isn't that interesting?"

"It certainly is. Did he say anything else? It sounded like you stopped it before the conversation was over."

"You heard the interesting part. I had to lie a little more about the money for the university. I didn't think you wanted to hear about that."

"Thanks for sparing me." The old prof would probably go to his grave wondering what had happened to Mullen's money.

"Oh, there was one other thing. He said that one of the gold coins was cut in half, and that it was real gold all the way through."

Pierce could barely hold back his excitement. He wanted to tell her about his day, but that could wait. "Did he say what happened to the coins?"

"That was the last question I asked him. He said they disappeared along with Mullen."

Chapter 11

"Litter boxes. Litter boxes. My little sweets have dirty, dirty litter boxes," Glenda Greenfelder babbled, as she peered into a compact mirror and touched up her arching eyebrows with her new pencil. "Mama's back from the store and she's going to clean them up right now, Malcolm. Then you can do your business in peace." She snapped the compact shut and deposited it, along with her eyebrow pencil, into the pocket of her housedress.

Glenda moved about the kitchen, unaware that Nigel Erickson was also inside the house, pressed against the sliding glass door just a few feet away. His black cross-training shoes protruded slightly from the bottom of the smelly green plastic curtains. He gazed through the slight opening between two sections of the drapery, but Glenda seemed too preoccupied with her feline friends to notice.

Erickson knew that clandestine operations meant field work, but he'd never suspected he'd be doing this sort of crap. It was part of the training, Martin had said. But breaking into a house and taking a cat was plain weird. Not just any cat, either. Martin wanted a black one with a white paw, and he had literally waded through cats to find it while Glenda was out. Good thing he was wearing gloves. The cat had bit him hard. He felt a bruise between his thumb and index finger, but the skin wasn't broken. Fortunately, the cat was declawed, or his arms would've been shredded.

As he handed Martin the struggling cat, she told him to wait until she came back. But the old lady had returned first, and he couldn't get the sliding door open to escape, so he'd ducked behind the curtain.

He had no idea why Martin wanted the cat or why he was supposed to be waiting in the house. For all he knew, Glenda might be one of the players, part of the training team. If that was the case, she was doing a damn good job of acting. She looked like a real cat lady to him.

"Now, let's get our babies some fresh litter."

She picked soiled newspaper and litter out of a plastic box just a few feet away from him, and carried it over to a trash can, taking care not to spill a granule of litter. As she leaned down to the second of the four boxes, a Persian cat wandered over and sniffed at Erickson's foot.

His heart pounded. This was not his idea of a good time.

But he had to admit that Martin did have a sense of humor. She'd said she was taking him to a cathouse.

When they'd arrived, they'd turned the directional mike toward the house and listened to Glenda talking to the cats. Martin said that the old lady went shopping every Saturday evening at nine o'clock. At two minutes to the hour, she'd left the house, right on time.

As soon as she was gone, Martin had led the way to the side of the house and showed him how to get past the locked slider by lifting it out of the frame. He'd followed her instructions, and it had worked. Maybe the lesson here was that breaking into someone's house was not above the ethics of a clandestine operation.

"Okay, sweetheart." Glenda poured fresh litter into one of the boxes. The Persian had moved away from Erickson's foot and was inspecting the old lady's work. The cat pawed tentatively at the clean box, then looked over at the old lady, shook a paw, and backed away.

"Oh, you're a fussy one, Malcolm. Typical Persian." She lifted the soiled newspaper from another box, and deposited it in the trash. She reached for a clean section of the newspaper, then paused, and looked around. *Had she heard him?*

"Now that's strange. Where do you think our friend Two Bits went, Malc? He's usually first in line to greet mama."

She smoothed newspaper into the bottom of the plastic box, then added litter. She was about to attack the last box when the doorbell rang.

"Now, who's that? I'm not expecting anyone. At least, I don't think I am." She brushed off her hands and picked up a tabby off the counter. Its ears were pressed back. "Don't you worry, Charlie. It's not a dog, I guarantee that." She set the tabby down on the floor. "Maybe someone is going home early. I bet that's it."

Glenda walked into the living room as the bell rang for a second time. "Cool your jets, kiddo. I can't be everywhere at once." She flipped on the outside light, unlocked the door and opened it as far as the chain would permit.

"Well, who do we have here?"

"Don't you remember my Felix, Glenda? I told you I was coming. Remember, I called last night."

"Oh, yes, of course. Felix. Felix. Come in. Oops. Let me get this blasted chain. I use it so the cats don't get out and I can still talk." She closed the door and slid off the chain. She stepped back, opening the door about six inches, and automatically scanned the room for any cats ready to bolt outside. "Hurry now. I'm already missing one of my boys."

Erickson stepped out from the curtain, and saw Martin holding a cage covered by a cloth. She'd wrapped her blond braid on top of her head, and in the pale light of a sixty-watt bulb she looked ageless, anywhere from twenty-five to fifty.

"How many friends will Felix have tonight?" Martin asked.

"Oh, dear. Fourteen, I think. No, let's see. One left earlier when there were fourteen. Then two arrived. What's that, fifteen? No, sixteen." She stared at the cage, then looked up at Isabel. "So how long will Felix be with us?"

"Oh, not too long."

Glenda took a step back. "I think I remember you, but ..." She was confused. "... but I don't remember Felix."

"Of course you know me, Glenda. I'm Isabel. That's part of the problem. You're just too snoopy for your own good, and now your tongue is getting too loose."

Erickson moved over to the doorway of the kitchen, impressed with the perfection of the scene. Isabel there, himself here, the cat woman over there. Everyone was playing their roles perfectly, he thought. He half-expected the two women to turn around and tell him what he'd done wrong. *But how could this be an act?* He'd seen Pierce enter this same house yesterday evening, and he'd listened to him and the old lady from his van with a directional mike.

Glenda shook her head. "I don't know what you're talking about."

"Then I'll spell it out. You told me that the gold quarter on Two-Bits' collar had been lost. But you had it, didn't you? And you put it back on the cat."

Was that what this was about, a goddamned coin? Erickson wondered.

"But it is lost," Glenda pleaded. "I don't know where it is. I don't even know where Two Bits is right now."

"Take a look!" Martin pulled the cloth away from the cage.

Glenda gasped, and her jaw dropped. She back away, her hands covering her face. "Oh, my God. Two-Bits. What did you do to him?"

"Payback, Glenda. You lied. The detective's got the gold quarter."

Glenda shook her head, still staring at the cage. "I didn't give it to him. What's wrong with Two Bits?"

The cat was slumped on the bottom of the cage. *Was it drugged or dead?* Erickson wondered.

Martin shook the cage and the cat's head rolled away from the body.

Glenda screamed, and rushed at Isabel, grabbing her around the throat, squeezing and screaming. Isabel tried to throw her off, but the old lady clung to her like a wild cat and kept screaming.

Erickson lurched forward, gripped the old lady by the arms, and jerked her back, away from Isabel. He slapped a hand over her mouth, silencing her. She thrashed, kicked and screamed against his hand.

"Jesus, what do want me to do, Isabel?"

"Shut up, Nigel, just shut the hell up," Isabel snapped, and plunged a knife into the old woman. She pulled it out, stabbing her again and again, as Erickson felt the life shudder out of her.

He couldn't take his eyes off Isabel. Her face glowed with rage.

"Don't think about it, Nigel," she told him for the third time, as they drove south through the night, along I-95.

"But you killed her."

"*We* killed her, Nigel," she corrected. "Both of us. You held her."

Erickson was in shock. But she'd gotten him out of the house. He'd left with her, and now she was in control. She would make him understand that he was compromised.

"I never thought this job was going to involve murder."

"It doesn't. This just happened."

"We've got to tell the police."

"Do you *want* to go to jail? We broke into the house. It would take a strong male to lift that slider from the frame."

"I don't know what to think," he said in a soft voice.

She thought she knew exactly what he was thinking. He was considering running, turning her in, and facing the consequences. She couldn't let him out of her sight tonight. Even if it meant that he'd see her in the morning, at her worst, when she felt weak and ill. But she had to work on him, and she'd make it worth his while tonight.

"Take this exit. Pull into the Holiday Inn lot. We'll get a room."

Chapter 12

Only a half dozen vehicles were parked along the Rickenbacker Causeway when Pierce arrived. Vance's Range Rover was facing the bay, not more than five feet from the water. The driver's door was open and Vance was seated behind the wheel. A sticker on his rear window showed a windsurfer and beneath the slogan: "Gone with the Wind."

Pierced approached the Range Rover, but Vance made no move to get out. A voice, surrounded by static, was broadcasting inside the vehicle, and Pierce thought that it was a police radio, until he heard what was being said:

"Tonight, the winds will be east to southeast at five to ten knots from Key West to the Dry Tortugas. Florida Bay will have a moderate chop and winds of ten knots."

Vance turned off the weather radio. "Damn high pressure front is stalled over south Florida."

"Is that bad?"

"It is if you want wind. But today's conditions are good for a first lesson."

"Do you want me to tell you where things stand before we begin?"

"Let's keep our priorities straight here. Windsurfing first. Business later."

"Fine with me. Where's your board?"

"I didn't bring one. I don't need it."

"What happens if I can't get back in?" Pierce asked warily.

"The breeze is almost directly on-shore. You'll just drift in."

Vance got out of the Range Rover and walked over to the Saab. "Let's see what you've got. Okay, this is definitely a beginner's board. Real floaty. Stable. And nearly impossible to sail in winds over fifteen miles an hour."

They loosened the straps and lowered the board to the ground.

"How much is it worth?" Pierce asked.

"Oh, nothing."

"What?"

"Just kidding." He ran a hand through his thick blond hair. His deep tan and firm muscles made him look like an aging lifeguard. "You might get a couple of hundred for it if you sold it complete with mast, boom and a sail. Two-fifty tops."

"That's all?" *Linder had owed him $600.*

"At the lower end, the equipment is pretty cheap. There's lots of used stuff on the market, at least in Florida. Okay, get everything out. Let's start piece by piece."

Vance talked about masts, sails, booms, extensions and bases for the next half hour, and showed Pierce how to assemble the sail, mast and boom. Then he explained the basics of sailing, from up-hauling the sail to tacking and jibing.

Pierce tried to keep it all straight, but got more confused by the minute, particularly as some of the things that Vance said seemed to contradict what he'd seen last night in the windsurfing video he'd rented.

"Don't worry if you can't remember everything I say. Three quarters of what you learn will take place while you sail and experiment. It's important to understand the techniques, but your body has to learn to sail and how to react to different circumstances. Then it will all come naturally."

Vance picked up the board with one hand, dangling it by a footstrap, and hoisted the mast with the other. He eased the board into the water and let the sail drop in after it. For the next few minutes, he demonstrated the techniques he'd been describing. Then it was Pierce's turn. "Okay, get out there and make a splash."

"Funny, Vance, very funny."

"We all fall down, Pierce. It's part of learning."

Pierce waded into the water, and tentatively stepped up onto the board. The bow immediately plunged to the bottom and he jumped off.

"Move back about eighteen inches," Vance advised. "You gotta get the feel of it, find your balance point."

He stepped up again. This time the board wobbled under his feet, but he managed to stay on.

"Okay, bend over and grab the up-haul line," Vance directed.

Pierce slowly crouched down, found the line, and pulled as he stood up. The line helped him to keep his balance, but up-hauling the sail was not as easy as Vance made it sound. He pulled in the line, hand over hand, until the sail lifted from the water. But before he was able to grab the boom, the mast came too far forward and knocked him off the board. He fell backward and the sail flopped over on top of him, pinning him to the bottom.

"You okay, Pierce?" Vance lifted the sail by the mast, and helped him to his feet.

Pierce glanced at a slender woman in a bikini nearby, who held the boom of her sail in her hands. She smiled at him, stepped on her board, and sailed blithely off.

"Just a case of wounded pride. She probably thinks I'm a klutz."

"Hey, she's probably just a lesson or two ahead of you. Everyone sailing today is a beginner, I guarantee it. This is not a windsurfing day, not even for long boards."

"I guess that's good news. How come she didn't have to up-haul?"

"She did a beach start. I'll show you that a little later."

For the next hour, Pierce practiced everything Vance had shown him. Once he'd managed to up-haul the sail and grab the boom, he then found it difficult to sheet-in the way Vance had explained it. He tended to bend forward, fearing that he would fall over if he leaned too far back.

It was close to five when everything finally came together. He up-hauled, sheeted in, and sailed away from shore. After going a hundred yards, he pulled the sail back, forcing the board to turn upwind. Then he carefully walked around the front of the board, completed the tack without falling over, and sailed back to shore.

He worked the sail forward and back, steering the board,

and hit shore just a few yards downwind from where he'd started.

Vance beamed. "Good show. You were sailing!"

"I'm slowly getting the hang of it." In spite of his lack of skill and knowledge, he was enjoying himself more than he had in a long time.

"Hey, it's your first time out. Hell, when I started, I must've gone out seven or eight times before I felt like I was actually sailing."

"Why so long?"

"Garity and I started together back when the sport was brand new. We had to figure it out for ourselves. We had no experience, no body of knowledge to fall back on, and besides that, the equipment sucked."

"So Jack Garity was a windsurfer, too?"

"Yeah, but he stopped a couple of years ago, said he didn't have the time or energy for it anymore. That was about the time his health was starting to deteriorate. You going out again?"

"I think that's enough for today. I really appreciate your help, though. "

"Glad I could introduce you to it. Let's break things down and get something to eat, and talk business. You know any restaurants nearby?"

"Yeah, there's a place out on Key Biscayne; it's casual and the food is passable."

A twelve-foot long Fanatic Mega Cat and a 7.7-meter sail, the largest Erickson had bought, was stowed in the back of the blue Chevy van. But he hadn't bothered to even take it out. The winds were too light, and Vance was just teaching Pierce the basics.

He peered out through the darkly tinted windows, glanced at his watch, noted the time.

He'd monitored their conversations as best he could with his directional mike, but the only thing he'd learned about Garity was that he'd given up windsurfing. *Martin wouldn't be pleased.* But he'd enjoyed listening to Vance's chatter about the sport, even though it was all basic stuff. He'd even considered walking over and joining in the conversation, but that might raise suspicions, especially on such a light wind day.

Anything to get the cat lady off his mind.

He kept seeing the old lady's face, the arched eyebrows, the surprise, the pain, and wondering if her body had been discovered yet.

As he saw it, Martin had only intended to threaten Greenfelder. If she'd planned to kill her, she wouldn't have bothered catching and killing the cat. But the old lady had gone bananas, and Martin had acted in self-defense. *Sort of.* That's what Martin wanted him to think, anyway, and when they were in bed together, anything she said made sense.

Last night she'd been incredible. It was as if killing the old lady had triggered something primal in her. She'd completely devoured him, and he'd forgotten about the evening's twisted events. But then it had all come back during the night, when he'd heard Martin throwing up again. *What the hell was wrong with her, anyway? And was it contagious?*

The cops would probably see the murder scene as a break-in that had gone bad. Maybe Greenfelder had come home and surprised a burglar, who had entered through a sliding glass door. They would know that a strong man was involved, one who could lift the glass door from its frame. They wouldn't suspect that a woman had committed the crime, at least not one working on her own. If he turned in Martin, he'd be turning in himself.

But maybe they were safe. They'd both worn gloves, so the chance of the police finding any prints were slim. They'd gotten away. But what the hell was this all about, and what would she want him to do next?

He knew he was in over his head, that he'd been swallowed by Martin and her madness. But if he ran, she might frame him, or even knock him off.

Would she do that? Would she?

He didn't know.

Forget about it; let it go, he told himself. After all, he didn't kill the old lady.

It never happened. The less he knew the better off he was.

Windsurfing was another matter. Martin didn't understand why Vance would waste his time teaching the sport to Pierce. But Erickson knew why. Vance didn't think about it as a waste of time. He was itching for wind, and if he could combine business with windsurfing, so much the better. Erickson felt exactly the same way.

It wasn't exciting watching Pierce fumble and fall, but it was a helluva lot better than following Carla Garity around to the shopping malls every day. 'Boring' didn't begin to describe that.

He started the van's engine as Pierce and Vance loaded the windsurfer onto the top of the Saab, then pulled out of the parking area and headed toward Key Biscayne. He knew the restaurant Pierce was talking about. He'd get there first and get settled at the bar. Vance might think that windsurfing was his strong point, but Erickson knew it was also his weakness.

The aging, weather-burnished wood-frame restaurant sat adjacent to a deep channel that allowed boats to reach its dock. Beyond the channel, a sea of grass spread out, seemingly to infinity.

Inside, the place was packed with people who had been out boating, fishing or diving. While Vance went in search of a table, Pierce headed to the restroom to change his clothes.

He washed off as much salt water as he could, then peeled off his damp swimming trunks and dressed in his fresh, dry clothing. He looked at himself in the mirror and combing his fingers through his hair. His year-round, South Florida tan had deepened to burnt brown, so that the color of his cheeks nearly matched his hair.

He felt better than he had for a long time. It wasn't just the exercise and being outside on the water. He'd never felt quite like this after a day at the beach, or even while scuba diving. It was something more, a sense of exhilaration that continued on past the actual sailing time. He could only imagine what it would feel like if he were skimming across the surface, leaning back against a strong wind and soaring off waves on a short board.

Vance had not only gotten a window table, but had ordered

a couple of beers. "Well, how do you feel after your first day on a board?"

"It's odd. Kind of euphoric or something."

Vance nodded knowingly. "You got a taste of it. That feeling is what it's all about. After a good day, you can bring back a bit of the rapture for days. It's a nice high."

"I don't think it'll last that long for me. Tomorrow I'll probably just be sore."

Vance laughed. "A little practice and some new equipment and you'll be out there in thirty knots, leaping a dozen feet in the air. And that's not just invigorating; it's orgasmic."

"I think I've got a ways to go before my first windsurfing orgasm."

"Transformation. That's a word that Garity used."

"About windsurfing?"

Vance nodded.

Transformational was an alchemical term. Pierce had seen it in Mullen's book.

Vance seemed to study him for a moment. "So you think you'll want a second lesson one of these days?"

Pierce sipped his beer. "Why not?"

"I can see it now. You'll be getting a harness, then a new board. You'll be water starting and jibing."

"You lost me. What's the harness do?"

"It used to be an optional part of the gear. Now, it's as essential as the boom. That's if you really get into the sport."

A waitress in a t-shirt and shorts arrived and they ordered two pounds of U-Peel-'Em shrimp and bowls of conch chowder.

"I think it's going to take me awhile to catch on to all of the finer points," Pierce confessed.

"Watch other people. Ask questions. Windsurfers are a friendly bunch. You don't see anybody laughing at beginners, except maybe other beginners. Of course, there are a few assholes, just like everywhere, but there aren't as many among windsurfers."

"Why's that?"

Vance shrugged. "I guess it's the nature of the sport—or maybe it's because it's a nature sport. Wind and water, you know. It's individualistic, but still nice to be around other people doing it. It's non-competitive, but it's fun to race, too. I don't know. You'll see."

Away from his headquarters and business and in the realm of his favorite sport, Vance was a different sort of man. Pierce liked him a lot more now than he had after their first meeting. Just the fact that he had taken the time to teach him the basics of windsurfing, when he had little to gain by it, impressed him.

"The main thing, Pierce, is getting out there and practicing. Next time I'll teach you how to beach start."

"Next time I'd like to see you out there," Pierce said.

"Pray for wind," Vance responded. "I haven't seen any since late April."

Their food arrived, and Pierce suggested they talk about the case.

"You mean, back to reality? Why not?"

Vance tasted his chowder as Pierce peeled a shrimp.

"I've come up with something I need to tell you about before I go any farther," Pierce began. "Does the name Lydia Mullen mean anything to you?"

Vance repeated the name. "Not offhand. Does she know how to jibe a short board?"

Pierce laughed. "I doubt it. She wrote a book on alchemy that I found in Jack Garity's house." He summarized what he'd found out about Mullen. "Garity was very interested in her at the time he disappeared. There could be some connection."

"You never know. She could be a windsurfer," Vance mused. "There are men and women in their seventies and even eighties out there. But anyhow, if Jack had files on this woman and they're missing from his house, then you might be onto something. As far as the alchemy goes, it doesn't really surprise me. Jack was always willing to consider ideas that others thought were off-the-wall."

"I didn't find his ex-wife very helpful. In fact, if Dawn hadn't stepped into the conversation, I wouldn't have found out much of anything."

"Carla's not one of my favorite people, " Vance said. "I've felt all along that she hasn't been telling everything she knows, and you've proven it. That's something the cops should know about her."

"What about you and Carla? Where does that fit?" Pierce asked.

A couple of beats passed. "You really are a detective, Pierce. Let me guess, Wayne Garity told you we had an affair?" Before Pierce could respond, Vance continued: "It never happened, and Jack believed me. But Carla was ready for a divorce, and she blamed me for Jack's lack of interest in her."

"Why you?"

"Because of the nature of the suntan lotion business. You know, a lot of young ladies hanging around. But that wasn't it at all. Jack hardly ever paid attention to any of them. He was in his own world."

"And you never had an affair with Carla?"

"You want to know what happened? I ran into her at a nightclub after she and Jack were separated. She was with a girlfriend. I swear the two of them were lovers, the way they were dancing together. When Carla saw me, I bought her a drink, and the other woman got mad and left. I ended up driving Carla home, and that's when she came onto me. But I just couldn't screw Jack's wife, even if they were divorced. I ended up walking away, with her cursing me. Somehow that became a so-called affair."

"Maybe Carla turned Drucker on you. He says you're a suspect, the only one as far as I can tell."

"I wouldn't be surprised."

"But Drucker sounds like he's got something of substance on you. Not just a rumor."

"Then he should arrest me. But he won't, because he doesn't have anything." Vance's expression turned defiant. "What have you got so far on Isabel? You're supposed to be investigating her, not me."

Testy, Pierce thought, and wondered if his involvement in the case was coming to a rapid close. "Nothing. Nobody seems to know if she even exists, or ever did."

"Do you think you're getting anywhere?"

Pierce took out his billfold, shook it, and the gold quarter clattered onto the table. He told Vance where he'd gotten it.

Vance reached into the collar of his t-shirt and lifted the chain bearing the gold half-dollar. "Just like this one. Jack gave it to me on my birthday last year. I started wearing it after he disappeared."

"What did he say about it?"

"Not much. It was just a memento." Vance turned it over in his hand. "Are you telling me you think Jack made these through magic or alchemy?"

"No, I'm not. According to the chair of the chemistry department at the University of Miami, that woman Lydia Mullen made eight of them. I think these are two of those eight, and somehow Jack came into their possession."

"You think the coins are related to Garity's disappearance?"

"Yeah, maybe Mullen's too. She went missing a couple of weeks after she made these coins in a semi-public performance."

Vance dropped the coin back under his t-shirt. "Okay, look into the Mullen angle. See where it goes." He smiled. "Follow the gold."

Pierce hesitated. He wasn't sure the Mullen trail would lead to anything but confusion. Vance, however, misinterpreted his equivocation for a concern about money.

"I'll have Wendy send you a check for another week."

"I thought your secretary's name was Diana?"

"That's over. She's gone. Wendy has replaced her."

Chapter 13

Elise sank deeply into the soft, yielding sofa as she waited for Umberto in the corner of the lounge outside the conference center. The place was crowded with attendees sipping cocktails before dinner. But no one was within ten feet of her, and she had a clear view of the double door at the entrance.

She and Umberto were going to dinner with several others, but they'd agreed to meet here a few minutes before heading to the dining room. She'd told him she had something she wanted to discuss with him privately.

Elise had surprised herself. She was actually enjoying the conference. It seemed that astro-archaeology had come into its own. A few years ago she'd attended another conference on the subject and only two dozen people had shown up. The presentations had been high-handed and monotonous. Many scholars then had doubted that the ancients knew much of anything about the movement of the stars, and they were intent on disproving the speculation about supposed astronomical observatories like Stonehenge and Chaco Canyon.

This conference was another matter altogether, with more than three hundred in attendance, enough to attract the press. The presentations were enthusiastic and emphasized a sense of wonder at the accomplishments of the ancients. Although a couple of presentations had attacked speculative archaeology and downplayed the importance and extent of the celestial knowledge of ancient peoples, the research seemed tainted by ideology. The presenters were both in the hierarchy of a well-known group of skeptics whose members, in their own way, were as adamant as fundamentalists about preserving their beliefs.

The conference was dominated by scholars who took advantage of satellites and computer technology, and their presentations showed that the ancients were indeed advanced astronomers and mathematicians. Some of the speakers had even gone a step farther and peeled away the scientific know-how of the ancients to explore the spiritual basis underlying the celestial knowledge.

Umberto's talk this afternoon on the Galactic Cycle of the Tzolkin was the highlight. Without a doubt it was also the most controversial speech of the conference. In a nutshell, he saw two futures, one which resulted in a virtual destruction of the planet through a combination of manmade catastrophes and natural disasters. In that future, the survivors lived a primitive existence. In the other future, the species evolved beyond the current 'high-tech, high poverty' condition of the planet to one of worldwide cooperation, harmony, and rapid spiritual growth in which national barriers and armies disappeared. What's more, he saw both futures being equally true. They would both happen in twenty to fifty years. Which future you experienced would be determined largely by your particular beliefs.

A few of the attendees, Elise among them, praised and congratulated Umberto on his ground-breaking research. Others said it made no sense. There could only be one future, because there was only one reality, and Umberto had taken the easy way out by saying there were two. Umberto had countered by saying that he'd actually simplified things; there were many futures, all equally valid.

She glanced at her watch. Umberto had agreed to meet here at six forty-five and now it was six fifty-five, and they were expected at dinner in a few minutes. She'd no sooner started fretting when he breezed through the doorway. He paused, his dark eyes slipping through the room and found her. He seemed, just then, like someone displaced in time, this handsome, exotic-looking man so visibly uncomfortable in a suit and tie. He belonged, she thought, among the Guatemalan ruins of his youth.

They chatted briefly about the conference. Umberto was pleased with his presentation, and surprised by the reaction. A reporter from the Miami Herald had wanted to interview him about what to expect in the remaining years of the Great Cycle, but he'd declined.

"Why don't you want your work and your ideas recognized by the public?" Elise asked. "I'm sure a lot people would be interested in them."

"They probably would. But I already know that the article would be something of a spool."

"Spool? Oh, you mean a spoof."

"Yes, that's it. I don't mind someone taking my ideas lightly, but the article this woman wants to write would make me seem like a crazy professor. You know?"

"I know what you mean, but you could always show the reporter your book. Let her see what you've done in the past."

Umberto had published a slender book called *The Waning Intensity: The Last Years of the Great Cycle*. It had predicted a worldwide trend toward decentralization of governments and a realignment of powers. It had seemed like fantasy but much of what he had predicted, based on interpretations of the Mayan calendar, had already occurred with one remarkable exception. As the Great Cycle came to a close, the center of world power would be based in South America, in a country that did not presently exist.

"It wouldn't do any good. Just more to ridicule."

He eyed the file folder on her lap. "So, you wanted to talk."

"It's about the notebook."

"Oh, I thought you wanted to discuss something personal."

She couldn't tell whether he was serious or not. "It is personal."

He smiled. "I know it is. Go on."

She opened the folder. "It turns out that Dad wrote the notebook in Tzotzil and then encoded it. You remember those four words you pointed out, the ones you said were the key? Take a look."

She showed him a sheet of paper on which she'd written the four cryptic words in a column. Next to each word was Umberto's suggested meanings: WARRIOR, OPPONENT, BATTLE, OUTCOME. To the right were Sabo's transcription of the code words: KOT, AVOT, K'OSHOSH, VAH.

Umberto looked at the words and laughed.

"What's so funny?"

"The key words all mean tortilla."

"Tortilla? You're kidding."

"But tortillas are an important part of the daily life of Mayans. So we have many ways of talking about them." He tapped the sheet. "What we have here is: *kot*, my tortilla; *avot*, your tortilla; *k'oshosh*, cooked tortilla; and *vah*, tortilla in a gourd."

Elise frowned, shook her head. "I don't get it."

A couple of beats passed. "I think I do. My tortilla is like me, the warrior. Your tortilla is the other person, the opponent. A cooked tortilla is near the fire—the battle; and a tortilla in a gourd is one that's ready to be eaten—the outcome.

"I like that," she said. "I guess dad was using his sense of humor."

"I wonder why he hid it in a code. Tzotzil would be hard enough to decipher."

She told him her theory. "He was just being careful this time, making sure no one like Andrews was going to be able to take that notebook and misuse it."

"He did the right thing. Is the entire notebook transcribed into Tzotzil?"

"Yes. Sabo had his students work on it." She handed the file to him and he paged through it.

"I just wish there were classes in Tzotzil so I could get it translated into English as easily."

Umberto frowned as he studied a page.

"What's wrong, more tortillas?"

"As you were talking, I was reading the interpretation of AKBAL-5."

"What is it?"

"Danger, darkness at the center. It reminded me of your Nick, and our dinner conversation the other night. How's he doing?"

"Fine, as far as I know. Is there something you're not telling me?"

He shrugged. "He's going to find the person he's looking for very soon. That's what I think."

"I'll tell him." She wasn't sure whether she was supposed to be happy for Nick or not. But maybe Umberto was just babbling.

He handed her the sheet of paper. "Don't worry. I'll interpret it for you."

"I don't want to impose on you. That's asking an awful lot."

"It's no problem. Señor Simms, your father, and I were very close, you know."

His steady gaze felt unsettling. It was as if he saw right into her. "I know. He often said you were like a son."

"We can do it together. I'll translate and you write everything down."

"That would be fantastic. When can we get started?"

He laughed. "You're impatient, aren't you? Rush, rush, rush."

"Sorry."

"Let's work on it tomorrow after the conference, at my place," he said, standing up.

"That's great."

Elated, she hugged him, and he held her close. A little too close. She caught her breath and stepped back, feeling awkward, tongue-tied, adolescent. The friendly gesture had nearly melted into a sensual embrace. 'Umberto, you know what? I think it would be better if we met at my office."

He laughed. "Of course."

Chapter 14

"Officer Horton, please."

Pierce leaned back in his chair, the phone to his ear, and picked at flecks of hunter green paint on his fingernails. He'd stopped painting after one wall. He could see the living room from his desk, and Elise was right. The color did make the room seem smaller.

"Horton."

"*Flaca.*"

"*Fulano, co-mo es-tas?*" She said it slowly, mimicking his accent. *Fulano* mean something like—'Hey, guy!'—but to Pierce it always sounded like she was calling him a fool.

"I'm fine. Glad you work Sundays. Got a special request to make." He reached across his desk to a gold-painted pyramid with drawers on each side where he kept supplies like paper clips and pens. He opened one of them, pulled out a pack of gum, and unwrapped a stick.

"*Un otro.* You don't want much. What now?"

"I hereby invoke Florida statute one-nineteen. I need the file on the case of Lydia Mullen."

"You don't always have to invoke that public records law with me. I'm not some tight-assed bureaucrat, you know. If the case is closed, you get it."

"It's from 1955. The woman disappeared that fall. I understand there was a big search for her." He spelled her name.

"Let me just check the computer, and see what we've got."

Horton was back in a couple of minutes. "It's in 'cold storage,' inactive, but never closed. Wow, five hundred and thirty-five pages. A big one."

"Oh, come on. What do you mean never closed? It's nearly forty years old."

"That's the status."

"Listen, it's related to the Garity case, and I've already got clearance on the records. Right?"

"That's a stretch, *fulano*. Are you sure it's related?"

"Definitely."

"Well, I'll still have to go through Drucker."

"Shit. Can't we do this without him?"

Horton laughed. "What, you don't like Detective Sergeant Drucker?"

"Not much. He didn't seem to care for you, either."

"It's nothing personal with him. He's just got a problem dealing with blacks, Latinos and women, and I happen to be all three."

"So how can I get the file without having to deal with him?"

"Tell you what, I'll inform Drucker of your interest in the file after you've had an hour with it. That way he knows about it, and you don't get cut out if Drucker and powers that be say you can't see it. How's that sound?"

"Great. When can I get it?"

"*Tengo que tipear una forma.*"

'Tipear' was Spanglish for 'to type.' Considering that the proper Spanish term was *escribir a maquina*, there was little doubt why *tipear* was preferred. "So how long will that take?"

"Come by this afternoon at two. I happen to know that Drucker is off today. That's the only reason I'm doing this."

He thanked her, and rang off. Now he had to kill a few hours. If he hadn't already sent Janet to look up the articles on Mullen, he would head to the library. He wanted to look up a few articles on alchemy to see what he could find. But it was probably just as well. The library was treacherous territory during the daytime hours. His ex-wife worked there, and just the thought of running into her made him feel uneasy.

But then he realized there was another library he could visit. In fact, it would be the one that Mullen had used herself at the University of Miami Medical School. He punched Elise's number and got her machine again. "It's ten o'clock on Sunday.

Must be a real exciting conference, if you're still there. I thought you didn't like those stuffy gatherings. Give me a call."

He dropped the handset back in the cradle and rubbed his hands over his face. Maybe Urella made it exciting for her. Maybe Urella had more in common with her than he did. Maybe she'd tell him tomorrow that she was moving to Guatemala with him. Hell, anything was possible.

A few minutes later, Pierce was on the MacArthur causeway headed toward the University of Miami and the medical library. A breeze was blowing and few white caps frosted the bay. He wondered if Vance would consider it a windy day, or just a so-so one. When he arrived at the visitor's parking lot, a campus cop was leaning against her modified golf cart and writing a ticket for the car next to him.

"We've got to watch out for her, Swedie." He stepped out of the Saab, and greeted the woman with a friendly good morning. The breeze carried a faint smell of perfume. She looked up briefly from her ticket book, muttered a vague greeting, and returned to her work.

"Which building is the medical library?"

She jabbed her pen over her shoulder. "Third building on the left."

"Thanks." He fed quarters into the meter until it registered three hours. He glanced at his watch, saw it was ten-thirty. He didn't plan to spend that long here, but no sense taking a chance.

As he crossed the campus, he thought about the questions that he wanted answered. Why did a chemistry professor write a text on a medieval practice from the viewpoint of a practitioner? And why would a chemist for a suntan lotion company take such an interest in that professor and her hobby three and half decades later? Finally, and most important, why did they both vanish and where had they gone?

When he arrived at the library, he headed directly to the book index. He found the microfiche card for AL and ran through hundreds of entries on alcoholism. He backtracked until he found a couple of dozen options for alchemy. He wrote down a few titles and noticed that Mullen's book wasn't listed. He moved over to the magazine index and added a few articles to his list. A couple of the books were in the stacks; the other books and articles were in the public sections. When he'd assembled everything, he piled it all on a desk, pulled up a chair, and began reading.

Alchemy was a mix of the spiritual and material worlds. It was also one of the most baffling mystical practices because it brought together mundane laboratory procedures and a spiritual quest. Science and spirit, after all, officially existed in separate domains—one of cause and effect, the other of belief. But with alchemy, change in the material world—lead to gold— required a transformation of the soul. As above, so below.

According to alchemists, all things were made of three substances: sulphur, salt and mercury. But the three substances were not the same as the chemical elements of the same name. Sulphur was an active, masculine force. Mercury was passive and feminine. Salt provided the means of union between sulphur and mercury, and was compared to the life force that united the soul and body.

An article from a journal called *The Skeptic* suggested that the term 'mad scientist' was derived from alchemy. The author argued that alchemists who raved about how their experiments had changed them had simply been poisoned while dabbling with toxic chemicals. Mercury was commonly used in their experiments, and repeated exposure to its fumes from improperly sealed receptacles caused delirium.

Yet, alchemy, he read elsewhere, was the only para-religious practice that ever contributed to knowledge of the physical sciences. Among the accomplishments of European alchemists were the discoveries of sulfuric acid, sodium sulphate, phosphorus, and benzoic acid. Alchemists produced tin monoxide, potassium lye, and zinc; introduced chemical compounds to the medical field and recognized the existence of gases. To his surprise, he learned that Isaac Newton, the father of modern physics, had dabbled in alchemy.

But did any of the experiments produce gold from lead? Most of the references were from ancient alchemical writings and were vague and esoteric. The Greek philosopher Proclus wrote: "Native gold, silver and every metal, like all other substances, are engendered in the earth under the influence of the celestial divinities and their emanations. The sun produces gold, the moon silver, Saturn lead and Mars iron."

The idea was that all metals were supposedly essentially alike. Some were more pure and perfect than others. Gold was the highest form, the end result of nature's transformation of the metallic realm. The cycle started with iron and was followed by copper, lead, tin, mercury, silver, and gold. Metals were considered to be like living things, and the alchemist who possessed the quintessence, the active life force, could greatly speed the transmutation and obtain gold.

Pierce wasn't sure how the esoteric stuff could help with his case. It was interesting to a point, but he couldn't justify charging Kurt Vance for his time unless he came up with something directly useful.

A book called *Fables of Alchemy* offered several formulas for struggling alchemists, but warned that with alchemy the state of the alchemist was as important as the chemical process. If an 'initiate,' and someone uninitiated into the esoteric craft, worked side by side with the same formula and chemicals, the initiate would produce the elixir, while the other person would fail or produce a poisonous, dangerous substance. The same could probably said about P.I. work, he thought. Sometimes it took a little magic by the investigator to get anywhere with a case. This one certainly could use some hocus-pocus to unravel the mystery of Garity's disappearance. If he didn't get anywhere with the Mullen lead, he was going to tell Vance that he was wasting his money.

Out of curiosity, he turned to the index of *Fables* and ran his finger down the page until he reached the letter M. His finger stopped on the entry reading: Mullen, Lydia. He quickly turned to the page indicated.

The reference was brief, and dealt with Mullen's association with someone named Fulcanelli. He turned back to the beginning of the chapter, and found out that Fulcanelli was a twentieth century alchemist, who disappeared in the 1920s after completing two manuscripts on alchemy. According to a French physicist, Fulcanelli reappeared in 1937 at the man's laboratory where he warned him of the dangers of nuclear power, and told him that releasing atomic energy of devastating force was easier than assumed.

Fulcanelli was subsequently pursued by the American government, and one of the people interrogated was Lydia Mullen, a sixteen-year-old French girl who was said to be his lover. Nothing was mentioned about Mullen immigrating to the United States or becoming a chemistry professor, or an alchemist. But now the implication was clear: Fulcanelli was her mentor, and he'd disappeared into the great void before her. Another disappearing act. That made three vanishing alchemists, he thought, and no cigar.

A short time later, Pierce hurried across the campus to the parking lot. Somehow, three hours had passed, and his meter had no doubt expired. He leaned into the wind that gusted between the buildings. A flag fluttered in the stiff breeze. If Vance was good to his word, he'd be out windsurfing right now.

To his relief, no ticket decorated his window and the cop was nowhere in sight. "Good job, Swedie."

He quickly tossed his stack of copied pages on the passenger seat and headed downtown. Horton should have the Mullen file ready. He would spend his allotted hour with it. Hopefully, it would be all he needed to find a lead or maybe even a link to Garity's disappearance.

There wasn't much spare floor space in Elise's cramped office at the university, but her desk was so cluttered that the floor was the only logical place for her to try out the divination system. She tossed a pair of running shoes in the corner and moved aside a box jammed with office supplies that had been in the same spot for several weeks. Then she set the stack of translated pages on the floor, and sat down. It had taken nearly four hours for her and Umberto to complete the task. But once they got started, they decided to see if they could finish in one sitting. Now that they were done, she wanted to see how it worked and so did Umberto. She crossed her legs, and placed a fast food carry-out bag and a notepad on her lap.

Inside the bag were thirteen nickels and twenty quarters.

Each one was numbered with a stick-on label.

"Okay, let's try you out," Elise said aloud. Right after they finished the translation, she'd read it over and focused on her father's instructions for performing the divination. He'd suggested painting names and numbers on stones and keeping them in two separate containers, but coins in a Panera Bread bag would have to do right now.

She looked up at Umberto, who was leaning back in her chair watching her. "Okay, I'm ready." She closed her eyes and thought about what she wanted to ask. She'd told Sabo, the cryptographer, that she would ask what she should do with the divination system. But she already knew the answer to that. She was going to put it to use, for herself and for anyone else who wanted to try it.

"Do you mind if I get personal?"

Umberto frowned. "You asking me or the gods?"

"I want to ask about Nick and me. Is that okay?"

"Of course."

"Good. What's going on with Nick and me? No, that's too vague." This was harder than she thought. Dad had written that it was important to be as specific as possible. "Okay. Where is my relationship with Nicholas Pierce headed?"

That was the crux of what she wanted to know. She closed her eyes again and repeated the question to herself. She reached into her bag. Several divination methods were suggested in the notebook, but she'd decided to use the one he'd emphasized, which had four simple parts to it.

She'd translated the four tortillas to mean: the surrounding influences, the past, the present, and the outcome. For each part she would draw a quarter designating one of the twenty sacred signs, and a nickel representing one of the thirteen numbers. If the tail side of the coin appeared, it meant the meaning was reversed. The notebook provided a brief analysis of every combination.

The first quarter she drew was seventeen, Caban or Earth. The nickel was number eleven. She wrote it down as Umberto watched. The second combination was Ik or wind, which was reversed, and the number two. The third was Chicchan or serpent and the number five. The last was Kan or Seed and the number four.

She looked up at Umberto. "You know what it means already, don't you? Well, don't tell me. I'm going to look it up. We'll see if it makes any sense."

Umberto didn't say a word.

She flipped through the pages of the interpretation section. The surrounding influence dealt with the earth and dissonance. Like an earthquake, she thought. Not exactly encouraging. The relationship was in danger of breaking up. She turned to the second combination.

For the past, there was some sort of gathering of people that affected the situation. The conference. The quarter had been reversed with the tail side up, indicating that the gathering had a negative impact. Right on the money, she thought. The number one indicated unity or a singular state. She had attended the conference on her own, separate from the relationship.

The present situation, the serpent, suggested energy, possibly sexual energy, and the five was the center. There was still that, the sexual attraction. Maybe it was at the center of their relationship, but there was more to it than that. She wasn't so sure she liked this oracle. How strange, she thought. Her father was dead, yet here he was advising her on her relationship with a man, something he'd never done in life. He'd even kept his personal life to himself, a matter that she was still trying to comprehend.

Maybe the oracle was saying that sex was all that was keeping them together right now. It was true. When she'd gone to his house and stayed the night, their relationship had mended, at least temporarily.

The outcome, the seed, the generative principal. Sex. More sex. But it was reversed. Sexual tension. Wonderful. But she'd forgotten to look at how the sign combined with the number four. She ran her finger down the page until she found the number. One word caught her attention: jeopardy.

Great. The relationship was in jeopardy. Or was Pierce in jeopardy? She remembered Umberto's comments about Pierce and danger. As if Pierce lusted after it. But if he was in jeopardy, then so was her relationship with him.

"I don't like it, Umberto. It's not telling me anything I want to hear."

"But maybe it's telling you something you need to know."

"If that's the case, then it looks like Pierce and I have had it. Finito."

"No. That's only the pattern you're in right now. It can change."

"How? Tell me how I can change it."

"I do it," Umberto said.

She shook her head. "No, I think it's best that you stay out of it. I know you mean well, but Nick wouldn't understand."

"You don't understand, either. There's something I have to tell you."

He was going to make things worse. He was in love with her. "Umberto, I really want things to work with Nick and me."

"I do too. But there's something you both should know. I told your father I would never say anything, but now I know it's okay."

"What're you talking about?"

He reached into a file folder in which he'd carried his copy of the notebook. "There's one page we didn't do." He held it up. There were five words in the center of the page. Elise had looked briefly at this page, thinking it was a title page. But now she realized it was a dedication page, and she knew enough Tzotzil to translate it.

"For my daughter and son."

Umberto leaned forward, his dark face straining at the seams of his jaw, and when he spoke, his voice was very soft. "You're my sister, Elise. My half-sister."

Elise laughed nervously. "You're kidding, aren't you?"

"It's true," he said softly.

Elise just stared at him, surprised, angry, hurt that her father had never told her. She tried to fit it all together, but couldn't. Too many pieces missing, she thought, too many years when she'd been in the States and her father had remained in Guatemala.

"I should have told you before," Umberto went on, speaking quickly now. "I wanted to. But I was afraid you would not understand, afraid you would think he didn't love your mother. I was conceived when they were still married."

Her eyes filled with tears then and she realized that what she felt most of all was joy. "It's great. It's just great." She leaped up and hugged him. "You're my brother. That's all that's important."

He pulled back from her embrace. "Tell Nick."

When Pierce arrived at the records office, Horton didn't return his jovial greeting. Her dusky curls famed her face as a she leaned over the count and her dark eyes telegraphed bad news. "*Fulano. Te vas a fearkear* when I tell you what I found out."

"I'm going to freak? *Porque, flaca?*" Pierce couldn't help laughing. He rarely heard anyone use 'freak' as a verb anymore in English, but it was one of those Spanglish street words that kept popping up in Miami. Not long ago, he'd heard Gloria Estefan use it in an interview on one of the Spanish TV stations, which he supposed legitimized it.

"You're not the only one interested in these old records," she said.

"Drucker's got it?"

"No, Frank Davis. He checked out the file two days before he died. It was never returned."

Pierce wasn't surprised that Davis had taken the file. After all, Dawn Garity had told the detective about Mullen. "Maybe it's still at his house."

Horton shook her head. "I called Davis' widow and asked her about it. She looked around, but she didn't think it was there. She's gone through everything, and would have seen it, she said. But that's not all she told me."

"What else?"

Horton lowered her voice. "The day of the funeral someone broke into the house. Davis's study was ransacked. Nothing was taken as far as she could tell."

"But she didn't know about the file, did she?"

Horton smiled. "Bingo, Nick-o."

Bingo, hell. He wasn't any closer to finding Isabel, which was what he was hired to do, than before. All he knew now was that Davis's scuba diving accident was sounding like murder, and if he really thought about it, he knew he'd suspected as much all along. "I'd like to take another look at the Garity file. I want to see everything Davis wrote about the case, especially during his last days."

"I can't do it, Nick. Not unless Drucker is here. That came from the chief."

"That figures. Drucker's got something he doesn't want me to see. It's about Kurt Vance, the guy who hired me."

"Oh, oh, *fulano*. You working for the bad guy again?"

"Not if I can help it. Where's Drucker now?"

"They assigned him another murder case. More punishment, I think. The house where it happened was full of cats, and Drucker hates them. I hear he won't stay in the house for more than a minute or two at a time, and the cats are gone."

"Cats? Where's the house?"

"Up in north Miami. Not far from the FIU north campus."

"Hundred and Fourth-Third Street?"

Horton turned and tapped a few keys on a computer. He already knew what the answer was going to be. "That's it. The victim's name is Glenda Greenfelder, age sixty-six. Happened sometime Friday night. They didn't find her until this afternoon. It looks like a botched break-in." She moved back to the counter. "You know something about it?"

"Sure do. I know that Jack Garity's next door neighbor is dead."

"*Carajo*," she said under her breath. "Maybe that's why Drucker's on it."

The light was blinking on his recorder as Pierce walked into his study. Probably Elise returning his call from earlier. He tapped the message button. "Nick, Vance here. We need to get together. Something's come up. Besides the wind, that is. Bring your board. Let's meet at 16th Street in Pompano Beach. It's a good place, protected by the reef. Say twelve-thirty. If that's any problem, let me know. Like I said, we've got to talk, and I don't want to do it on the phone."

There goes tomorrow afternoon, he thought. Pompano was

another fifteen minutes north of Fort Lauderdale. He hoped Vance wasn't just looking for a windsurfing buddy.

The recorder beeped with another call. "Nick, it's Elise. Where are you? I've got some very interesting news. I'm at the office now, but I'm heading home in a few minutes. I'll give you a call when I get there."

She sounded up, he thought, but wondered what she was doing at her office on a Sunday.

The doorbell rang. Maybe she'd changed her mind and decided to stop by. He tried to think who else it would be, if not Elise. He answered the door. Janet. Dressed in a pale blue cotton skirt and a pink t-shirt with shoulder pads. Holding a file folder. "Well, hello. What's going on?"

She smiled, looked embarrassed. "I hope I'm not intruding, Nick."

"No, not at all. What is it?"

"I had some time this afternoon so I went to the library and looked up what I could find on Mullen."

"Janet, you didn't have to do that."

"I wanted to."

"C'mon inside." He led her into the living room, and she took a seat on the couch. "Something to drink?"

"A glass of water would be fine."

He poured two glasses of ice water, amazed by his new secretary's enthusiasm. Maybe she didn't have anything else to do. Maybe she wanted to impress him in her first week so he'd keep his promise about sponsoring her. He knew one thing. She was acting more like a partner than a secretary. He handed her the water and sat in the chair next to her.

"Thanks. I was so intrigued by what Professor Kaufmanus said about Mullen that I wanted to follow up on it." She tapped the bulging file folder on her lap. "Anyhow, I think you'll be interested in seeing this stuff."

"Tell me about it."

"Do you know that Mullen was once involved in cancer research?"

"Nope. Didn't know that. There's a lot of things I don't know about her. Or about Garity. But I'm thinking whatever happened to him wasn't an accident. Either someone wanted Garity to disappear or he intentionally got lost to get away from someone."

He told her about Glenda Greenfelder.

"That's awful. Why would anyone kill her?"

Pierce thought about the gold coin tucked in his billfold. "Maybe she knew more than she let on. I don't know. But now I'm wondering about those detectives who died. Maybe the deaths weren't accidental at all."

"Maybe not. What an interesting and mysterious case. But where does Mullen fit in?"

"That is looking more and more like the key question." He realized he was straying from her research. "I'm sorry. About this cancer research. What did she do that got so much attention? I know she didn't find a cure."

"No, but she got in some hot water. It seems she gave a talk to a fundraising group, and said that cancer was created by the mind of the individual. I guess that kind of talk didn't go over well in the fifties. She lost her research grant, and turned to other things."

"Like alchemy?"

"So it seems."

"I'll have to read it over. What else did you find?"

Janet flipped through the file. "There're several articles on her disappearance and the investigation, and some others on her work." She stood, handed him the file. "I'll let you go."

He gazed into her blue eyes. "Listen, I appreciate your effort."

"Nick?"

"Yeah?"

"I just want to thank you for getting me involved in a case right away." She shrugged. "If there's anything else I can do, just let me know. It doesn't matter what time, either."

"Janet, I know you want to be an investigator, but you don't have to break your neck your first week. Besides, you've got to keep in mind that primarily I want you to man the office."

"*Man* the office?"

He laughed. "I guess that's not the best way to put it."

"Well, I'm glad you noticed." She extended her hand. "I better be going."

How could he not notice? He took her hand, didn't exactly

shake it, just held it and got lost in those eyes. He felt a nearly magnetic attraction pulling him toward her. He would kiss her; they would tumble onto the couch and it would be all over. Did she feel it as strongly as he did? Her fingers tightened over the back of his hand and they leaned toward each other at the same instant.

Then the phone rang. He quickly released her hand. "Excuse me." He walked over to the phone.

"Nick, it's me. Did you get my message?"

"Hey, Elise." He glanced at Janet. "Yeah, I got it."

"Well, you could sound a little more curious."

"Sorry. I'm just preoccupied with this case. How was the conference?"

"As a matter of fact, it was a good one. And guess what? I got Dad's notebook translated into English from Tzotzil."

"How'd you do that?"

"Umberto and I finished it today, at my office."

"Oh. Good."

"I want to tell you all about it, and something else, too. It's a surprise. Can we get together tomorrow for lunch?"

"I'll be windsurfing."

"I thought you were going to do that Saturday."

"I did. Vance and are going again. He likes it."

"Do you?"

"Well, I'm willing to try it again."

"Be careful. It might be windy tomorrow."

"That's the idea."

"You know what I mean." She sounded glum.

"I'll give you a call."

"Okay. Bye." She hung up. Maybe he should've asked her what the big surprise was. But hell, she seemed more interested in spending time with Umberto, anyhow.

He turned to Janet, feeling awkward now. "That was Elise."

"I know. I'll see you tomorrow."

He walked her to the door. She paused a moment, gave him a small, secret smile, then walked off. Jesus. Working with Janet was going to be a different sort of challenge than he'd faced with his other secretaries. And that was an understatement.

Chapter 15

At first he thought it was the alarm. Pierce's hand patted the top of the clock, but the ringing continued. The telephone. Christ, what time was it?

He squinted at the clock, Quarter to seven. Who'd be calling him now? He cleared his throat. "Pierce."

"Good morning, Nick-o. Wake up call."

Horton. *Flaca*. For chrissake. What the hell's going on? You on a new shift?"

"No. I'm still at home. I didn't want to call you from the office, but I had to tell you I found out what the asshole is hiding from you."

Pierce was confused. "Which asshole?"

"You must know a lot of them, huh? Drucker, *fulano*. I'm talking about Drucker."

He rubbed his face, clearing away the sleep. "Right. I'm just waking up."

"I can tell. Well, this will open your eyes. Before I left yesterday, I got a peek at the Garity file."

"I've already seen it, remember?"

"You haven't seen all of it."

"What do you got?"

"A letter from a woman name Isabel. She apparently was involved with Garity, but split when he disappeared."

Pierce was suddenly wide awake. "Hang on." He grabbed a pad and pen from the nightstand. "What's it say?"

"She says she's hiding because she's afraid of Vance. She says Garity told her he was worried that Vance was going to kill him. It was over some disagreement about a new drug Garity made in his lab at Vance's factory. Vance wanted commercial control and Garity balked. So how do you like them beans?"

"How old is the letter?"

"Drucker got it about a week before you showed up to see the file. But that's not all. Isabel followed it up with a short note. She pleads with Drucker to stop Vance. She thinks he's going to kill her if he finds her. That arrived the day before your visit. So I hope you're not looking for this Isabel for Vance."

"Christ. What a mess. That explains Drucker's behavior."

"Like hell it does," Horton barked. "He's always that way."

"I need some coffee. Oh, where was the letter mailed from?"

"All the way from Miami. She's right here in the Greater Miami playground."

"Thanks, *flaca.*"

"Whatever you do, don't say anything to Drucker about the letter, or my ass is grass."

"My lips are sealed, *flaca.*"

He started the coffee and looked out the kitchen window. He glimpsed a slice of the bay. Waves, a trace of white caps. The leaves and branches of the trees in the yard were fluttering. A good day for windsurfing, and now he had a good reason to go. He'd confront Vance head on.

As he ate breakfast, he read a couple of the articles from the Mullen clippings, then decided to play the windsurfing video again. This time he actually knew what they were talking about, and he picked up a couple of pointers. He imagined Vance learning to windsurf years ago with no teacher, no videos. It was amazing that he'd persisted.

Outside, he loaded the windsurfer on the roof rack, and decided to spend a couple of hours at the office before driving to Pompano. He'd just locked the door of his apartment when he heard the phone and realized he'd forgotten to turn on the recorder. Maybe it was Elise. He'd call her tonight. Someday maybe he'd get a car phone. But truth of the matter was that he liked not having one. Driving still provided a small corner of privacy where no one could impinge on his thoughts.

He entered the Edison Hotel lobby, the Mullen file under his arm. The elevator door opened and Gibby rolled out. "Morning, Gib."

"There you are." Gibby's curly hair was wild, and his eyes were bulging more than usual. "Talk to your secretary right away, Nick. You've got a present up there. You better call the cops, too, if she hasn't already."

"What're you talking about?"

"Go see for yourself. I don't want to spoil my appetite talking about it."

Pierce took the stairs two at a time to the mezzanine offices. He hurried through the travel agency, heads turning his way. Whatever it was, everyone knew. Not even nine o'clock and his day was raging several knots ahead of the wind.

A box lay on the floor a few feet inside the door. A towel covered it. "Janet?"

She walked out of the bathroom. "Nick, I called you a few minutes ago. You must have just left."

"What's going on?" He set the Mullen file on the corner of her desk, and took a couple steps toward the box. "What is it?" He lifted the towel. "Jesus Christ." A headless black cat lay in a dried pool of blood. No, the head was under the tail, its lips drawn back from its teeth, its mouth half open. The corpse stank.

"One of the travel agents found the box outside the main door when she got here. It had your name on it. I brought it into the office. I wasn't going to open it, but the smell made me suspicious."

He took another look, then tilted the box so that the body flopped over. The right paw was white. "Shit. It's Garity's cat. Two-Bits."

"You mean the one..."

"The one that had the gold quarter. Greenfelder said it was his good luck charm. I guess the luck ran out, for both of them." He suddenly felt guilty about taking the quarter.

"But why would anyone...?" Janet shook her head. "Do you think it has something to do with that quarter?"

"I've got the feeling that it does."

He'd only told a few people about the coin. Janet, Vance,

Dawn and Carla Garity, Elise and Umberto. He could discount the last two right away. Carla and Dawn had left town and were supposedly in North Carolina. That left the man who had hired him, who had a gold coin around his neck, and Pierce's own secretary. But what about Judge Garity? What did he know about the gold coin?

"Janet, would you call Judge Garity's office and see if he's in? And also find out who flies out of West Palm Beach to Asheville, North Carolina."

"I'll get right on it. Do you want me to check with the airlines to see if Carla and Dawn Garity were passengers on a flight on Saturday?"

"Don't even bother. That sort of information is almost impossible now to get from the airlines. Unless you got connections."

"I get it," she answered. "The travel agency."

"You catch on fast."

There was a sharp rap at the door. "Oh, I already called the police."

Pierce dropped the towel over the box, and reached for the knob just as the door swung open. "Hiya, Nick. How are ya?"

Larry Linder, the furniture magnate, smiled broadly. At the moment, he was the last person Pierce cared to see. Even though it was at least eighty degrees out, he wore a three-piece suit. His trademark cigar stuck out of a corner of his mouth, unlit.

"Mr. Linder."

"Call me, Larry, Nick." He slapped Pierce on the back as he moved into the office. He eyed Janet up and down, nodded and winked. Janet walked into Pierce's office and went to work on the phone. He couldn't blame her.

"What's up?" Pierce asked. "I thought you were all through with me."

"All through nothing." He leaned his butt against Janet's desk. "You were right about the lie detector test. It's bogus. I hired another guy and he found half a dozen of my people in on the theft, including my mother-in-law, who works part-time in accounting, and a new salesman who was living in Cleveland or some place like that when all the thieving happened. No way those two were stealing from me."

Pierce shrugged. "Yeah, well, that's too bad."

"So I want you back on board. You can pick up where you left off."

"Sorry, Larry. I'm all tied up with another case right now. I can't do it." Actually, he had no problem handling two or three cases at the same time, especially now that he had Janet with him. But he wasn't about to work for Linder again.

"You're kidding me. Come on, Nick," Linder cajoled.

"Sorry."

Linder's eyes dropped to the floor. "Something stinks in here. What'ya got in the box?"

"Nothing." He scooped up the box, carried it into the bathroom with it. "I gotta go, Larry. See ya around." He pulled the door closed, shutting out Linder. He was the sort who would hang around and whine if he didn't cut him off.

"Gotta go where?" Linder called through the door. "Oh, I get it. You gotta take a crap."

Yeah, Linder was a class act.

Pierce set the box down and leaned against the door. Great. Stuck in the bathroom with a dead cat. He'd give Linder a few seconds, then escort him out of the office.

Now Linder was talking to Janet. "I know you. Sure. I never forget a face. I couldn't place you at first. But now I remember. You were looking for a bedroom set about a year ago."

"I didn't live in Miami a year ago," Janet answered.

What was Linder doing, trying to pick her up? Pierce opened the door just as Linder handed Janet his card. "You must have seen my ads on TV. Linder furniture."

She shook her head.

Linder shrugged. "Maybe I'm wrong. You *must* be new in town if you ain't seen my mug on TV."

"Larry, we've got work to do," Pierce said. "I'll have to ask you to leave."

"All right All right. I get your message. I think you're making a big mistake, though. From a business stand point, you never turn down a customer."

"You do if you can't help him," Pierce snapped. "I told you I'm busy."

Linder headed toward the door. "Hey, I saw my windsurfer on your car around back. I guess you got time for that."

"Good-bye, Larry."

"You didn't even thank me."

Pierce took a step toward Linder, his jaw set. "Did I hear you say you wanted to take it back and pay me the six hundred you owe me?"

Linder smiled, and backed out the door. "I don't think so. We made a deal."

Pierce turned to Janet when he was sure Linder had left. "One of my former clients. Sorry if he harassed you. Linder isn't known for his tact."

"So I gathered. But now I know how you got your windsurfer."

"Yeah. Did you get hold of the judge?"

"He's in court. I'll try calling him later and set up a time when you can talk with him. I found out that Delta flies to Asheville. Do you want me to talk to Gibby to see if he can get passenger info on last Saturday's flight?"

"You better let me handle that one." Gibby had the right contacts, but was more likely to help with a direct request from his ex-partner than from Pierce's new secretary.

"I get it. If he thinks you're too busy to make the request yourself, then maybe he's too busy to check on the names."

"You are a quick study," Pierce remarked with a laugh. "You've already got his number down.

He headed into his office with the Mullen file and started paging through the articles. One of them seized his attention: "Outspoken Chemist Abandons Cancer Research."

He stared at the picture accompanying the article. Lydia Mullen appeared to be in her mid to late thirties, a serious-looking woman with curly, dark hair and glasses. Although her sullen expression made him initially think she was homely, he realized that she was actually quite attractive.

The article, dated Dec. 15, 1954, started out by saying that Mullen was a biochemist who had left her promising career a year earlier. She was characterized as being 'difficult' by colleagues, which was probably true for any woman in the 1950s who said anything controversial and stood by it. Her academic background and accomplishments were described in glowing terms, no doubt with the intent of showing how peculiar it was that she had forsaken her career.

She explained that she still stood by her statements about cancer, but that her intent was never to blame cancer patients for their disease. "Of course no one would wish cancer on himself," she said. "But the mind works at levels we barely understand. Our thoughts and emotions are related to our physical well being, and anyone who says differently has never looked deeply inside himself."

Strong words, Pierce thought, and read on. When asked if she missed her research, she said there was nothing to miss. She continued to teach and conduct research, but now she was free to pursue new avenues. Her goal, she said, was to create an elixir that not only protected against diseases and viruses, but greatly extended the normal life span.

"What I'm talking about is the inverse of what I've said about cancer. The mind creates disease, but with proper preparation and the help of the elixir, the mind can create health and extend life indefinitely."

If Jack Garity was interested in Mullen's research, he might've been attempting to produce the drug she'd been working on, Pierce thought. He flipped through the articles, looking for anything related to a new drug. He paused at an article proclaiming: "Controversial Prof Admits No Magic in Gold Coins." It described the experiment he'd already heard about through Janet, but now Mullen was saying it was a gimmick to attract attention to the 'disappearing study of alchemy.'

A month later, Mullen herself disappeared. Now Garity. Maybe it wasn't about gold at all, but about a magic bullet, a new wonder drug, Mullen's so-called elixir. Maybe Garity wasn't the only one interested in Mullen's work. If Garity had been attempting to make a life-prolonging drug, then Pierce may have found a motive for the chemist's disappearance. Or for his murder. And more and more it looked as if Vance was at the heart of the matter.

"Knock, knock," a deep voice said from the doorway, interrupting his thoughts.

Now what? Pierce looked up, half-expecting to see Linder again. But it was Drucker. "Where's the cat, Pierce?"

The wind was blowing about seventeen or eighteen knots out of the northeast when Erickson arrived at the beach. Vance's Range Rover was parked a couple spaces away, but Vance was nowhere in sight, and neither was Pierce. He spotted a half dozen sails bobbing above the waves, a couple of them more than a mile from shore. It was the first day of the season for short boards and Erickson was itching to catch a few puffs. He needed to clear his head, to release the anxiety he was feeling.

He quickly unloaded his gear and carried it over to a small park adjoining the beach. He would have preferred windsurfing without the complications. But he had to keep in mind that he had a job to do. He was expected to start a conversation with Vance. Nothing serious. Just light banter. Find out how much windsurfing he was planning on during the coming weeks. Easy stuff. But Martin had made one other request, an odd one, and it bothered him. Bothered him deeply.

Thanks to Drucker, Pierce was late getting to Pompano. The homicide detective had questioned him for nearly an hour about the cat and Glenda Greenfelder. Pierce did his best to sound helpful, and told him about his two conversations with Greenfelder. But he didn't say a word about the gold coin. Drucker, after all, wasn't exactly forthcoming with his leads.

It was nearly one-thirty when he eased down 16th Street looking for a parking space. He found a tight spot between a pickup and an old Camaro with a home-made trailer designed for hauling windsurfing gear. It was a weekday, too windy for lying on the beach, yet there was hardly a parking space left on the street. Vans and sports utility vehicles predominated, most of them with roof racks. Vance's Range Rover was among them, but Pierce didn't see him. He was probably out on the water.

The surf looked choppy, but the waves breaking on the shore were reassuringly small. Maybe a couple of feet. He watched several windsurfers skim across the surf, winged creatures, mercurial. He'd stick close to shore and practice. No sense getting into trouble. Besides, the main point of the trip, as far as he was concerned, was talking to Vance, not windsurfing. He unstrapped his board, and lifted it from the roof rack. The wind caught the bottom side and nearly ripped the board off his shoulders. He bent his knees, and tilted the board toward the wind. But now the wind drove him downward and he nearly lost his footing.

"Can I give you a hand there, buddy?"

"Sure." Pierce couldn't see who was talking to him, but it didn't matter.

"Take the nose. I got the tail," the man said.

Pierce lifted the nose over his shoulder, and the two of them carried the board down to the shore. "Thanks. I appreciate it."

"No problem. That's a long, heavy board. You could have some serious trouble sailing that one today." The man was several inches shorter than Pierce, lean and muscular, with a crew cut and a pierced ear.

"I'm just learning. A friend of mine is going to give me a few pointers. That's all." It was odd calling Vance a friend, but it was the simplest thing to say.

"I'll give you a couple of quick ones," he said. "Rig your sail up on the grass, not down here in the sand, and don't go out too far or you may end up with a long walk back."

Pierce laughed. "You mean a long sail back, right?"

"Nope. I mean a long walk back dragging you board and rig." Crew Cut picked up his board and sail as if the entire rig weighed five pounds and waded into the surf. A moment later, he stepped onto the board and sailed away, rising over one wave after another.

Pierce had just finished rigging his sail when Vance showed up. He wore a glistening wet one-piece black and yellow wet suit that reached to mid-thigh. Around his waist was a harness with a hook in front similar to what Crew Cut was wearing. His hair was slicked back, water rolled in beads down his face.

"There you are, Pierce. I was wondering if you were going to make it."

"I'm here."

"It's sort of windy for you today, but it'll be good experience. Like I told you before, you gotta put your time in." He got down on one knee and loosened the line Pierce had just tied at the base of his sail. "You need more downhaul. You don't want your sail flapping around like wet laundry."

"You having a good time out there?" Pierce asked.

"After five months of no windsurfing, the answer is a definite yes. A great time."

"You never go out in the summer?"

"Not unless there's a hurricane warning, and the past summer was quiet. I didn't even get down to Aruba or D.R. this year."

"So the windsurfing is good in the Dominican Republic?"

"Some of the best. There's a windsurfing village on the north coast called Cabarete. You ought to go there sometime. Catch those summer winds. It's not too pricey, either."

When Pierce co-owned the travel agency with Gibby, he was constantly offered FAM trips to virtually every tourist destination in the Caribbean. He turned them down every week. But now he'd have to pay full fare like any other tourist.

"Sounds like fun. Listen, we've got to talk."

Vance's expression hardened. "I told you, Pierce, I don't mix business with windsurfing. It'll wait. The wind won't. It could die any moment. It'd be a damned shame if we wasted that gift."

The wind was a gift, the wind dying. He'd never thought of it that way. He carried the sail down to his board; it looked like a great white whale next to Vance's trimmed down version that was covered with pink graphics and the name, Fanatic, on the bow and Ultra Rabbit near the center of the board. "So this is one of your short boards," Pierce said.

"One of my longer short boards. It's got a lot of volume. It's for light wind conditions."

"I thought you said the wind was strong."

"For you, it is." Vance laughed. "It's all relative, you know. Stop talking and get out there."

Pierce attached the mast to the board and awkwardly lugged the board toward the water, dragging the sail behind him.

"Hold it. There's an easier way to do that," Vance said. He took the rig by the mast with one hand and one of the foot straps with the other and guided it into the water. "Always hang onto the mast and board, and keep the clew of the sail leeward."

"I feel like a baby learning to walk."

"No, you're learning to sail, Pierce." The waves crashed above Vance's waist and the ebb was at his knees as he lowered the into the water. "Another thing. Watch out so you don't drop the fin on your foot. You can snap a toe or two very easily. And stay on the windward side of the rig or it'll crash into you."

Pierce nodded, trying to keep track of everything Vance was telling him and what he'd learned his first time out. He took the board from Vance, and waded a few more steps.

"Just climb on and try uphauling," Vance advised. "And be glad we're not in Lauderdale."

"Why's that?"

He pointed off-shore to the northeast. "The reef is breaking the waves. In Lauderdale, the waves right now would be breaking over your head and you'd be pounded into the sand."

"I'll take your word for it." Pierce climbed onto the board, started to stand up, but a wave knocked him off. A second try ended the same way.

"You're drifting in." Vance called to him. "Walk it out to where it's up to your shoulders. The waves are tamer out there."

He did what Vance told him and was about to climb onto the board when he heard a shout. "Look out!" Vance yelled from shore.

Pierce glanced up just in time to see a board skipping over the waves, headed right at him. He glimpsed Crew Cut an instant before the crash. He start to duck below the surface, but suddenly the on-coming board and sailor were airborne, rising over Pierce's head, over his board and rig.

The board touched the water ten feet away. It carved a U on the crest of a wave; the sail snapped around, and Crew Cut darted away as abruptly as he'd arrived.

"That son of a bitch," Vance shouted and leaped on his board and took off in pursuit.

Chapter 16

"Can I help you?" Janet asked as she answered the phone on the first ring.

"I hope so. This is Judge Garity's secretary again. Is Mr. Pierce in?"

"I'm sorry. He's out for the rest of the afternoon. Can I take a message?

The secretary sighed. "Did he get the judge's message from this morning?"

"I gave it to him as soon as he arrived this morning, and I told him there was another one on the machine from last night."

"Then why hasn't he called the judge? She snapped. "I said it was important."

"I don't know. I'm his secretary, not his conscience. I just give him the messages."

"I'm sorry if I'm being short with you, Janet. But it's extremely urgent. Judge Garity must speak to Mr. Pierce today. As soon as possible. Will you beep him for me, please."

"I wish I could, but Mr. Pierce doesn't use a beeper, and he's very busy today. I doubt that he'll be back in the office before tomorrow."

The secretary didn't respond, and Janet could literally feel the woman scowling at her. "Could you hold a moment for the judge?"

"Of course." Janet studied the contour of her nails, and copper-cinnamon polish. No chips, no cracks. Perfect.

"Good afternoon, Janet. How are you?" Garity's voice was deep, melodic, affable, as if they were old friends.

"I'm fine."

"I seem to be having a problem reaching Mr. Pierce." Not a hint of annoyance or apprehension in his voice. "Can you tell me the situation?"

Janet repeated what she'd already told the secretary. "I see." An inkling of irritation rippled through his voice. "Could you give me his home number? I'll call him this evening."

"I'm sorry. I'm not allowed to give that out. But I'll be glad to leave a message on his machine at home."

"Please, do that. Tell him I'll be at Viscaya this evening for a concert. It starts at seven-thirty. Tell him to meet me there, if he can, and say that I've found out who Isabel is."

"How should he dress?"

Garity laughed. "Casual dress."

Janet hung up and knuckled her eyes. She needed to go outside for some air. She was driving herself too hard. But it was her choice—her only choice. It wouldn't be long now.

If Pierce had any doubt that Vance was an accomplished windsurfer, it instantly vanished. Crew Cut was fast, but Vance was gaining on him. They were half a mile out when Vance pulled alongside of him. Their sails appeared to touch as they raced over the waves. Then Crew Cut's sail slammed down, and an instant later Vance's dropped into the sea.

Pierce couldn't see a thing. The two men could be strangling each other for all he knew. The boards would eventually float to shore and later, the bodies. He wished he could jump on his board and race to Vance's aid. Hell, he had to try. He couldn't just stand here. He crawled up on the board, concentrated. Keeping his balance, he uphauled the sail. He was about to grab the mast when a wave knocked him onto his back.

He tried again. This time he crouched slightly, as he'd seen in the video. He took hold of the mast. Following Vance's instructions, he kept his gaze on the horizon rather than on the board or sail. He reached for the boom, gripped it with both hands and sheeted in. He leaned the sail forward somewhat, and moved back a couple of feet on the board. He was doing it, Jesus, he was sailing on the ocean.

He rose up over a swell, plunged into the trough, rose up

again. He wasn't going anywhere near the speed of Vance or Crew Cut, but he felt the surge of adrenaline that he'd experienced on Key Biscayne. The exhilaration, the goddamned high. He tried to pick out the two men and their rigs, but he wasn't sure any longer where he'd last seen them.

The moment that he shifted his attention the board headed into the wind. He pushed the sail forward, but was too late. The wind caught the backside of the sail, and slammed him into the water. He was stunned by the suddenness, the violence of the wind. The sail pressed down on him. He clawed at it. Finally, he found the mast and pulled himself around it. His head broke the surface; he gasped air, but a wave crashed over him and he gulped salt water. Sputtering, he broke through the surface.

Water and sky. That was all he could see. The board was his life preserver, riding the swells as he clung to the mast. He looked back toward the shore and saw that he was about a quarter of a mile out, and a couple hundred yards to the south of his starting point. He studied the shapes of the houses and condos on shore so he wouldn't lose track of his launch site.

The board pointed toward the wind, the mast toward shore. He worked his way around the board, climbed onto it, uphauled the sail, grabbed the mast, then the boom. He sheeted-in, headed toward shore. There was nothing he could do about Vance and Crew Cut. He'd been a fool to even try. He couldn't get out to them, couldn't even find them.

Then he realized he wasn't going to make it back to his starting point. He'd drifted too far south. He needed to go out farther and try again. With a better angle, he could make it. At least, he would be closer.

Recalling what he'd learned about tacking, he pulled back on the boom, turned the board into the wind. Holding the mast, he stepped around the front of it as the board pointed at the eye of the wind. But the wind caught the back of the sail, and the mast drove him into the water. Now the board was turned to sea, and so was the mast. He recalled something from the windsurfing video about how to rectify that situation, but he couldn't think. He was breathing hard, losing his strength, felt the first flutter on panic in the pit of his gut.

Maybe he should go back in. He climbed onto the board, uphauled the sail. Something was wrong. The wind immediately slammed him into the water again. That was it. The sail had been laying to the windward side.

At least now the sail and board were aligned in the same direction, even if it faced out to sea. He climbed onto the board, sat on it, rested. He counted three sails moving across the water to the south, one directly to the east and a couple more to the north. Nobody seemed to having any problems. And where was Vance?

After a couple of minutes, he uphauled again, and carefully grasped the boom. He sheeted-in, pushed forward, forcing the board away from the wind. He just wanted to sail, to stay out of the water. He was heading downwind and out to sea, but for now it didn't matter.

He glimpsed a sail and glanced over his shoulder. Vance was sailing up to him, holding his boom with one hand, motioning with the other. "Tack! Go back to shore," he yelled.

He wanted to ask what happened out there, but Vance was already sailing away. He concentrated on a starboard tack. This time he remembered the easy way. The board passed through the eye of the wind, then he walked around the mast to the starboard side. Rather than holding the mast, this time he held the uphaul line and let the tail of the mast drop down. It was easier that way. He uphauled, sheeted in, headed to shore. Then he realized that none of the buildings along the shore were familiar. He looked north and still didn't recognize any of them.

He turned upwind, but the board nearly stopped dead, and he knew he was in danger of being slammed again. He turned downwind, determined to work his way to shore. It was futile to try to regain his lost ground. He wasn't looking forward to dragging the heavy board along the beach, but he didn't have much choice. Suddenly, Crew Cut's comment to him made sense. It was going to be a long walk back.

When Pierce hit shore, he pulled the rig onto the beach and collapsed face down on the board. After a minute, he sat up. He hadn't realized how exhausted he'd gotten. Finally, he stood up, lifted the mast with his right hand and tucked the nose of the board under his left arm. He headed up the beach, dragging the board behind him. He'd gone barely a hundred yards when he heard honking. Vance's Land Rover was parked at the edge of the beach between two hotels. He stepped out the door and wave. "You want a lift, Pierce?"

Vance met him halfway. They detached the sail, and carried the board to the Land Rover. "Walking this sucker all the way back would've been a helluva penalty to pay," Vance said. "You probably never would've sailed again."

"You might be right."

"Don't get frustrated. The better you get, the easier everything is. It's actually pretty amazing that you were sailing on the ocean after one lesson. I didn't really think that you would get away from shore."

"I guess I was motivated," Pierce said as they walked back to the sail. "What happened out there, anyhow? I saw you two go down and I thought....I didn't know what to think."

"You mean you were going to come out and save my ass?" Vance laughed, and clasped a hand on Pierce's shoulder. "You got heart, Pierce. You don't know what you're doing out there, but you plunge right into it."

Suddenly, Pierce realized that he hadn't seen Crew Cut. "What did you do to him, anyhow?"

They stopped next to the sail. "Do to him? Nothing. Break down your sail and I'll tell you who that was."

"You know him?" Pierce asked as he loosened the downhaul line.

"That was Nigel Erickson. He's one of the top fifty windsurfers in the world, or at least he was when he raced. He qualified for the Olympics five years ago, but decided to become a cop instead."

"How do you know him?"

Vance shrugged. "Just from following the sport. He's done a lot of sailing in south Florida, and he's been featured in the trade magazines."

Pierce took off the boom. "So I guess you must be pretty good yourself, Vance. You caught up to him."

"Bullshit. He slowed down and waited for me." Vance held

the mast as Pierce pulled the sail off. "He apologized. He didn't see you until he was already committed to the jump. Then he hit his duck jive and the were was no reason to stop, as he saw it."

"So you guys were just talking out there."

"What did you think we were doing, drowning each other?" He laughed. "This is windsurfing, Pierce. It's not like hockey or wrestling. We don't go getting into fights with each other. Although we do exchange a few words from time to time with regular surfers. But they're usually the ones who start it, because they think they own the waves."

Pierce rolled up the sail and carried it to the Range Rover. Vance took the boom and mast. A couple of bikini-clad teenagers were showering a few steps from the vehicle, and Pierce and Vance walked over to wait their turn.

"Don't forget to wash the salt off your gear when you get home."

Pierce nodded, but his thoughts were elsewhere, and it wasn't on the girls. "We've got to talk, you know."

"Don't worry, I haven't forgotten about business." He gazed after the two girls as they walked away. "There's a little restaurant down the beach. We'll transfer your gear and load up mine, then go for a beer."

Twenty minutes later, they were seated in the shady veranda of a beachfront hotel-restaurant. In the distance, windsurfers darted across the deep blue waters, their colorful sails bobbing like butterfly wings.

"I read about Glenda Greenfelder's murder in the paper this morning," Vance said after they ordered drinks. "Do you think it's linked?"

"No doubt." Pierce told him about Garity's dead cat and where it was delivered.

"My God. Well, I've got an alibi if Drucker thinks I did it. I had company that night. And I certainly wouldn't give you a dead cat."

Pierce studied him a moment. "I don't know what Drucker thinks. I did find out, though, why he's interested in you." He told him about the letters from Isabel to the cops. He expected Vance to deny that he had been involved with Garity on a new drug patent or had threatened him. But Vance didn't react at all. He looked past Pierce, watching the windsurfers and probably wishing he was on the waves with them.

"Well, is it true?"

Vance shifted his gaze back to Pierce. "Garity had developed a drug, and yes, we did get into an argument over it. It had nothing to do with rights or money, though. I told him that if he wanted to continue working for me, he had to stop making it and taking it."

"Taking it?"

"That's right."

"What did he say the drug was for?"

"He'd been worried for months about his health. He told me the drug would help him. He kept calling it an elixir, made it sound like some sort of potent vitamin. He even had a name for it. The Fifth Essence."

"How did it affect him?"

"At first, it seemed to help. But then I noticed that he was changing, getting more introverted. He wasn't fun to be around, and his work was suffering. Finally, I threatened to fire him. I was pissed off. He'd developed this drug in my lab, on my time. I didn't know what it was. I told him that he was endangering my business with his experiments. You know, if word got out that he was making drugs at the lab, it was all over. I'd be shut down."

"I'm guessing it wasn't long after that argument that Garity disappeared."

"You got it. Just a few days."

Their beers arrived and Vance raised his glass. "A toast to the wind and to coming days of clear sailing."

They tipped glasses, but Pierce was still intent on getting more out of Vance. He couldn't understand why Vance was so blasé. "You can see how this doesn't look good for you. The argument, then hiding the information about the drug."

"Yeah, I know, I know." He leaned forward and spoke in a low raspy voice. "I didn't have anything to do with the drug or with his disappearance. But now it's looking like both matters are falling on me."

"Why didn't you tell the cops about the drug?"

Vance sighed. "Because I had visions of the investigation turning into a TropicTan witch hunt. At the very minimum, the neighbors on the island would make me move my operation. Anyhow, I didn't think it had anything to do with his disappearance. But I'll tell you, I had a key to his house and I snuck over there a couple of times late at night just to see if he'd left anything behind about his work at the lab. I wasn't taking any chances."

Pierce recalled that Glenda Greenfelder had seen a man going into the house. "What did you find?"

"Nothing. If he had any files about the drug, they were gone."

"So it never came up."

"The cops cleared me right away. They never thought I was involved in his disappearance. Not until this Drucker came along."

"Did you take Garity's files on Lydia Mullen?"

"No, and I didn't threaten his girlfriend, either. Like I told you before, I've never even met the woman."

"But you wanted me to find her."

Vance slammed his half-empty glass on the table. "Damn it, Pierce. You keep turning it around on me. Don't you realize that's what she wants? She's out there. She's manipulating you and Drucker."

"Why?"

Vance sat back in his chair. "I don't know. Maybe she was after the drug, too. But that doesn't explain his disappearance, unless she killed him."

"How long had he been taking it when you found out about it?"

"A few months, I think. To tell you the truth, I didn't follow much of his esoteric reasoning or his chemistry. But I knew right then that he was heading for trouble. I warned him. For awhile, I thought he'd dropped it, but then he started talking about prolonged life, saying he thought he could live to at least a hundred and thirty-five in good health. I just laughed and told him he was turning into a fruit cake."

"Did that make him mad?"

"No, just sort of sad. He said that Isabel was the only one who understood him."

"What did he say about Lydia Mullen?"

"I already told you. Nothing. He never mentioned her name to me. Besides, as I see it, she's not the point. It's Isabel. The bitch must have knocked off Detective Davis because he was getting too close to her, and she killed the cat lady because she was afraid that she knew too much. Who's she going to do next?"

Pierce finished his beer, gathered his thoughts. "I don't think it's just Isabel. There must be others involved. Drucker said he thought at least two people broke into Greenfelder's house. And Detective Davis. He was getting too close to the truth. If she knocked him off, she definitely had help."

"So what are you saying, Pierce?"

"It's larger than Isabel. Maybe she's part of a company or an organization that wants the drug. Maybe Garity found out about it and ran. Or maybe he knew about it and turned against them. It's got something to do with the gold coins. I'm almost sure they came from Mullen. Maybe Isabel gave them to Garity to win his confidence. She wanted him to make the elixir. I'm just talking off the top of my head now."

"So you're telling me that Garity might still be alive?"

Pierce recalled what the Guatemalan Urella had seen in his black beans. "Yeah. He might be alive and hiding."

Vance beamed at him. "I knew I didn't hire you to investigate me. What else?"

"I think Isabel is nearby. She knows what's going on. She knew that I had the gold quarter. That's why she went after Greenfelder."

"So who knew about the quarter?"

"I told you, of course. I told Carla and Dawn, but unless they were lying they had left town by the time Greenfelder was killed. I told my lady friend, Elise, and her friend Umberto. They might be having an affair, but they're not killing a cat lady over a quarter."

Vance guffawed. "Maybe it is Carla, and the trip was a ploy."

Pierce shook his head. "That doesn't make sense. If Garity

was seeing Carla again, he wouldn't call her Isabel."

"I suppose not. Who else? There's got to be someone else."

Suddenly, it fell together. "Oh, shit."

"What?"

Pierce recalled Larry Linder saying that he'd seen Janet in his store a year ago at a time when she was supposedly living in St. Paul. Janet who was perfect. Janet whose credentials had checked out right down the line. She was the consummate secretary, impeccable. But now, ironically, he realized her flaw: she was flawless.

"I think Isabel works for me. She's my secretary."

Chapter 17

One more call and her life as Janet Howarth was over. She tapped Vance's number and Wendy Spenser answered on the second ring. "It's very convenient that you're answering the phone now yourself."

"I think you've got the wrong number."

"Oh, so you can't talk. I'll keep it short. Don't let Vance be seen anywhere this evening. Keep him home. Give him a good reason to stay there."

"That's the number, but there's no one named Esther here."

Isabel Martin hung up. Esther, which sounded like yes sir, was the name they'd agreed to use in such situations when the answer was affirmative. If she'd said Norman, it was negative.

At four-thirty, she locked the door of the Pierce Agency and headed down the hallway. Gibby was talking with someone in the main office of the travel agency as she passed by.

"See you tomorrow, Janet," he called after her.

"Sure thing."

She wasn't thinking about tomorrow. Tonight was what mattered and she was looking forward to her evening with growing anticipation.

"Oh, Janet."

Now what? "Yes?"

"In case you see Nick before I do, tell him there were no Garitys—Carla or Dawn—on any Delta flights to Asheville all weekend."

"I'll tell him. Thanks."

A woman opened the door to the travel agency just as Isabel reached it. Wide-set eyes, high cheek bones, attractive in an off-beat way. The woman stared at her a moment, then moved on. It was a look of recognition, she thought, and paused in the doorway. Then she heard Gibby spout: "Hi, Elise. He's not here. I haven't seen him. You just missed Janet, his new secretary."

Isabel let the door close. So that was Pierce's honey. The anthropology prof. She'd better keep her nose out of Pierce's business, or she might lose it.

Ten minutes later, Isabel parked her red Cherokee in the lot between an old warehouse and a decrepit boarding house on the northwest side of downtown. A couple of blocks away a concrete maze of curving overpasses and interstate entrances served as a home for the homeless. She walked quickly through the lengthening shadows of late afternoon and approached the main entrance to the warehouse, the key already in her hand.

The place looked as if it had been deserted for decades. She unlocked the door, stepped inside, set the lock. A dusty directory was covered by a fissured piece of glass. It listed half a dozen companies that had probably vacated decades ago. She unlocked an inner door, flipped on a light switch and strode down the hall. She pulled open the gate to a freight elevator, stepped inside and rode up to her fourth floor apartment.

Tall windows, high ceilings and space. A sculptor had used it as a live-in studio for a few years. When she'd moved here, she'd renovated the place, modernizing it with exuberant black, red and yellow floral wallpaper, black metallic halogen light fixtures and matching ceiling fans. So much space. She loved it. Her bathroom was larger than the reception area at Pierce's agency, and her walk-in closet was larger than Pierce's office.

She kicked off her high heels, slipped the dress off over her head, stepped into the closet. A pyramidal skylight twenty feet overhead filtered the sun's rays into the spacious closet. She picked out a long white scarf, a pair of sandals, and a pale blue cotton dress appropriate for an outdoor concert on a warm Florida evening. She walked into the bathroom, carelessly pulled off her dark-haired wig, and shook loose her long blond hair.

She studied her features in the mirror. Her skin was tight on her face, accenting her cheekbones. Still good looking, she thought. Maybe a little gaunt. She'd lost eight pounds in the last two months. Without even trying. Most women would love it. But she was worried. She walked into the bedroom and flopped down on her king-sized bed. She needed to rest, to gather her strength for the evening.

The office door was slightly ajar and light filtered into the dusky hallway when Pierce arrived at five-thirty. So she was still here. En route from Pompano, he'd puzzled over how he would deal with Janet. His initial impulse was to surprise her by calling her Isabel.

Vance suggested he go directly to Drucker with what he knew, but Pierce doubted that the detective would take him seriously. He would probably figure it was a decoy to protect Vance. Even if Drucker did investigate Pierce's claim, chances were good that he'd just tip off Janet by questioning her.

No, he wouldn't go to Drucker yet. He'd play it by ear and look for more evidence. He'd find out what Janet or Isabel was up to. That was the puzzling thing. If she had stolen the files on Lydia Mullen from Garity and Detective Davis to protect herself, why had she been so helpful in providing him with articles and information on Mullen? Maybe it was just to prove herself so he would trust her, and let her in on details of the investigation. But who the hell was she, and what was the large picture? Who was *she* working for?

He gently pushed the door with his fingertips. He hadn't really been expected to find her here, but now he had to act as if he didn't suspect her. He saw a pair of feet crossed at the ankles, protruding from the side of his desk. "Janet?"

"She's gone home, Nick. It's me."

"Elise, what're you doing here?" He was relieved, then irked. "Waiting for you."

"Was she here when you left?"

Elise leaned back in his chair, her hands folded behind her head. A light from a lamp in the corner of the office silhouetted her slender figure. "Why do you ask? Are you afraid that she'd say something you didn't want me to hear?"

He didn't answer her.

"I'm sorry," she said. "I used the key you gave me to get in. You just had this weird, suspicious look on your face."

"I'm full of suspicions today." He glanced around the office, almost expecting to find Isabel standing in a dark corner, ready to pounce. Everything looked the same, but the place felt different.

"You're sunburned. You really did go windsurfing."

"Of course I did."

"How was it?"

It irritated him that she was acting as if everything was okay with them. "I hear it gets easier." He opened a file drawer. Everything was neatly organized, and alphabetized. He found Janet's application; picked up the phone, punched her number.

"You want me to move?" Elise asked.

He held up a hand, silencing her. The phone was answered by a recording. In a business-like tone, Janet gave a typical answering machine reply. Nothing fancy, nothing funny: it revealed nothing about her. He hung up, looked at the application again, then put it back.

He felt Elise's gaze on him. "I've got to make one more call." He flipped through his Rolodex, then punched a number.

"Garity residence," a woman said.

He asked for the judge.

"He won't be home until late." Pierce realized he knew nothing about the judge's personal life. He introduced himself and asked if she was his wife.

The woman laughed. "I'm his housekeeper. Wayne isn't married. I'm glad you called. Do you know he's been trying to reach you?"

Pierce scanned his desk for pink slips of paper with phone messages. There were none. "No, I didn't."

"He's out with friends this evening, a concert at Viscaya. It's a fundraiser for the sheriff."

"Tell him that he can call me at home anytime this evening."

"He said that he'd like you to meet him in the Viscaya parking lot at about 9 PM. He said it's important."

Pierce turned to Elise as he ended the call. "Shit. I can't believe this."

Elise didn't answer. He looked at her as if seeing her for the first time, and realized that she was miffed about something. He couldn't think. His concern about Janet was complicated by his confusion about Elise. "So what's wrong?"

"Well, for starters you didn't say hello," she snapped. "You didn't hug me. You're acting like I'm a piece of furniture that's in the wrong place."

"Sorry." He shouldn't have asked. Why did she have to be here now?

"It's Umberto, isn't it? You think I'm sleeping with him. Well, I'm not. In fact, if you want to know something..."

"I didn't say that."

"Well, I could feel it."

He crossed his arms. "Look, things are getting very weird in this case, and I've got a lot of things on my mind right now."

"Oh, I see. You're pushing me away. You want me to leave."

"Wait." He touched her arm as she stood. "I was just surprised to see you here. That's all." He pulled her to him, kissed her gently. "I love you," he whispered. "I'd hate like hell to lose you."

She drew her head back, green eyes studying his face. "I was worried that you were falling for that new secretary of yours, the perfect woman."

"I don't think you have to worry about that. C'mon. Let's get out of here."

"You taking me to dinner?"

"Why not? But first we're going to Janet's apartment."

"What? Why?"

"I'll tell you on the way."

Isabel rode the freight elevator down to the third floor. After a half-hour nap, she felt refreshed. She stepped out into a modern, windowless suite of offices that could be anywhere. She owned the warehouse, and Aurum rented office space. A sweetheart deal. Although only a fraction of the offices were needed, Isabel had renovated the entire floor. When she was finished in Miami, she would put the building on the market and leave it there until she made a killing.

Erickson was due back at six. He'd better be on time. She was anxious to get going. She crossed the carpeted floor and stepped into her office, where she booted up her computer and checked her e-mail. There was a day-old message waiting from Roscoe, her senior agent in Washington.

Randall contacted Judge Garity. Told him that Isabel Martin was the chief agent of Aurum. He called it a "secret government agency of the occult."

Roscoe was monitoring Randall Forrester and Heath Bingham, her last two young associates. Randall had driven the boat when she and Bingham had scuba-dived down to Detective Davis. Isabel typed a terse response.

SILENCE Randall immediately.

The capital letters would make it clear that Randall was not to talk to anyone again. Ever. Roscoe wasn't a killer, but he followed orders. He would hire a professional and Randall would be dead within twenty-four hours.

Now she knew where the judge had gotten his information. She couldn't take any chances with him. He knew about Aurum and that was knowing too much. He wouldn't stop even if Randall was killed. He was the type who would persist, and force open doors that were best left shut. Aurum's success was based on its secrecy. Besides, she was so close; the essence was almost within reach. She could feel it, and she needed it badly.

She heard the groan of the elevator and glanced at her watch. Erickson was a few minutes early. She walked toward the outer office and met him as he entered. He wore baggy khaki shorts, deck shoes and a t-shirt. She was fascinated by his looks, the crew cut and earring, but was more interested in what was going on inside of him.

He was cautious around her, but she thought she had him under control. He was concerned about Greenfelder's murder, but he'd been a cop and he knew that the code of silence applied to intelligence as well as police work. You didn't snitch on a fellow cop, and you didn't turn your boss in to the bureaucrats, either. Still, she wasn't going to take him with her this evening. She'd handle tonight's chore all on her own.

"How're you, Nigel?"

"Fine." He looked around as he always did, as if he were thinking the office was big enough for thirty people, but there was never anyone else here.

"How was the windsurfing?"

He fidgeted, shifting his weight from one foot to the other. "It was a good day for it." He reached into his pocket and pulled out a length of blue-striped cord.

"What is it?" she asked.

"What you wanted. Something of Vance's that fits in a pocket. It's line from his windsurfer."

She ran her fingers along the cord. "Good choice. Does he have more of the same kind?"

"Probably. Yeah, I'm sure he does."

"You're certain that it's Vance's?" she asked, watching him closely.

"I found it wrapped around his roof rack."

"Thanks." She touched his arm, leaned forward and kissed him lightly on the mouth. "I've got to go, Nigel, but I'd like you to meet me back here at eleven. We'll go upstairs and relax."

"All right."

"Well, you could sound a little more enthusiastic. You're a fortunate young man, you know."

He smiled. "Yeah, I know."

"Listen, I just want to tell you again that Friday night wasn't supposed to happen that way. I didn't expect that sort of reaction."

He nodded. "Can I ask you a question, Isabel?"

"Go ahead."

"What're you going to do with the line?"

Her hand dropped away. "That's my business. Don't worry about it."

Revelations. Elise had her own, but she decided to wait until they sat down to dinner before she told Pierce. Besides, his was more immediate, more threatening. As they crossed town en route to Coral Gables, she listened closely to everything he said about the woman who called herself Janet.

"Nick, you could be in a lot of trouble. I think you better go to the cops."

"Not yet. I need more on her."

"What're you going to say to her?"

"I don't know. I'll play it by ear. Maybe I'll tell her you're jealous and you want to be reassured that nothing is going on between us."

"Don't you dare say anything of the kind."

"We'll just take a look. I know she drives a red Cherokee. We'll see if it's parked outside first."

Pierce turned left onto 37th Avenue and headed south. When he reached Miracle Mile, he jogged over one block to Aragon Avenue. "Let's see. Two-ninety-six. It should be on the next block."

He slowed to a stop in front of a building. "It's a bookstore," Elise said. Immediately, someone honked at Pierce.

"All right. All right." He stepped on the gas and pulled to the curb half a block away. He looked at the address again. "Maybe I wrote it down wrong."

"You know what? I bet there's an apartment on the second floor."

"Let's go see."

They walked to the corner and found a door adjacent to the bookstore. Pierce tried it. Locked." He reached for the buzzer, but Elise grabbed his arm.

"What're you going to say?" she whispered.

"We were in the bookstore, and I realized she lived upstairs." He hit the buzzer. Waited. No answer. He pressed it again.

"Who is it?" a woman asked. A crackly sound distorted the voice.

"Janet, it's Nick."

A couple of beats passed. "Nick who?"

It didn't sound like Janet. "Pierce."

"I don't know you."

"I'm looking for Janet Howarth."

"That's my name. Who're you?"

"I guess you're not my secretary."

"I'm eighty-two years old, young man. I'm not anyone's secretary."

"Sorry to bother you."

"It looks like your suspicions were correct." Elise said as they headed back to the car.

"Yeah, and I've got the feeling my peerless secretary ain't gonna show up for work tomorrow."

"That's the least of your concerns."

"Let's go to the Grove," Pierce said. "We'll eat there. It's close to Viscaya."

"Calliope's?" she asked, hopefully.

He wrapped his arm around her shoulder. "I was thinking more on the line of fast food, but I guess we've got time."

Erickson didn't know what the place was or why Martin had turned into the long entry drive. He continued on for a block, made a U-turn, and headed back to Viscaya. It seemed that he'd heard the name. He took a closer look at the sign as he turned into the entrance. A museum, that was it. He wasn't much of a museum-goer, and he doubted that Martin had come here out of curiosity or boredom. Everything she did had a purpose. She didn't waste time.

The driveway was bordered by a thicket of tall trees and underbrush, a natural barrier from the outside world. He slowed to a crawl. He didn't want to surprise Martin or, worse, have Martin surprise him. But if she caught him spying on her, he was ready with an excuse. He wanted to find out more about the project. After all, she'd said herself that a clandestine operation meant knowing as much as possible about everyone and everything involved. But Martin also had said that you don't get caught. He didn't know what the repercussions would be, and he didn't want to find out. He was certain she wouldn't be amused.

To his relief, the drive led to a crowded parking lot with forty or fifty cars. A dozen or so people were moving toward a gate where others stood in line buying tickets. Martin was among them. He stepped out of his Camaro. Just act like everyone else, he thought.

A few people were dressed for a cocktail party, but most everyone wore casual attire. He'd fit right in with his shorts. But what were they doing here? He could fake his way through anything, but he had to know what he was faking. As he approached the gate, he saw a poster with drawing of a cello, a couple of violins. Maybe one was a viola. Whatever. It was chamber music. A concert. Then he saw the ticket price on the poster.

Twenty-five bucks. His stomach tightened. He almost turned around. He didn't know anything about chamber music, except that it wasn't going to be anything like the Springsteen concert he'd seen last month.

"How many, sir?"

"Just one." He paid for the ticket. Now he was committed.

He strolled down the path leading into the estate, and kept an eye out for Martin. He neared a stucco mansion, and saw that the crowd was walking past it, into a garden. Incredible. The grounds were immense and well cared for, and there seemed to be as many statues and fountains as there were trees. A stage with overhead lights was set up in an open area across from a couple hundred folding chairs. About half of them were occupied. On stage were four chairs and two cellos, but no musicians.

Erickson didn't dare walk over to the seating area. He moved away from the path and stood by a hedge at least fifty yards from the stage. A fountain sprayed water several feet in the air and partially blocked his view. But he could see most of the seating area through the mist. The chairs were filling rapidly, but he couldn't find Martin. Her hair had been loose when he'd met her at the office, the first time he'd seen her without a braid. She should be easy to pick out.

Then he saw her, walking down a path toward another part of the estate with a gray-haired man. From a distance, he thought, she looked remarkably like Wendy. A moment later, she was out of sight. He hurried after them, relieved that he'd spotted her in time.

Erickson followed the path until he was near the east side of the building. He saw a patio that led toward the bay, where a cove had been created by jetties of land extending out from the shore in the shape of a horseshoe. In the center of the horse shoe, several yards off shore, was a massive sculptured stone barge. Isabel and the man were walking out to it on a floating wooden walkway. From the way it bobbed on the surface, it was apparent that the walkway was a temporary addition, and not a permanent bridge to the island.

Erickson moved as close as he could, and ducked behind a bronze statue of a woman with one bare breast. One of her hands was extended, palm turned up, as if checking for rain. Isabel and her companion stepped onto the rocky structure and out of his sight. He wished he could get closer to hear their conversation, but it was too dangerous to go out to the islet. Even if he made it to the walkway without being seen, it would be difficult to stay out of sight. Maybe this was a waste of time. He wouldn't learn anything, not unless he waited for the gray-haired man to leave. He could get his license plate and trace it.

But then he heard a sharp cry from the islet. The cry of a seabird? No, it had sounded human. The music began, the cello and violins sounded distant, dreamy, weaving a thread of dark enchantment across the palatial estate. Had she just killed him? He sidled alongside a hedge, backtracking, but unwilling to turn his gaze away from the islet. He bumped into a three-foot-high statue of a black cupid, nearly toppling it over. He shouldn't have left himself so vulnerable.

But then he found an opening in the shrubbery, and ducked into it. He heard a cawing above the music and looked up at a dozen crows sweeping low. A murder of crows. It wasn't only the ironic symbolism of the moment, though, that caught his attention. Just as his brother told him six years ago that their father had died on a fall from a scaffolding on a construction site, the sky had filled with cawing crows, and he'd never forgotten that startling merger of events.

He caught his breath as he glimpsed Isabel strolling onto the walkway, her oversized handbag casually slung over her shoulder. Erickson waited, but the man didn't follow her. She was alone, and he swore he saw a slight smile on her lips.

Chapter 18

If Coconut Grove was considered upscale living, Calliope's was at the top of the scale. Ambiance, service, beautiful people. But tonight Pierce just wanted to eat, and to be on his way. He rapped his fingers on the table as he waited for his fettuccini Alfredo. He'd figured the meal would arrive in a few minutes, but then Elise had ordered half a roast duck.

"What're they doing, hunting your duck?"

"Calm down, Nick. It's only seven-thirty, and Viscaya's just five minutes away.

"I don't want to be late."

Elise peered at him, an amused look on her face. "Well, this is a first. You actually want to be early, don't you?"

"It's important. Besides, Garity doesn't know I'm coming. He won't wait around. Weren't you going to tell me something?"

She sipped her wine. "I've been waiting to get your attention."

He pulled his chair closer to the table, folded his hands, and leaned toward her. "Okay, I'm all here, all ears."

"I want to tell you about my weekend. You didn't even ask about the notebook."

"You already told me that you and Umberto spent the weekend together working on it."

"Nick, that's not true. We spent almost four hours on Sunday translating the Tzolkin. It was tedious work, but I wanted to get it translated."

Pierce shook his head. "What's going on between you two?"

"I told you before there's nothing going on." She sounded exasperated. "I like him. You know that. We're very close. In fact, and here's my surprise for you, he's my brother, my half-brother."

"*What*? You never told me that."

"I didn't know myself until Sunday. It was in the notebook, the dedication."

Pierce didn't know whether to be suspicious or overjoyed. "Are you sure it's true?"

"Umberto has known for years."

"And your father didn't tell you?"

"I'm still getting over that part. It's silly, but I guess he didn't want to hurt me."

Suddenly, Pierce felt as if his bulky windsurfer had been lifted from his back after a mile hike on the beach. "You know, I didn't think Umberto looked like a full-blooded Indian. Your brother, your goddamned brother."

She touched his hand. "You're not going to be jealous anymore, are you?"

He drew back. "Who said I was jealous?"

"Oh, nobody. Here comes our dinners."

An hour later. "I've got a funny feeling about this whole thing," Elise said as they neared the turn off for the museum. "I don't know what it is, but it reminds me of that night we went to the Coral Castle."

Pierce guffawed. "I don't think we'll be doing any digging tonight. At least I hope not."

That night she and Pierce climbed over the wall of the Coral Castle and had dismantled a rock altar where, as they'd suspected, a crystal skull had been hidden. But as they'd left, Raymond Andrews and his thugs had shown up. Andrews was so captivated by the legend of the skull and its twin that he'd sacrificed everything to bring the two skulls together. Nothing else mattered to him. The remainder of that night was blurred in her memory, a nightmare she didn't want to remember.

Viscaya and the Coral Castle: Elise had never thought of the two together, but there were certain similarities. While Vizcaya wasn't as eccentric as Coral Castle, a monument featuring colossal coral rock furniture, towers and walls of cosmic symbols, both places represented one man's singular vision expressed in stone.

Both were also places associated with heartbreak. Everything in the Coral Castle was dedicated to its builder's Sweet Sixteen, a young woman who backed out of marriage at the last moment. Vizcaya was built by John Deering, the magnate of International Harvester. It took several years to build, and was completed in 1916. But Deering only lived in it for one year. It was built for him and his wife, but Deering lost interest in the estate after their divorce.

Elise had been here many times and knew the place well. The ten acres of gardens and statuary were as fascinating to her as the seventy-room Italian Renaissance palace itself. While the Coral Castle was made of the native coral rock, Vizcaya was known for its imported art and architecture that even included the tremendous seventeenth-century gates made of pink marble and Istrian stone. The grounds were enclosed by a pink concrete wall that bore carved, primitive designs and were festooned by bright red bougainvillea and flaming vines.

As they reached the end of the long driveway and eased into the parking lot, Elise saw police cruisers and crime scene vans. She and Pierce looked at each other, then got out of the Saab and quickly walked toward the gate where a dozen officers were congregated. Several of them were interviewing people who had attended the concert. A line of people waited behind them.

A man in jeans and Miami Police windbreaker walked up to them. His dark eyes gave her the creeps. He had a roundish face with pocked cheeks and a receding hairline. "You want something, Mr. P.I.?"

"Drucker, what's going on?"

"You must know or you wouldn't be here." Drucker glanced at Elise, but didn't nod or greet her.

"I don't know a thing. Guess you'll have to tell me about it."

Drucker laughed. "I don't have to tell you nothing, Pierce."

"We're here to meet Judge Garity," Elise said.

Drucker took a closer look at her. "Is that right? Who're you?"

"Elise Simms."

"You work for Pierce?"

"She's a friend," Pierce said. "Any other questions?"

"Yeah, a few. C'mon with me. Both of you."

"What happened to Judge Garity?" Elise asked.

They passed through the gate, followed a path onto the estate. Drucker didn't say a word to them as they moved through the warm night. The mansion loomed in front of them, but they kept going in the direction of the bay. Bright lights illuminated the stone barge that rose out of the cove.

They ducked under a yellow crime scene ribbon and followed Drucker along a temporary walkway to the barge where a police photographer, forensic people, and detectives were at work. Elise glimpsed a leg and a hand of a body sprawled on the stones, then Drucker stepped in front of her.

"Wait here," he said and stepped over to a uniform. "Keep an eye on those two. They're not to go anywhere."

"He's dead, Nick," Elise whispered. "It's him."

"I know."

Drucker conferred with one of the detectives who glanced in their direction. He handed Drucker something and the detective examined it a moment.

"Why's he acting so nasty?"

Pierce shrugged. "He's not acting. I hear that's the way he is."

Drucker ambled back to them and held up a plastic evidence bag. A blue and white striped cord was inside it. "You recognize this Pierce?"

At first, she thought he was going to say no. Then he replied, "It looks like polyester line that's used on windsurfers."

"Have you ever seen this particular style and color?"

He nodded. "Kurt Vance has a spool of it in his garage where he keeps his windsurfing gear. I think it's the same color."

Drucker studied Pierce a moment. "Well, aren't you forthcoming. Why so cooperative?"

"Simple. Vance didn't kill Judge Garity."

"Who said Garity's dead? Maybe that's someone else laying over there."

"I don't think so," Elise replied. "Why else would you bring us over here?"

"Who asked you, lady?"

Color rushed into Elise's face. "You know, Detective Drucker, you're not a very good representative of your species, and I don't mean cops. I mean humans."

Drucker laughed and leaned toward Pierce. "I like your lady friend. She can hold her own."

Pierce ignored the comment. "I was with Vance this afternoon in Pompano Beach. He was going out to dinner with a woman named Wendy this evening."

Drucker slipped out a note pad, jotted something down. "Wendy's last name?"

"I don't know."

"What's Wendy look like?"

"Tall, long blond hair."

Drucker smiled. "Your client is not going to like you much when you testify against him in his murder trial."

"What're you talking about?"

"A tall young woman with long blond hair approached Garity before the concert began. He walked off with her and headed in this direction."

"There are a lot of tall blondes," Elise said.

"Sure there are." He turned back to Pierce. "Why did you want to see Garity this evening?"

"He's been trying to reach me."

Drucker shrugged. "Why not just leave a message?"

"Because he said it was important. Besides, I had something to tell him, too. I found Isabel, Jack Garity's missing girlfriend."

"If you had information about a criminal suspect, why didn't you come to me?" Drucker looked tense and irritated.

"I told him he should," Elise answered. "But he wanted more evidence."

"Okay, who is she?"

"My secretary."

"Your what?"

"She used the name Janet Howarth when she applied for the job. She's about thirty-five, tall, maybe five-ten, slender, attractive, blue eyes, dark brown hair about shoulder length."

"What makes you think she's Isabel?"

Pierce hesitated. "I don't know for sure. It's more of a feeling than anything." Pierce knew that telling him about the gold quarter wouldn't prove anything.

"We went to the address she gave Nick on her application form, but somebody else with the same name lives there," Elise said.

Drucker threw up his hands. "So you've got a secretary with a false address, and maybe a false name. I still want to know why you think she's Isabel."

"I don't know for sure," Pierce said.

"Then stop wasting my time," Drucker snapped.

"Okay, does that mean we can go?"

Two men in white coats lifted the body onto a stretch. "Not until I'm through. Now tell me why you came here."

"I already told you," Pierce said.

"Tell me again."

The questioning went on for another half an hour before Drucker told them to leave. "If I were you, Pierce, I'd drop your client real fast. Don't even call him unless you want to be charged with aiding and abetting. That bag of shit may have money, but he's going to jail, and as I see it, you're on real shaky ground yourself."

She noticed the deep furrow on Pierce's brow as they headed toward the parking lot. "Don't let him get to you, Nick."

"I'm worried about Vance. Drucker's going to try to pin the murder on him and Wendy. Maybe I should go talk to him."

She clasped his arm. "That would be a bad idea. You heard, Drucker. C'mon, Nick, let's go to my place tonight."

As they drove out of the parking lot, Elise couldn't help recalling her divination. Surrounding influences: Earth— Dissonance. Shaky ground.

Elise's house. It was a cottage, actually. Small and quaint. Varnished wood floors. Wood everywhere. It was what Coconut Grove had once been all about, and was now not much more than a memory.

"Did you lock the door?" he asked.

"Of course. Glass of wine."

"Actually, I'll take a Scotch on the rocks, if you got any."

"Sorry."

"Probably for the better. I'm going to call Vance."

"Are you sure you want to do that? Remember Drucker's warning."

"Yeah, aiding and abetting. My guess is that he already has company. They've probably taken him in for questioning."

"If they've found him," Elise said as she slipped a CD on the stereo. He recognized Enya. He'd first heard the recording here nearly a year ago. When she returned with two glasses of red wine, she lowered the volume, then reached into her leather shoulder bag that served as a book bag, briefcase and purse all in one, and pulled out a black velvet pouch. "I want you to try Dad's Mayan divination system."

"Is that what's in the little bag?"

"Part of it."

He opened the bag as if he were inspecting a bomb. "Coins. I was hoping for a Genie to pop out."

"Maybe one did."

He shook several of the quarters and nickels into his palm and saw they were numbered. "I don't get it."

"I'll show you how it works." She pulled a spiral notebook from her shoulder bag.

It seemed an odd time to play a game, but he knew that her father's fortune-telling system was important to her, and hell, maybe it would help relieve the stress of the evening. The combination of the shocking revelation about Garity's fate, combined with Drucker's dark insinuations, had left him feeling stunned and angry. "Okay, so what do I have to do?"

"Think of a question."

"Got it."

"That was quick. What's the question?"

"Do I have to tell you?"

She crossed her arms. "Of course you do. I'm not a psychic."

"But I thought this was fortune-telling."

"It's a process of drawing on the subconscious mind, bringing to the surface what you already know a deeper level."

He peeked into the bag again. "These coins do that?"

"No, you do it. The coins are a tool. So what's your question?"

"I want to ask about the Garity case."

"I'm not surprised."

"Yeah, the judge is dead and Isabel turned up in my office. That makes it damned personal."

"Say it as if you're asking a question."

"Am I going to get to the bottom of the Garity case?"

"Don't ask a yes or no question. It doesn't work that way. Rephrase it. Ask a 'how' or 'what' question."

He leaned back into the couch and rubbed her neck. The skin was damp, a little cool. He thought of a better way of ending this evening. "Let's go into the bedroom and forget all this. We'll leave this wretched scenario at the door."

"Ha. Let's do this first."

"Okay, let's see. How do I get to the bottom of the Garity case? That's really what I want to know."

"Now, reach into the bag and pick out a quarter and a nickel. One each. And tell me if the quarter is face up or down when you pull it out."

Pierce reached into the bag. "My quarter is face up and it says number one. The nickel is thirteen."

"Let's see. That combination represents the surrounding influences. We'll interpret when you're done. Take two more." He slipped his hand around her neck and loosened the top button of her blouse. "Hey, what're you doing?"

"Just creating some of my own surrounding influences."

"Be serious."

"I am."

She couldn't help smiling. "Think about your question and take two more, a quarter and a nickel."

"Oh, oh. My quarter's showing tails this time."

"It's reversed and it means something different."

"It doesn't mean I'm going to get some tail?"

She burst out laughing. "You sound like you're in high school."

He picked up a nickel. "Ten for the quarter. Three for the nickel." He leaned over, kissed her gently on the lips, and worked another button open on her blouse. She was his alone. Umberto was out of it. He still couldn't get over it.

"C'mon now. Let's finish this."

"Okay." He sat up straight, picked two more coins. The

quarter was reversed again. He reached for her blouse, but she slapped his hand. He selected a nickel, and read the numbers.

"One more time. Think of your question."

"Okay. Oh no, tails again. I must be cursed."

She wrote down the number as he picked the fourth nickel.

"Seriously, does this mean terrible things?" he asked.

"Not necessarily." She opened her notebook. "Let's see, the first pair of coins. Surrounding influences."

"I think you should take off your blouse for this."

"Be quiet and listen. You can wait."

"I was thinking about naked divination. Or is that a separate technique?"

She paged through the notebook, then looked up, frowning slightly. "Do you think sex is at the center of our relationship?"

"You asking me or the coins?"

"I already asked the coins about us."

"And?"

"There was something about sex being the main focus."

"That's not true. We haven't had sex for...for days. Besides, I think you interpreted that wrong. It's love, not sex."

Her clear blue eyes met his. "I hope so."

"Come on. Let's get to my question."

She turned another page of the notebook. "*Imix.*"

"What?"

"That's the name of the sign. It's symbolized by the dragon, and it's related to the source of life. But it's combined with the number thirteen. Secrets. The secrets of life."

"How's that fit my question?"

"I'd say alchemy is the surrounding influence."

"Hm. It does involve the elixir of some sort. What else?"

"The next combination is the opposition you face regarding the case. It's *Oc* Dog. It means faithfulness, loyalty. But it was reversed."

"Janet wasn't loyal."

"*Oc* was combined with three, which relates to the rhythm and the pattern of things. So you could say that when Janet or Isabel was working for you it was part of a larger picture or pattern for her."

He wasn't quite sure he followed her logic, but the conclusion made sense. "What's next?"

"The present." She turned a couple of pages of the notebook. "*Chicchan*. Serpent is related to energy. Combine with eight, it means…this is interesting…it's related to the manifestation of occult energy. Again it sounds like alchemy. But yours was reversed."

"What does that mean?"

"It shifts to fear, darkness."

He touched her leg, lifted the hem of her skirt. "I don't see that as my present situation."

"We're talking about the case. Maybe it relates to whatever's at the center of the case."

"Like Jack Garity, and his elixir?"

"Could be."

"So what's the outcome? That's the last one, right?"

She nodded. "I got this one, too. Seventeen is *Caban*, Earth. It's related to timing of events, and the number two is polarity. *Caban* is reversed. Poor timing. Things or people being pulled apart."

"That doesn't sound very good. What happened to happy endings?"

Elise frowned at the notebook. "I'm not sure what it means, Nick. But I've got the feeling we're going to find out."

Chapter 19

The scent of coffee woke him. Morning sun streamed through the window of Elise's bedroom. "Morning, Nick. Coffee and a newspaper. How's that for service?"

He reached for the cup of coffee she offered. "I like it. What's the catch?"

"Take a look at this."

She dropped the morning paper on the bed, he sat up, and his breath caught in his throat at the sight of a headline in the bottom corner of the front page. *Judge murdered at Vizcaya.* His gut tightened as if he'd been punched. The evening's events flooded back as he read the brief article. It mentioned an unidentified blond woman meeting him. There was no mention of any suspects. Garity had been knocked unconscious, then strangled.

"He must have been killed with that windsurfing line," Elise said. "But if the murderer left it at the scene, it means that she was either in a big hurry or wanted it to be found."

"Namely to implicate Vance." Pierce sipped his coffee, feeling more disturbed by the moment. He glanced at the bedside clock. "Shit, eight-thirty already. You kept me up last night."

"In more ways than one," she said.

He grabbed for the oversized t-shirt she was wearing, but she scurried out of his reach. "Nope. It's late, remember?"

He threw his legs over the side of the bed, took another swallow of coffee. "I'm going to go see if my wonderful secretary showed up at the office."

"Why don't you call the office and see if she answers?"

"Good idea." He leaned over the bedside phone and punched the number. He heard the answering machine click. Silence. "Hello, hello. Janet, you there?"

He exchanged a look with Elise, waited until the recorder cut him off. "The machine was on, but her message was erased."

"Interesting. She doesn't want any evidence of her voice on tape."

Pierce was already punching another number. "Flaca, *como andas?*"

"Nick, I'm not surprised you called. No time for bullshit. Do you know about the judge?"

"Yeah. Anything new?"

"A woman named Wendy Spenser and Kurt Vance, both of Fort Lauderdale, were arrested at two-thirty this morning. Vance is being charged with murder one, but they're letting the woman go. Word is they cut a deal with her."

"Thanks. Anything else?"

"No, I gotta go."

"What is it?" Elise asked.

He told her as he headed for the shower.

"That doesn't make any sense, Nick. A woman was spotted with Garity before he was killed, not Vance."

"I know. But that's not the whole story. At least not how they're going to play it out."

"Maybe Vance was involved."

"I don't buy it. I'm wondering now if Vance's secretary and my secretary were in on it together somehow."

"Jesus. The secretarial service from hell," Elise called after him.

Wendy's eyes were red and her hair was tousled. She looked rumpled; she looked like hell, Erickson thought, and opened the passenger door of the van for her. "Are you all right?"

"No, I'm not."

Erickson drove away from the downtown police station. "Do you want to talk about it?"

"I'm not supposed to say any...anything to you." Wendy

tried to sound tough. But her voice failed her. It cracked, her shoulders shuddered.

"C'mon, Wendy. What happened?"

"That's it. I don't know what happened. Suddenly, there were cops in the bedroom. It was horrible. God, I was scared. They said we killed a judge. It was crazy."

In the bedroom. He didn't want to think of her with Vance. He had the urge to run away and take Wendy with him. They'd never look back. But how far would they get before Isabel or the law caught up with them?

"We hadn't even done anything yet," Wendy said. "Vance isn't at all like the image he projects of some big playboy. He'd been with Diana for a couple of years, and she was really nasty to him. I saw it. I took advantage of it like I was supposed to do."

"What happened after you were arrested?"

"I just kept saying I didn't know what they were talking about." She swiped at her eyes. "Then about five o'clock this morning a lawyer showed up. He'd been sent by Isabel. He said I wasn't to worry, that everything was going to be all right. All I had to do was sign a paper, and I could leave. I just wanted to get out of there so I did. Then they put me back in a cell for four hours until you showed up."

"What was the paper?"

"It said that I agreed to tell what happened and in return I wouldn't be charged. But there's nothing to say. We spent the evening together by ourselves. That was what Isabel wanted me to do."

Erickson stopped at a red light. "She told me to pick you up and take you to the lawyer's office."

"I want to go home and go to bed."

"Not yet." He drove ahead, not liking what he had to tell her next. "Isabel told me what you've got say. You lured Garity away from the crowd because Vance told you he wanted to talk to him in private. But he didn't think Garity would go with him. So you told him you had some information about his brother and to come with you. Once you were alone, Vance jumped out of hiding, knocked him out, and strangled him."

"That's all a lie."

"I know, but you've got no choice but to frame him. If you don't, you're going down, too."

Wendy shook her head. "Nigel, what's this about? What's going on?"

A few days ago, he'd thought Wendy knew all the answers, and he was in the dark. Now it seemed to be the other way around. "I don't know what she's after. But at this point, you better do what the lawyer says."

She ran a hand through her hair. "I can't do that to Vance. He's innocent."

Erickson turned into a downtown parking ramp and the morning sunlight was replaced by a dingy gloom. "Look, you've gotta be realistic. If you don't go along...."

"Yeah, I'll go to jail, but the truth will come out. Isabel will be exposed. I'm sure she's responsible for Jack Garity's disappearance and now the judge's death. You can help me."

He pulled into a parking space, shut off the engine, turned to her, touched her arm. "Wake up, Wendy. If you fight her, you won't go to jail. You won't make it that far. You'll be like the judge. Dead."

Pierce and Elise were headed to South Beach where she'd left her car. "Listen, Nick, I don't care what the divination said about polarity. I'm canceling my classes today and staying with you."

Pierce smiled. "Oh, I thought you were a believer."

"Sometimes you can change things if you know about them in advance. At least, I think you can," she added uneasily.

Pierce pulled into the alley behind the Edison and parked next to Elise's Cabriolet, which now had a ticket on the windshield.

"Sorry about the ticket. I forgot about getting your car out of here."

"I thought about getting it, but I just wanted to go home after that scene at Vizcaya."

They headed around the side of the building, entered the hotel, and took the stairs to the mezzanine level. "I'll tell Janet you're my bodyguard in case she asks."

Elise paused outside of Gibby's travel agency. "You really think she's here?"

"I doubt it. But let's go see."

"What are you going to do if she *is* here?" Elise asked.

He didn't answer. He didn't know. They entered the travel agency and headed toward Pierce's office.

"Hi Nick," Gibby called out. "Elise, back again?"

"She wants to meet my new secretary," Pierce said, dryly. "She's heard a lot about her."

"You'll have to wait until another time. Janet's been here and gone already," Gibby called after them.

Pierce spun around. "She was here this morning?"

Gibby wheeled his way between a couple of desks. I got here just after eight and she was in the office. I didn't see her leave, but your door is locked now."

"Thanks, Gib."

He slid the key into the lock, opened the door slowly, uncertain what he'd find. Land mines. Booby-traps. A crazed secretary with a knife.

"Be careful," Elise whispered.

"Of what?" Everything looked as he'd left it. He stepped inside. The offices and bathroom were empty. "There's no one here except the cockroaches."

"Nick, look here."

Elise handed him a note. It was typed. *Nick, something's come up. I can't make it in today. Hope that's okay. I'll call you.—Janet*

She's covering her ass," Elise said. "She's good."

"Yeah, she typed her note, erased her recording, and probably wiped her prints off everything," Pierce said.

"You've got a call on the recorder."

"Probably my own. Janet must have been here when I called."

He walked over to the machine and pressed the playback. He heard his voice asking for Janet, and ran it fast-forward. A beep indicated another message. He hit play.

"Is this an answering machine? I'm calling Nicholas Pierce's office."

The female voice was vaguely familiar. He heard her breathing. Then he heard a faint voice in the background. "What is it, Mama?"

"I don't know." She spoke into the phone in a business-like voice. "If this is Mr. Pierce's office, I would like him to return my call. This is Carla Garity. He has my number."

Pierce turned off the recorder and reached for the Rolodex. "So Carla's back in town. If she ever left. Shit, I forgot to ask Gibby what he found out about the flight to Asheville."

"Who was that in the background?"

"Dawn, her daughter. The college girl. She lives in Gainesville, and supposedly went on the trip with her mama."

Pierce found Carla's number, and picked up the phone. "You don't have to stick around, Elise." He punched out the number.

"I think I'll go use one of Gibby's lines to call my teaching assistant."

Pierce watched Elise leave. Carla's phone rang and she answered on the second ring. "It's Nicholas Pierce. How was your trip?"

"We need to talk. It's important. Can you meet me at the airport at the Sundial Air counter?"

"When?"

"In an hour. Dawn's heading back to Gainesville."

"Do you know about Wayne Garity?"

"Yes, but this is about Jack."

"I'll be there."

Elise returned to the office, and Pierce quickly summarized the conversation.

"Gibby just told me they didn't fly Delta to Asheville," she said. "And don't you think it's rather odd that Dawn would leave campus and take a trip at the beginning of the semester?"

Pierce shrugged. "I hadn't thought about it, but I guess that is a little peculiar."

"We better get going. I don't know Sundial Air. Do you?"

"Nope." He made no effort to get up.

"What are you waiting for?"

"Elise, two weeks on the job and you'd find out why I don't rush to get to places early."

"Why not?"

"Because nobody else does, and there's enough waiting around involved without creating more of it."

"I'd probably hate all the waiting. I'm hating it right now. Let's go. I rather wait there."

"All right."

Pierce locked the door and suddenly Gibby wheeled to the doorway of his adjacent office. "You guys leaving already?"

"Gotta meet somebody at the airport, Gib. You ever heard of Sundial Air?"

"Sure. You should know who they are."

"Afraid not."

When he and Gibby were partners, Pierce had known all about the airlines, who was promoting what destinations, who was offering the best rates, who was sponsoring what FAM trip. But since he'd left the travel industry, it seemed that airlines came and went and changed names every week. He didn't keep track of them, didn't give a damn.

"Well, ol' partner. It used to be Tropic Air."

"Oh, great," Elise groaned.

"I shouldn't have asked," Pierce said. Tropic Air had been owned by Raymond Andrews. A part of his empire. No matter how much he wanted to forget about the renegade financier, the reminders kept cropping up.

"They've down-sized now, just doing short jumps around the state and to the Bahamas," Gibby said. "Cheap flights, no service."

"Gotcha. See ya later."

Isabel listened to Carla's conversation with Pierce for a second time. She'd heard everything: from the phone conversation with Carla to the exchanges between Pierce and Simms. She'd tapped his phone and wired his office. A three-inch long transmitter was fixed above a ceiling panel and sent every spoken word to another transmitter on the roof of her warehouse where it was re-directed to a tape recorder in her office.

She'd made the right decision to work for Pierce. He was like a magnet. Everyone he'd talked to reported back to him, and he'd figured out a lot. But not everything.

She wondered what Carla was going to say. Would she tell him the truth, that she knew Isabel, that she'd been in touch with her since Garity's disappearance? She doubted it. Carla had something else on her mind. Isabel wished she'd kept closer tabs on the mother and daughter, but she couldn't be everywhere. She'd chosen Pierce as her best bet, and she didn't regret it.

Isabel turned off the recorder and picked up the phone. She punched in a number. She needed to bolster her office staff today. "Fritz, good morning. We've got a situation developing. Can you have two men here in an hour?"

After a short conversation, she hung up, and walked over to Erickson's office. He was seated at his desk in a coat and tie, reading a windsurfing magazine.

"Nigel."

He closed the magazine, and looked sheepishly up at her. "I was just boning up on some the new equipment. It might help when I see Vance again."

"Don't worry about Vance. We're going to the airport. You drive the van."

Pierce flowed into the river of traffic entering the airport. He passed a sign bearing the names of airlines and watched for Sundial.

"There it is." He spotted it near the end of the terminal and turned into short-term parking.

As they crossed the street from the parking lot to the terminal, Pierce said, "Why don't you hang back when we get inside. I don't want her to clam up."

"You mean I came along for nothing?"

"No. If it seems okay, I'll call you over."

He found Carla and Dawn waiting in front of the counter. Dawn looked glum; Carla was angry. "We were about to leave for the gate without you. Dawn's plane takes off in twenty minutes."

Dawn picked up a carry-on bag and the mother and daughter moved off. Pierce followed close behind. "Sorry. Traffic was heavy."

Neither one said anything. They moved quickly along the concourse and Pierce glanced back and saw Elise trailing after them. It was probably a mistake that she'd come along, but there was nothing he could do about it now. When they reached the gate, there were no passengers waiting to board. An attendant stood behind a mobile counter.

"Mom, I want to stay."

"I said no. It's too dangerous."

"It's horrible about Uncle Wayne, but Gainesville's dangerous, too," Dawn sulked. "I want to be here. I want to..."

"That's enough." Carla kissed her daughter on the cheek.

Dawn turned to Pierce. "Please help my father. He's alive. But he needs help very badly." With that, she turned and ran to the ramp, her ticket flapping in her hand.

Chapter 20

"Let's go to the lounge," Carla said. "I need a drink."

"What was Dawn talking about?"

"I'll explain everything."

Pierce caught Elise's eye when they passed her on the concourse. He shook his head. He didn't want to take any chances.

When they reached the lounge and found a booth, Pierce asked if she wanted lunch. Carla shook her head. She ordered Scotch and water. Pierce ordered a club sandwich and iced tea.

"Dawn made it sound like your ex-husband is still alive."

"I think he is."

"Why do you say that?"

"We didn't go to North Carolina. That was a ruse. We didn't want any interference. But let me backtrack. There's a lot you don't know. When I met Jack twenty-two years ago, he was actually more interested in my father than me."

Pierce nodded, wondering why Carla was digressing two decades.

"Is the name Fulcannelli at all familiar to you?"

Fulcannelli, Pierce knew, was the guy who had been linked to Lydia Mullen; he was her mentor. "An alchemist, right?"

"Probably the best known one of the twentieth century. During the forties, Mani was assigned to find Fulcannelli."

"Who?"

"My father's name was Manfred Winchell, but everyone called him Mani. It seemed that Fulcannelli had approached a French nuclear physicist and revealed his knowledge of the secret research underway to develop the nuclear bomb. Mani was a scientist and a major in the army. He was assigned to find out what Fulcannelli knew and who he was working for. That's how it began."

"And Jack was curious about it," Pierce said.

"He'd read about Mani's exploits during the war. But Mani disappointed Jack. He wouldn't say anything about his search for the alchemist. He wouldn't even say whether or not he thought Fulcannelli was still alive."

"Did your father's search for him end after the war?" Pierce asked.

"No. But it shifted directions. Several sources had told him that Fulcannelli had successfully transmuted lead and other base metals to gold. So Mani expanded his search. He dedicated himself to tracking not only Fulcannelli, but other legitimate practitioners of alchemy."

Pierce sipped his iced tea as Carla continued her story. As far as she knew, he had given up the search in the early sixties when he retired from the army without every finding the enigmatic alchemist. He spent the last thirteen years of his life working in the intelligence branch of the Department of Energy. He died of brain cancer in 1985.

"Did Jack tell you why he was interested in Fulcannelli?"

"It was Lydia Mullen, of course. He had found evidence that she had been a student of Fulcannelli's in the forties before coming to the United States."

"Why didn't you tell me about this before when I asked you about Mullen?"

"I had my reasons," she said evasively.

Pierce's lunch arrived and he offered half of his club sandwich to Carla. She shook her head, and ordered another Scotch. "So tell me about your trip."

"I'm getting to that. Jack called me about a month before he vanished, and asked me to visit him at the house. He wanted to talk to me about Isabel. At first I refused, but he insisted I was the only one he could talk to about her."

An eerie thought occurred to Pierce. Carla was going to tell him that Mullen, who would be an old lady today, and Isabel, who should've been born about the time that Mullen disappeared were one and the same. Alchemy.

"Why would he want to talk to you about Isabel?"

"Well, I was the one who had introduced her to Jack. She'd been my friend. I met her through my father. She worked with Mani in the Department of Energy. She was a chemist."

Another nice little fact that she'd hidden from him and investigators. "Oh, yeah?"

"Isabel was having a profound influence on him. I'm well aware of the effect she can have on a person."

"Why didn't you tell the police about her?" He spoke more harshly than he had intended, and she drew back from him.

"Okay, I'll tell you," she said after a moment. "We were lovers, and I didn't want to lose her. But right now I'm just afraid of her."

He remembered Vance's comment about meeting Carla and a woman in a nightclub. "I'm a little confused. I thought she was Jack's girlfriend."

"I had an affair with her for the last two years of the marriage. Then everything fell apart when she and Jack started up. But after he disappeared, Isabel and I patched things up. I know it sounds strange, but Isabel is a very persuasive woman."

Pierce knew what she meant just from the short time he'd spent with Isabel in the office. He wasn't quite sure where to go with his questions.

"We were talking about her and Jack," Carla said, rescuing him. "I think Isabel also provided Jack with money to buy the equipment he needed to perfect his elixir."

"What was her interest in the drug?"

"Jack told me that he was convinced that he'd found Mullen in Isabel. He thought they were one and the same."

Pierce looked toward the entrance. No sign of Elise. "I've got a big problem with Isabel being Mullen. But for the fun of it let's say it's true. Why didn't Isabel just tell Jack how to make his elixir?"

"That's what I asked him. He said that it didn't work that way, that you had to uncover the secret yourself by trying over and over again. The process was as important as the ingredients."

"Why does he call it the Fifth Essence?"

"Fire, earth, air, and water are the four essences. The fifth is the distillation of the life force or spirit, the quintessence. That was the way he described it."

Janet the secretary; Isabel the girlfriend. And supposedly Lydia the alchemist. A lady of many faces. "But did Jack actually believe she was Mullen?"

"He desperately wanted to believe it, and she encouraged it. As proof, she gave him several coins, quarters and half-dollars that Mullen had supposedly transformed in the fifties."

Carla's drink arrived. He glanced over at the people standing at the bar and seated in the booths. He was looking not only for Elise, but anyone who was taking an interest in them.

"Didn't Jack realize that the coins could have been minted in gold in a very normal way?"

"Maybe he did in the end. He found out who she really was, and fled."

Another face? "Who was she?"

"I've learned quite a bit about Isabel in the last few days."

Pierce waited for her to continue. She was finally going to talk about her trip. "I'm all ears."

"Two days before you and I met, Dawn got a call from a man who said he had information about her father. He said it was important that he meet her. She was to go to the town of Cassadaga in central Florida that Saturday, check into the hotel there, and wait for him to contact her. Do you know anything about Cassadaga?"

"It's a spiritualist community, isn't it? I've read about it in the paper from time to time." Usually around Halloween.

She nodded, and continued. "Dawn immediately called me and I told her to come home so we could drive together to Cassadaga and meet the man."

"He didn't give his name?"

"No. He was very cautious. He said he would introduce himself when she got there."

"Did you tell Wayne about it?"

She shook her head. "He would've contacted the police, and the caller had said if the police were contacted there would be no meeting. So when Wayne called me and asked me to meet you, I told him we were about to leave for North Carolina. I didn't want to see you, but he pressed me. I agreed just so he wouldn't get suspicious."

"What happened when you got to Cassadaga?"

"We waited. No one showed up until the third day. We were sitting on the porch of the hotel yesterday morning, wonderings if the call had been a prank, when a silver-haired man of about fifty or so introduced himself as David Fletcher. He said he was the one who had called and he'd made us wait because he wanted to be certain that we weren't followed."

"Was he helpful?"

"He told us about Isabel."

"Let me guess. She's not Mullen."

"Isabel Martin is the chief field officer for an obscure federal agency called Aurum. It's part of the intelligence branch of the Department of Energy. I found out for the first time that my father had started the agency himself."

"You didn't know that?"

She shook her head. "When I was a child, Mani told me about alchemy and Fulcannelli, but after I was an adult he never spoke of it. I thought it was all in the past."

"A government agency searching for the secret of alchemy," Pierce mused. "Well, I've heard stranger ways of spending tax money. So how did Fletcher know about Aurum? Who is he?"

Tears suddenly welled in Carla's eyes. She found a Kleenex in her purse and dabbed them.

"Are you okay?"

She struggled to contain her tears, lost the battle, and shook her head. "Sorry, I, uh, this is difficult for me, Mr. Pierce."

"Take your time."

After a minute, she continued. "Fletcher knew all about Isabel and my father. She wasn't just his associate. She was his lover during the last ten years of his life. That sickens me. It was bad enough when she started up with Jack, but...." Her voice faded. "When I heard that...my own father...." She shook her head, clenched her fist. "I could kill her. I know I could." Carla drained her scotch. "Find her, Nick. Stop her. That's all I ask." She pushed away from the table and abruptly stood up. "Do whatever it takes."

"Hold on," Pierce said. "What about Jack? Did you see him? Where is he?"

"He only wanted to see Dawn. She said he looks terrible. He's very ill, but he won't go to a doctor. He's at Fletcher's place." She walked off.

In the restroom, Elise ran a brush through her hair. Coming here with Pierce had been a mistake. All she could do was watch him and Carla, and that had gotten boring real fast. Now she knew what Pierce meant when he said that following someone was the least interesting part of his job.

"That's an unusual necklace? What is it?"

Elise glanced at the blonde at the next sink who had spoken to her. Elise touched the odd-shaped gold pendant that had fallen out of her blouse. "Oh, its from Guatemala. I grew up there."

"You don't look Guatemalan."

Elise felt like saying, *So what.* She hated it when a total stranger asked her to explain her heritage. "My parents were Americans." She headed out the exit, and down the concourse toward the lounge. She wondered how much longer Pierce would be. She didn't like the idea that he was eating lunch without her. She was hungry, too, but she hated eating alone, even at airports.

"Say, you dropped something."

Elise turned around and saw the blonde again. In her hand was a coin, a gold one. "That's not...mine..."

"No, it's mine." The woman's hand quickly slid inside her beige leather purse. "I've got a little Derringer in my purse, and I'll use it, Elise. I think you know that."

Elise's heart slammed against her ribs. She was standing face to face with Isabel. The hair was different, but it was the same woman she'd passed as she entered the travel agency yesterday. "What do you want from me?"

"Turn around and start working."

Elise turned. They moved side by side toward the end of the

concourse, and passed by the metal detectors as they moved into the main terminal. Now she wondered if Isabel really had a gun. "How did you get the gun through?"

"It's all high-grade plastic, except for the steel barrel. The gun comes apart into six pieces and no one has ever identified it yet. It takes me about three minutes to assemble in a bathroom stall. Take a look in my purse."

Elise glanced over and glimpsed the weapon in her hand. Maybe it was a toy gun, she thought. Maybe it wasn't loaded. Did she have plastic bullets, too? But if Pierce was right about Isabel, it wasn't worth taking any chances with her.

They left the terminal and crossed the street to the parking ramp. "Where's Pierce's car?" Isabel hissed.

Elise hesitated. She felt the barrel of the Derringer pressed hard against her spine. "If I pull the trigger now, you'll be paralyzed for life if you don't die. Where is the car?"

"Over there. Row N."

"Go to your left."

They moved away from Pierce's Saab and passed a couple of dozen cars. Everything was a blur. "What are you going to do to me?"

"Shut up."

Isabel grabbed her arm and turned her toward a dark blue van. The side door sprang open and a man with a crew cut and an earring crouched inside the doorway. He looked at Elise, then Isabel.

"Get inside," she barked. "Now!"

The man reached for her arm, but Elise pulled it away. "Hel...!"

Isabel clamped her hand over Elise's mouth, and shoved her inside the empty back of the van. She struggled, but was quickly overwhelmed. Within seconds, she was lying face down on the floor, her eyes and mouth taped, her ankles bound to her wrists.

Pierce walked out of the lounge and into the concourse to look for Elise. He'd expected her to show up as soon as Carla left, but there was no sign of her. Maybe she was mad at him. He walked down to the nearest gates and moved past row after row of chairs with passengers waiting for their flights. Elise wasn't among them. He headed in the other direction and checked a bookstore and gift shop. No Elise.

He was at a loss. He wandered around the concourse near the lounge for a few minutes. Then he realized there was one place he hadn't looked. She'd probably gotten impatient and decided to wait by the car as if that would speed him along. She'd be miffed. No doubt about that.

He braced himself for a verbal assault. It would be sharp, but brief. She'd turn silent, then say she was sorry. But when he reached the car, she wasn't there. "I don't get it, Swedie. Where'd she go?"

"Hello, Nick."

He spun around. "Janet." A man was behind her. He looked like someone Pierce had met, but where and when?

"Real funny. Let's not play games. You can call me Isabel. You remember Nigel, don't you? A fellow windsurfer."

Nigel Erickson, windsurfing pro. How did he know her? "What's this about?"

"It's about the case, Nick. You know, the Garity case. We're wrapping it up. You found Isabel, now we're going to follow Carla's instructions and get Jack and his elixir."

"What makes you think Carla knows anything?"

She smiled. "I don't think she called you just to chat about her trip to North Carolina. We both know she didn't go to Asheville. So you can tell me all about her last few days. Her missing days. Let's go."

"I'm not going anywhere with you except to the police station."

"Funny, very funny. But you're not dealing with an amateur, Nicky-boy. If you want to see your girlfriend alive again, you'll do exactly what I ask of you."

Pierce's fingers curled into fists. "Where is she?"

"I'll show you. Turn around and start walking. We'll be right behind you."

Pierce knew he had no choice.

"It was very thoughtful of you to bring Elise along," Isabel said from behind him. "I figured it would be you and Carla, but it's much better this way. Carla's a pain. Too emotional. Her anger devours her common sense. She would be more trouble than help."

"Where's Elise?"

"Keep going, a little further. Okay, turn to your left and walk over to the rear of the dark blue van."

Erickson slid open the side door. Elise was lying on the floor with her hands tied behind her back to her ankles. Surgical tape covered her mouth and eyes. Pierce spun around, but Erickson was ready for him. He clamped a hand on Pierce's neck and pressed a gun to his head. "Get in. On your face."

Elise's head twisted back and forth as she struggled against the bindings. "Take it easy, Professor Simms," Isabel said. "I don't want to make this any messier than I have to."

Pierce's hands and ankles were bound, and his eyes were taped shut. But he wasn't gagged; he was supposed to talk.

"Put these headphones over Elise's ears, Nigel," Isabel said. "I don't want her to hear anything she doesn't need to know."

"Where are you taking us?" Pierce asked.

Erickson turned on the as the engine and Isabel turned in her seat. "Just answer my questions. If you cooperate, you'll live. If you don't, you'll end up like Judge Garity." The van pulled out of the parking lot and headed for the airport exit. "You can start by telling me where Jack is hiding."

"I don't know. Why don't you ask Carla?"

"Because I'm asking you. I'm sure you don't want to see Elise harmed just to protect Carla's little secret."

Pierce grimaced.

"I'm waiting, Nicholas."

"Okay. I'll tell you what she said, but then you let us go."

"No deal. You don't have any bargaining chips. You talk or you die. Simple as that. But I'll let you go when I know you're telling me the truth."

Isabel was in control of the situation, but Pierce knew where Garity was. He doubted she would kill Elise while she needed his cooperation. "Let Elise go, and I'll take you to Garity. I think I know where he is. Otherwise, forget it."

"Well, we're getting closer. We're going to drop her off at

a safe place and if all goes well, she'll be released unharmed. That's a promise. So where is Garity?"

He didn't know if her promise was worth anything, but there was nothing he could do. "All right. He's in Central Florida, near Orlando."

"I bet it's not Disney World."

"Cassadaga."

"Never heard of it."

"I know it," Erickson said. "They worship spooks there."

"What?"

"You know, those people who talk to the dead. Mediums, that's what they're called. It's a whole town of them. Small town. A bunch of us from college drove over there one Halloween from Stetson, where I went to college, and raised hell."

"How clever," Isabel said. "So Jack is hiding with spiritualists. I think I read about the place. The mediums are divided and fighting each other. Something like that."

"Are we going there?" Erickson asked.

"As soon as we drop off Simms."

Chapter 21

The van slowed to a stop, accelerated, slowed and stopped. He heard honking, an occasional voice from the street. About half an hour had passed since Pierce had been confronted in the parking ramp. Just about enough time to drive downtown and get stuck in heavy traffic, he thought.

The van stopped again and this time the engine shut off. "Elise is getting out here," Isabel said. "She will stay here until we're finished with business."

The side door slid open and he heard the sound of fast-moving traffic in the distance. The interstate. Erickson clasped Elise's arm and she murmured into the tape. "You hurt her and I'll kill you," Pierce said.

"Keep your mouth shut, Pierce, or we'll tape it shut," he snapped.

"No one will hurt her, Nick," Isabel assured him. "Everybody cooperates and nobody gets hurt."

The side door slammed shut, Elise was gone. Pierce strained at his bindings, but they only tightened around his wrists and ankles.

"Don't try yelling for help, Nick," Isabel said. "There's no one around, but if I hear you, Elise will pay for your indiscretion."

With that, Isabel closed the front passenger door and he was alone.

Two Latin men greeted them at the door of the Aurum offices. One of them, who looked about forty, wore a dark sport coat over a navy t-shirt. The other was in his twenties and wore a black jacket over a paisley shirt that was open at the neck. Erickson had never seen them before and they definitely didn't look like office workers. More like hired thugs. Bulges under the left side of their jackets confirmed his suspicion.

"Let's put her in the back," Isabel said and led the way to one of the rear offices that was empty of furniture.

He was getting deeper and deeper into something that he didn't understand, and didn't like. Isabel acted as if they were invincible, that they would never be caught. She'd told him that clandestine operations existed outside of conventional laws, and he was privileged to have an inside look, even if he would never be able to talk about anything that he saw. He could understand why. If people knew that part of their government operated like the mafia, they'd be enraged.

After Simms was taken to the room, Isabel told the guards to remove the tape from her. Then she turned to Erickson. "Wait for me by the elevator."

When Isabel joined him a couple of minutes later, they stepped into the freight elevator and descended to the first floor. "What's going to happen to her?" he asked.

"Relax, Nigel. You don't have to get involved in any more unsavory activities."

He didn't like her answer or her patronizing tone. "But she'll go to the police after this is over. They both will."

"By then it won't matter. We'll be long gone. You and Wendy will get your full bonuses and you'll be reassigned. So don't worry."

He lifted the gate as the elevator stopped. "Well, I am worried. Vance recognized me from my windsurfing career, and he probably told Pierce about it. Now Pierce knows I work with you."

She paused outside the elevator. "I'm sorry to hear that, Nigel. Very sorry." She headed down the hallway toward the door, and Erickson hurried after her. "Now we'll have to take care of Pierce to save your ass."

Elise stood close to the door and listened to the men conversing in Spanish. One of them was talking about Isabel, saying how much he would like to get her alone. "She's probably real hot, clawing your back and moaning real loud."

"You're dreaming," the other man said. "She don't go for guys like us. She's a smart bitch. She runs this outfit."

"That don't matter when you get them in bed. I got more experience than you. You'll find out that you can get all kinds. Bitches like her are as hungry for it as any of them. They just try to act like they don't want it."

That was the older one, Elise thought.

"What do you think of this one we got?" the younger one asked.

"It don't matter what we think." The man's tone turned gruff. "This is business. I don't fuck a woman I may have to kill. That's not professional. That's what psychos do. We are professionals. Remember that."

"So we treat her like a lady until we kill her?" the younger one asked, then laughed.

Christ, oh Christ. How did I get myself into this mess? What an idiot.

"Let's see how she's doing," the older one said.

Elise jumped back as the door opened.

"Hello, sweetheart," one of them said in English. She guessed he was a Cuban who'd been in Miami since he was a kid. His English was unaccented. "Can we get you anything?"

"No, no, thanks."

"Don't be so nervous, honey. Nothing is going to happen to you."

"Then let me go."

"Oh, she is very forward," the younger one said.

"I didn't do anything to either of you. Let me go. I'll pay as much as you're getting paid. More."

"Sorry, lady," the older one said. "It don't work that way." He was a suave looking man, but a dark cast to one of his eyes added a coldness to his features. The younger one was lean and hyper with a thin face and long nose. He was staring at her legs. The last thing she wanted was to be left in this room with that one for more than ten seconds.

"Why not?"

"It just don't. But if everything goes all right, you'll be home tonight."

"I'll escort you," the younger one said and laughed.

They'd been on the road for more than four hours. Rock music blared on the rear speakers most of the way, and Pierce hadn't been able to hear much of the conversation in the front seat. They'd stopped twice on the turnpike for coffee, and each time one of them had remained in the van with him. They didn't give him any coffee, which was just as well since they didn't let him use the restroom. His hands were free now, and he was seated in a comfortable captain's chair where he'd dozed from time to time.

They passed Deltona. They were close. Isabel turned down the volume of the radio as Roy Orbison crooned *Pretty Woman*. "Where's Jack staying in Cassadaga?"

"I don't know."

"Nicholas, you've been cooperative so far. But don't change your mind now. All I have to do is call Miami and give an order and Elise is dead. It's that simple."

"Just like the judge, right?"

She didn't answer.

"Are you with the mafia or something?" He wanted her to think he knew virtually nothing about her.

She stared blankly at him. "You don't know?"

"Hey, until a day ago, you were my secretary."

A glance from Erickson; Pierce realized he was just learning what was going on himself.

"Answer my question. Where is Garity staying in Cassadaga?"

"A guy named Fletcher knows the answer. William Fletcher."

"Is Garity staying with Fletcher?"

"Maybe. That's where Dawn saw him. Garity didn't want to see Carla."

"What exactly did Carla tell you about Garity?"

"Not much. Just that he's ill."

Isabel's mouth turned down. "What did she say about me?"

"She said you'd been friends. Close friends."

Another glance from Erickson.

"What else did she say?"

"She said you messed up her marriage."

It wasn't what Isabel wanted to hear. She spun in her seat and aimed a Derringer at him. "Don't play games with me, Pierce."

"Sure. No problem."

She turned her back to him and abruptly ended the conversation.

In spite of the fact that Isabel seemed to make all the right moves at the right time and was capable of controlling a complex situation, there was a sense of desperation about her. She wasn't looking for Garity because he could make gold out of lead. She had supplied the gold coins. It was the drug that she was after, and it was more than her job. It was something that consumed her life, and he wondered why.

A few minutes later, Pierce saw a sign for Cassadaga, and Erickson eased off the interstate. They followed a two-lane rural highway shrouded in tall pines that curved and rose and fell through hills. That in itself was unusual. Pierce had never seen a hill in Florida that wasn't man-made.

They continued on a few miles until the town appeared. An old Mediterranean-style hotel, probably built in the early years of the twentieth century, faced the main street. The town itself was located on a network of narrow, tree-lined streets behind the hotel. They drove slowly along the streets, passing wood-frame houses with white picket fences.

"Quaint," Isabel said.

"It doesn't look like anything in Florida," Erickson commented.

Small signs near the gates announced the residence of one reverend-medium after another. Isabel told Erickson to drive slower and read the names on his side of the street. They probably missed a few of them, but of the ones they saw none indicated the home of William Fletcher.

"I hope you're not lying, Nick."

"I hope Carla wasn't lying," he replied.

They drove by a chapel called the Colby Memorial Temple,

then passed a small park with a gazebo and a pond. As they drove up a hill toward the hotel, Isabel noticed another road. "That way."

At the top of the hill, they turned to the right and headed downhill away from the hotel. They passed several houses, but none of them had a sign posted proclaiming the residence of a medium. At the end of the pavement, a winding, dirt road led into a heavily wooded area. "See where that goes," Isabel said.

Erickson followed the road for a quarter of a mile where it ended at a lake bordered by tall thick pines. There were a couple of picnic tables, but no one in sight. "Very picturesque," Isabel said, glumly. "Okay, go back to the hotel."

Erickson found a parking space, but before they approached the hotel, Isabel's gaze slid across the side street toward a long white wooden building with a porch. Posted above the door was a large sign that read: Southern Cassadaga Spiritualist Camp Meeting Association.

"That's the headquarters for Spooksville," Erickson said.

Elise pounded on the door. They'd given her a hamburger, fries and a coke, food she never ate. But she hadn't eaten since breakfast and gobbled it down. It tasted edible and was filling, but now the after-effects of the greasy dinner hit her stomach. She remembered that nutrition wasn't the only reason she didn't eat fatty, fried foods.

"What is it?" one of the men grumbled.

"I have to use the bathroom. Right now I feel sick."

The younger guard opened the door and grinned at her. "You making trouble?"

"I said I have to go to the bathroom."

"I'll have to watch, you know."

"No, you don't."

He laughed. "I'm just joking lady. C'mon." He held out his hand. "I'll show you the way."

She stepped through the doorway, brushing past the man, ignoring his out stretched hand. She smelled his sweet after-shave as he patted her butt. "Keep your hands to yourself," she snapped.

"Hey, can't a guy have some fun. You can call me Hans. My partner is Lars."

Hans and Lars. It sounded a comedy team. Fake names. A joke. Whatever.

She was led down a hallway. The place looked like a modern office building with partitioned space for secretaries and private offices, but there was no sign of anyone working.

"To your left, end of the hall. I'll be waiting."

She looked for an escape route on her way to the bathroom, but saw nothing. She closed the door behind her. The wall was bare brick, an older building, she guessed, possibly a converted warehouse. No windows, no way out. Not that she could see. There had to be at least one stairway besides the elevator. Somewhere. Then she saw another possibility.

A couple of minutes later, she opened the door and leaned against it, her right arm slightly behind her. "Hans, could you help me? I...I don't feel well. That dinner didn't agree with me. I've go a bad stomach ache."

The guard moved forward. "Just put your arm around my shoulder."

The second Hans stepped in front of her, she jerked up her arm, aimed a can of aerosol freshener, and sprayed him in his eyes. He yelped, his hand flew to his face and he lunged at her.

"You bitch!"

She sprayed again, jumped out of his way as he dropped to his knees, shrieking and clawing at his face.

She ran down the hall and ducked into one of the modular offices. She heard Lars charging down the hall in response to Hans' bellows. She dropped to the floor, rolled under a partition, and leaped to her feet. She sprinted away, darting between offices in a zig-zag route.

Where's the stairway? Where? She was lost in a maze of tiny offices, uncertain which way to go. Hans and Lars plowed into the network of offices. Hans stumbled over a chair and cursed loudly. "I'm going to kill you, bitch. Wait till I get my hands on you."

She ducked around a corner, into an office. She pressed against the partition, heart pounding in her chest, and Lars ran by, passing within three feet of her. As soon as he turned the corner, she dashed out and down another hallway. A steel door was straight ahead. *Be open. Please, be open.*

She pushed the bar and the door swung outward. Stairs. She scrambled down two flights and reached another door. Locked. Shit.

She hurried back up the stairs, kept going past the doors to the offices. The stairs led to a landing and another locked door. She kept going up. The stairs ended at a red door. She grabbed the knob. It turned, she pushed, stumbled out onto a roof. Light. Late afternoon. Maybe she could yell for help. But how long would it take for the guards to track her here? They'd probably find her before the police or anyone else could respond to her screams.

She struggled to orient herself. Tall buildings. She was near downtown. A deserted warehouse district, a tangle of interstate to her right. She recognized the Omni Mall in one direction, and the Miami Heat stadium in the other. She was on the edge of Overtown, a few blocks west of Biscayne Boulevard

She raced over to the edge of the building and looked over the side. Christ. Oh, Christ. She was four or five stories above an alley. No balconies, no fire escape. She dashed over to the rear of the building. Did fire escapes ever reach the top of buildings? She didn't think so, but there was always hope for a first. She looked over the side. The same thing. No way down. She checked the other side, then the front. No fire escapes.

A pyramid of glass rose several feet from the roof near the center of the building. She darted over to it and tried to peer through the glass, but it was too opaque. She walked around it. There was no way to open any of the large triangular window panes. She picked up a broken brick laying nearby, tapped against a glass pane, tapped until it cracked. A harder tap expanded the crack into a Y.

Elise hit a corner of the brick against the glass, knocking a hole in it. Kneeling, she peered through it, trying to see what lay below.

"Okay, lady, we got you now. C'mon out!"

Hans, on the roof. *Do something. Quick.*

She pressed her back against the glass, trying to meld with it. *Go away. Go away. You don't see me.*

She heard a screech and felt something move beneath her, and suddenly the glass gave way and she crashed through it, glass showering around her as she fell.

Chapter 22

Isabel climbed the steps to the porch of the long wooden building that was a bookstore and the public face of the camp. She opened one of the double doors, stepped into an entryway, placed a hand on the wall for balance. She felt dizzy. Shake it off, she told herself. *Okay, that's better.*

Directly ahead of her was another pair of doors that led to a meeting room. They were open and about twenty people were seated inside where a woman was speaking from behind a podium. Isabel heard a few phrases and sentences: "Higher, positive, universal forces...connection with cosmic powers... The guide, Michael, initiated contact between myself and the conscious mind of the etheric realms, which we know as the spirit world. He is loving, joyful energy."

To her left, another door led into the bookstore. Inside were a couple of browsers, and a woman of about fifty who scrutinized her as she entered. "Can I help you with anything, ma'am?"

Isabel shook her head. "Not yet."

The shop was small and its stock of esoteric books and pamphlets was aimed at a specific audience, visitors to the spiritualist community. Much of it looked self-published. There were shelves dedicated to books on crystals and their mystical applications, channeling, prophecy, others on American Indian mysticism. The shelves in one of the corners were stacked with tapes of New Age music and on the counter near the cash register were several baskets of crystals and semi-precious stones.

Isabel spotted a couple of familiar titles on alchemy. The books were published by Aurum, the agency's publishing front. The authors were both flakes who portrayed themselves as modern day alchemists. Isabel had edited both manuscripts when Aurum was headquartered in St. Paul. Their books were almost impossible to understand. But that was the history of alchemy, indecipherable, coded manuscripts, hidden information only accessible to initiates. Unfortunately, too many manuscripts were simply a jumble of confused thinking.

Several pamphlets and a couple of books on Cassadaga were displayed at the front counter. She picked up one of the pamphlets and perused it. Cassadaga was founded by George R. Colby, who was led into the interior of central Florida in 1894 by two spirit guides, Seneca the Philosopher, and the Unknown. The official definition of spiritualism, as written in the 1920s, was "the science, philosophy and religion of continuous life, based upon the demonstrated fact of communication by means of mediumship with those who live in the Spirit World."

The words began to blur and Isabel gripped the counter and closed her eyes. Her head was pounding. "Are you okay?" the clerk asked.

Isabel straightened up, smiled. "Yes, I'm fine. Just a little tired from the long drive from Miami."

"That is a long ways. Can I answer any questions for you?"

"Maybe." Isabel took out two dollars to pay for the pamphlet. "I'm looking for William Fletcher. I believe he lives here."

The woman hesitated, but only for a moment. "No, there's no one by that name here," she said firmly.

"But a friend of mine was here last week and saw him and his friend Jack Garity."

Neither name had any impact on the woman. "Is he a medium?"

"I assume so. My friend didn't come here for a manicure."

"Then he's probably with the ones across the street. I don't keep track of them." Her tone was curt, and suddenly she was no longer interested in Isabel. She turned to a box of books she was sorting.

Isabel was confused, then recalled the feud she'd read about. One group of mediums was associated with the spiritualist organization, the establishment. The others were psychics who had moved into the area, but didn't play by the rules of the old order. "Where do I look across the street?"

"Try the house on the corner with the tacky signs."

She stepped out onto the porch. There was a post office on the corner, and beyond it, the house in question. Signs were posted on the lawn and nailed to the wall of the two-story structure. All of them advertised psychic readings and there were several promises that someone was on-duty right now, ready to read your future. The gaudy display was no doubt part of the squabble.

She stopped at the van and asked Erickson if everything was okay. "Fine. Are we going to stay here tonight?"

"I don't know yet. I'll be back in a few minutes." She crossed the street to the placard house, and walked up to the door. She hesitated, not knowing whether to knock or simply open the door. She opted for the latter, and walked into a reception room. A man who weighed close to three hundred pounds was watering a potted plant under a window. "Good afternoon. How can I help you today?"

"I'm looking for a medium named William Fletcher. Do you know where I can find him?"

The man gave her an amused look. "You mean, Mrs. Fletcher, don't you? She's the medium. At least, that's what I hear."

"He's not?"

"I'd say he was more like me. An extra large." He laughed, but Isabel just stared at him. "Just a joke, you know. Medium, large."

"Where do I find Mrs. Fletcher? I want a reading with her."

"If you want to save time, you can get a reading right here."

"No thanks. I want Mrs. Fletcher."

"I tell you what, go down to the bookstore and ask Iris about her. I don't know anyone who's had a reading with her lately. She might not be doing it anymore."

"I was just over there. The clerk didn't know the Fletchers."

"Then you were at the wrong bookstore. There're three in town. Used to be four. One closed. Still not bad for a town of three hundred."

"Where's the one with Iris?" Isabel asked impatiently.

"Two blocks down. Same side of the street. If it doesn't work out, I've got two psychics available here for another hour or so."

Isabel started to leave, then stopped. "Do you know Jack Garity, a friend of the Fletchers?"

"Can't say I do. Is he staying with them?"

"I was hoping you'd tell me. Thanks again."

Erickson was standing outside of the van. She motioned at him, he crossed the street.

"Any luck?"

"I've got a lead."

"You want us to go with you?"

"No. It's time to get rid of Pierce."

"What do you mean?" Erickson asked.

"Drive down to the lake. Take him for a walk and put a bullet in his head."

"You want me to kill him?"

"That's right. Then wait for me at the bookstore down the street."

"But, Isabel…."

"Did you expect to make seventy grand windsurfing for me? You may be my lover, but you still have to work. So get to it, Nigel. Right now."

For several seconds, Elise didn't move. She felt something trickling on her wrist, and held up her arm. She'd gashed her palm and the blood was bubbling out. She tested her arm, her legs, neck and back. She was in one piece, bruised, bleeding, but there were no broken bones. She'd struck something, maybe a shelf, and now she lay on a floor, surrounded by a jumble of boxes, hangers, clothes. It was a closet, a huge closet, nearly as large as her office at the university. Woman's clothes. She found a white silk blouse and wrapped it around her injured hand.

"I'm not jumping down there. I'd break my neck."

Elise squinted up toward the shattered skylight, and saw two heads staring down at her. "Don't move!" Hans aimed a gun at her.

She rolled across the clothing, scrambled up, and nearly collapsed. Her knee, Christ, she'd wrenched her knee. She limped toward the doorway and Hans shouted. "She's trying to get away!"

"Don't shoot!"

A shot rang out and wood chips flew from the doorway inches from her head. "I said don't shoot," Lars barked.

She hobbled into the next room, a bedroom. Someone's apartment. And no one was home. She spotted a heavy steel door just outside of the bedroom, started to unlock it, but realized it was the same one that she'd passed on the stairs.

Desperate and unsteady, she hobbled as quickly as she could through the apartment, holding her injured hand up to stop the bleeding. She barely felt any pain; her mind was focused on fleeing.

It was a warehouse, but it looked as if no expense had been spared in decorating the apartment. A black metallic entertainment center featured a wall of high tech electronics, and opposite were black leather couches and chairs. A well-equipped gym took up another area. A counter with a butcher block top set off a kitchen where cast iron pots and pans hung from hooks in front of cupboards with glass windows.

She spotted another door near the kitchen. She grabbed a butcher's knife from a hook, and wrapped a dish towel around the blood-soaked blouse. No sense leaving a trail. She unlocked the door, then hurried out into a hallway, closing the door behind her. At the end of the corridor was the freight elevator. She moved quickly over to it, was about to push the call button, then hesitated. The elevator had to go up one floor to reach her. If the guards heard it, she'd be trapped. They'd be waiting for her.

Hide. That was the only option. A narrow passageway to the left of the elevator led to a wooden door. She tried the knob. Locked. But it was a cheap lock, the kind you could open with a credit card. Or a butcher's knife. She wedged it between the frame and the door, pressed the latch. The door popped open.

She peered into a cramped storage closet. She turned on the light switch, closed the door behind her, locked it. Her last stand. If they found her here, it was over. The butcher's knife gave her a sense of security, but a false one. It wouldn't help much against a gun. Not unless she could catch one of them alone. She tried to imagine herself jumping out and slashing someone with a butcher's knife. She didn't know if she could do it.

She quickly cleared a spot, stacking several boxes on top of one another. She turned off the light, and felt her way to her hiding place. She pressed back against the wall, waited. After a couple of minutes, the tension began to ease. Were they inside the apartment now, searching for her? Or downstairs waiting for her to take the elevator?

She slid down the wall, set the knife on the floor, thinking. A plan took shape. She would wait another five minutes, then carefully sneak back into the apartment and call 911. If she'd known the guards weren't coming right after her, she would've called right away. But what had slowed them down? The drop to the closet floor or something else?

She wondered who lived here. And why? From her brief glimpse of the apartment, it was someone with money who certainly didn't have to live near an interstate. Maybe it was an artist who needed the space, but she hadn't seen a studio or a single easel. She crept over to the door, found the light switch. *Careful*, she told herself. *You know what they say about curiosity.*

She opened one of the boxes. Books. She picked one up and looked at the title: *Anima Magica Abscondita*, by Eugenius Philalethes. Then another: *Centrum Naturae Concentratum*, by Alipili. She frowned, dug for a third volume. The book was entitled, *The New Light of Alchemy.*

"Uh-oh," she muttered. She opened the cover and read the inscription. *To Isabel with love and admiration—As always, Truth lies hidden in obscurity. Eternally yours, Mani.*

She snapped the book shut. She was in Isabel's apartment. She'd no sooner made the connection when she heard the groan of the elevator. She grabbed the butcher's knife.

The elevator stopped, she flicked off the light, heard the gate creak open. She crept slowly back to her hiding place. *Go away. Go away.*

She held her breath. A minute passed, two minutes. They

must be inside the apartment. *Get your ass out of here. Make a break for it.* She gripped the butcher's knife tightly and moved cautiously toward the door. She opened it, then tiptoed to the end of the corridor. The elevator was there, waiting. She peered around the corner. The apartment door was partially open.

She lifted the gate, winced at the sound of the gate creaking. The knife slipped from her hand and clattered to the floor.

"Freeze! Police!"

She raised her hands. "Police?"

"Turn around real slow."

She did as she was told, then burst out laughing, a shrill nervous sound. Two uniformed cops were crouched, pointing their weapons at her.

As Erickson parked the van near the lake, dusk settled over Cassadaga. "What're we doing here?" Pierce asked from the front passenger seat.

"Waiting while Isabel handles business," Erickson said. "We don't want to look too conspicuous."

Pierce wasn't sure what would be considered conspicuous in this place. It was unlike typical small towns in central Florida. This was Bible-belt country, and he wondered what the people in neighboring towns thought of this eccentric village of mediums.

From what he'd seen of it, the town looked a bit rundown. The mediums could use a few diligent carpenters and handymen among their populace.

Erickson opened his door. "Let's take a look around."

Pierce got out, stretched his legs. "Did she find Fletcher?"

"Maybe."

"What's she going to do, kill him?"

Erickson ignored the comment. "Let's take a look at the lake."

Sure. Just a little walk by the lake while killer-lady is planning more mayhem. And what are you up to, Erickson? Keep a close eye on him.

"Isabel is unpredictable," Erickson said as if attempting to start a conversation.

"I don't think so. She uses people, then kills some of them."

Erickson looked uneasy as they walked to the lake. But at least he was talking now. He hadn't said more than a few words to him on the entire trip.

"So how'd you think this lake would be for windsurfing?" Pierce asked as they stopped at the shoreline.

Erickson looked at the body of water as if seeing it for the first time. "It wouldn't be bad if you had a steady wind from across the lake. At least good for a beginner to practice."

"Why from over there?"

"Because it's flat and open on the other side. Not many trees to block the wind. Any other direction, forget it. Hills, trees. It wouldn't be any good."

"Might be gators in here," Pierce added.

"That too. I hit one once in a lake near Tampa a few years ago. I didn't know what it was. The fin hit it and I went flying. Luckily, I scared it off."

"And you kept sailing?"

"Not for long. I went back to shore and someone with binoculars pointed it out. I packed up. I don't need that sort of challenge."

Pierce felt like telling him to wake up, that Isabel's bite was as bad as any gator's. "What were you doing in Tampa?"

"Visiting a high school friend."

Just a couple of guys talking by the lake.

"You know, you don't strike me as the kind of guy who goes in for killing," Pierce said. "Did Isabel recruit you or seduce you?"

"You want to know what kind of guy I am? I'll show you."

Erickson dropped down to one knee, pulled up the leg of his jeans, and reached for a snub-nosed .38 strapped to his ankle. Dumb move. Pierce kicked Erickson in the side of the head, knocking him over, and raced for the trees.

"Stop!" Erickson yelled. The gun fired.

The skylight in Isabel's apartment had been wired with a silent alarm. It was part of an extensive security system that protected the apartment. The cops had responded, and one of them called for a backup after she quickly told them her story. The cops searched the apartment, but didn't find anyone hiding. She figured the guards must've suspected the place was secured and fled. Several more cops arrived and spread out to search the building.

Elise sat down on a stool at Isabel's butcher block counter and repeated her story to Detective Adele Harrison, while a medic bandaged her hand. Harrison, a middle-aged woman in street clothes, could've been a soccer mom, but probably wasn't. Elise told her about Pierce and how he was in danger. But she had no clue where he'd been taken. When she mentioned Judge Garity's murder and Drucker's investigation, she called into headquarters and left a message for her fellow detective. Elise thought she'd seen a smirk on the woman's face when she'd mentioned Drucker's name. No doubt he had an issue with female detectives.

The medic, a diligent guy who looked young enough to be one of her students, told her not to get the hand wet for a few days, then went on his way.

While she waited, Elise thought of Pierce's divination. The outcome had been polarity. She'd been confused by it, but here she was in a warehouse in Miami and Pierce was God knows where. He was in trouble and it seemed all she could do was wait and hope.

Unless.

She slid off the stool as Harrison moved into another room to confer with her colleagues. She picked up the phone, dialed directory assistance, got a number. Seconds later, she called it and reached an answering machine. She waited for the message to end, then said:

"Umberto, it's Elise. Are you there? Please pick up if you are." After half a minute, she set the headset back into the cradle.

Damn it. But what could Umberto do, drive her around looking for the van? Comfort her? That was about all she could expect, and she wasn't even going to get that. She paced around the kitchen area, and thought of the clutter in her own house. Here everything was neat and orderly. Isabel covered her madness with tidiness. But there had to be something around here that would reveal her true identity.

She slipped away to the rear of the apartment where she'd seen a desk behind a partition. No one was back there so she sat down in Isabel's chair and opened a file drawer. The files were coded: M-1, M-2, M-3. She ran her fingers through them. M-14, M-15, M-16. She pulled one out, and paged through it. Indecipherable notes. Chemical formulas. She saw the name Mullen, then saw it again and again.

She turned to M-1. A title page. It read, *The Fifth Essence*, by Jack Garity. It was a manuscript about Mullen and her work and each file was a chapter. The title page was followed by a lengthy introduction. Elise began reading:

The Fifth Essence is the key ingredient of the Philosopher's Stone, and is composed of the Three Spirits—the spirit of salt, the spirit of mercury, and the spirit of sulphur. Sulphur is the fiery, positive masculine, the sun. Mercury is passive, negative, feminine, the moon. The marriage of the two is necessary to produce the Fifth Essence. And the marriage must be witnessed by salt, the Earth principal, the priest.

She paged through the text. Much of the introduction dealt with the difference between male and female aspects of alchemy. It was wordy and hard to follow. It seemed that the male quest was related to immortality and the female to healing. He seemed to be saying something significant about that, but she couldn't tell what it was.

She closed the file. Was it fantasy, based on Mullen's ideas? Or was Garity someone who saw conspiracies in everything? She shut the drawer and opened a wide, narrow drawer in the center of the desk. The usual stuff, pens, paperclips, a stapler. She reached into the back. Her fingers touched a leather casing with a snap on it. She pulled it out and opened it. A journal.

She flipped through it. Isabel's journal. She stopped at a page dated two weeks ago. *Paid P.B.D. 20K. 2ⁿᵈ payment. 30K total. Should shut him up.*

Elise stared at the initials, puzzling over them. She turned a few pages ahead. *Started in Pierce's office today. Kinda fun. Making headway.*

Her fingers tightened on the journal. Just the sight of Pierce's name in the killer's journal sent a chill through her. She turned the page. *Two days now with Pierce. Oddly enough, I like him. Hope to kill him with love.*

Elise bit her lower lip as she read the next entry. *Almost caught him in the right mood at his house this evening, but Elise called and ruined the moment. Getting real close. Can't wait.*

She cursed under her breath. Pierce never said anything about Janet going to his house. There was more to the entry.

Later, when I've got the essence, I'll send him a note. Guess what, Nicky-Boy. You've got the virus, but I got the cure. See you in the obits.

The virus. What virus? Then she knew: a sexually transmitted one. *Nick, damn you. You didn't. Please, no.*

She couldn't read the next entry. She was afraid what the answer would be. But she knew what Isabel was about. She was infected and feared she was dying. For some reason, she was convinced that Garity's drug, the essence, was the cure.

Chapter 23

Pierce stopped dead. Raised his hands. The warning shot had brought him to his senses. He couldn't run. Even if he got away, Erickson would alert Isabel who would call Miami, and Elise's body would be found floating in the bay, or buried in a dumpster. This was his mess, not hers. His only option was to overpower Erickson, then get to Isabel. He'd force her to make the call to free Elise. Then he'd go to the police.

"Turn around," Erickson snapped.

Pierce did as he was told. Erickson pressed the muzzle of the gun against the back of his head. "C'mon, you don't want to do this, Nigel. You're a windsurfer, not a killer."

"Shut up, just shut the fuck up."

This was it. One shot through the brain. He knew if he moved, Erickson would pull the trigger. But if he didn't move, the results would be the same.

A murder of crows suddenly swept across the lake, cawing loudly. He felt the muzzle shift slightly as if Erickson was distracted by the sight. Pierce whipped his hand up and snatched at the gun, pulling Erickson's hand forward. The gun fell to the ground and Pierce kicked it away. He turned and ducked as Erickson threw a punch that bounced off the top of his head. Pierce reacted by driving a fist into Erickson's gut. Stunned, Erickson staggered back a couple of steps and Pierce dived for the gun, but Erickson quickly recovered, tackled him around his thighs, and rolled him away from the weapon. Pierce's outstretched hand grazed the barrel, but only for an instant.

Erickson lunged for the gun. Pierce grabbed him by the

collar, but Erickson snatched the weapon, tumbled over and slammed the butt at his head. But Pierce managed to knock his arm and the blow hammered his ribs. Erickson scissored Pierce with his legs, flipped him onto his back and pressed the gun to his head.

"Okay, fucker! Don't move." Erickson pushed off him, stood up.

Pierce knew it was over. He's lost the fight for the gun and now it was pointed at his chest.

"I'm not going to hurt you."

Pierce gasped for breath. "That's not what that gun tells me."

"Look, I'm supposed to shoot you. Those are my orders." Erickson held the snub-nosed weapon flat on his palm, as if it were a rock. "But I was going to throw the gun in the lake when you kicked me and ran off."

"Oh, yeah. Is that why you took a shot at me?"

"I've had it. I'm through with her. I'm driving that van straight to Washington to my old boss, and turning her in. He's honest. He'll stop her. Why don't you come with me?"

Erickson sounded sincere. "No, if we take off, Elise is dead, and who knows how many more people."

"I don't want any part of this insanity. I'm done with it. I don't know what she's doing or why she's doing it."

Pierce thought a moment. "You gotta go back to her. When she asks, tell her you killed me. Play along. Walk in the water, get your pants wet and say you dumped the body in the lake and it sank."

Erickson walked out until the water reached his hips, then retreated to shore, the water dripping from his pants, his sneakers squeaking with each wet step. "What about you?"

"I'll be around," Pierce said. "And when I show up, make damn sure you're ready to defend yourself."

Against who?"

"Who do you think? Isabel."

Elise had to read more from the journal. She couldn't blank her mind and act like she hadn't read any of it. She heard footsteps, a door slamming. She slapped the journal shut and stuck it into the rear waistband of her jeans and moved away from the desk.

Detective Harrison approached, scowling. "You shouldn't be wandering around. I thought you might've left. We're not quite finished yet." Her gaze fell to the bandage. "How's your hand?"

Nice of her to ask. "I'll live."

"Good. Come with me." They walked over to the teak table near the kitchen area and Harrison pointed to chair, then sat across from her.

"What else do you want to know?" Elise asked as she subtly adjusted the journal deeper into the rear of her slacks.

Harrison glanced at her notes. "You said that when you tried to escape, the first floor door at the bottom of the stairs was locked. Right?"

She nodded. "That's the way we came in. One of them had a key."

"So they were familiar with this place and must've known about the silent alarm system."

"Apparently not enough to turn it off or cancel the security check."

Harrison tapped a pen to her notebook. "They were Latin males, right, but named Hans and Lars?"

Elise was getting annoyed. "That's what one of them said. Hans is probably Juan. Lars is Laro, or something."

"Okay, while we're waiting for Detective Drucker to get here, let me go over a couple more things. You said that the woman who lives here was connected to the murder of Judge Garity."

"I think she killed him."

"Why did she take you hostage?"

"Because she's nuts. Because she's got PMS. How the hell should I now? Look, she's got my friend, and I'm afraid she's going to kill him unless someone does something fast."

"Please. Calm down." Harrison raised her hands, patted the air. "We'll do everything we can with the limited information we have. I've already asked the dispatcher to put out an APB on the van."

"What'll that do?"

"Any officer who sees a dark blue van with a license plate

beginning with JH-2 will pull it over. If they're driving around or even parked in a public place, they'll be caught."

Elise hoped she was right. "I'm sorry. I need some air. Do you mind if I step outside?"

"Don't go far. Detective Drucker should be here shortly."

"I'll be looking for him. We've met already and I didn't care for his attitude."

Harrison snickered. "You're not the only one. But he's a good detective."

Elise took the elevator to the first floor, followed the corridor to the entrance, went outside. She slipped the journal from her jeans, walked over to a bus stop bench under a glass shelter, and sat down. She found the last entry she read, and turned the page.

Leaving Pierce now. Farewell, dear Nicky. I'll catch up with you later. Moving on to the judge tonight.

The words burned into Elise's mind. But she caught her breath as she felt the presence of someone nearby. The scent of a musky male deodorant tickled her nostrils. *Oh my God. Have they been right outside waiting?* She raised her gaze and slowly turned her head to see a well-built Latino man in his mid-twenties. His chest and biceps looked as if they were about to pop the seams of his black t-shirt. He wore matching pants with a crease and shiny round-toed shoes. She felt a sense of relief—a cop.

"Detective Harrison asked me to keep an eye on you, just in case the trouble-makers are in the area."

"Thanks." She smiled, turned back to the journal, and re-read the brief entry. Her gaze settled on two words: *Dear Nicky.*

Did that mean she'd fucked Pierce? Would he do that? She didn't think so. But on second thought, Pierce had convinced himself that she was having an affair with Umberto. Would he use a condom? Probably not, if it was on the spur of the moment.

Christ.

She closed her eyes. She and Pierce had reconciled after the weekend and made love without protection. Nothing. She'd been safe. Like hell. She felt like screaming, hurling the journal. She wished she'd never read the damned thing. But that wouldn't change anything.

Polarity. The word took on new meaning. It was more than distance separating them now.

Across the street from the warehouse, a Lincoln Town Car with darkly tinted windows eased down an alley between two buildings. Seated behind the wheel was Lars, and next him, Hans. "There she is, and she has a guard," Lars said. He turned onto the street.

"Isn't that sweet. We'll do 'em both." Hans touched the button to open his window. He lifted his Mach 11.

"Put it down. *Rapido.* There's a cop car coming up behind us."

Hans lowered the automatic pistol as the window whispered closed. "That lucky bitch."

The second Cassadaga bookstore that Isabel visited was three times the size of the first one, a combination lecture hall, bookstore, and reading room. But in Cassadaga a reading room was not a place to read a book. It was where futures were told, where past lives were divulged, where one's fate was laid out. At the front of the bookstore a dozen rows of folding chairs faced a vacant podium. A checkout counter was on the far side of the chairs, and in the rear of the shop purple cloth hung across two doorways.

Isabel walked toward the back and pretended to take an interest in the books on the shelves. Behind one of the purple cloths, she heard a woman speaking in a soft, but authoritative voice. Isabel moved away, heading directly for the counter where a clerk handed change to a customer. She turned to Isabel. "Can I help you?"

"I'm interested in seeing Iris."

"She's in a reading right now. Would you like to wait or would you prefer a reading from someone else? We have another reader available right now."

"I'll wait."

She nodded.

Isabel handed her two twenties. Forty bucks, four hundred, four thousand. Anything, she thought, just to get closer to Garity and the essence.

She felt exhausted and nearly collapsed onto one of the folding chairs. She concentrated on her breathing: in, out, in, out. That always helped relieve the headaches. She had to get the essence soon. She was losing energy, fading. It was taking an effort to stay focused. If she didn't get it, she knew that in a couple of days, a week, a month or two she would check into a hospital and be diagnosed with brain cancer, like Mani, or some other horrid disease. She could feel the disease settling around her, preparing to ravage her body. The Fifth Essence was her only hope. It had worked while she was taking it, and it would work again.

A few minutes later, Erickson walked into the bookstore just as a balding man vacated the back room. Erickson, paused, glancing around. His gaze settled on her, then he casually moved over to her. "It's done," he whispered.

She stood up, looked him over. "Get out of here in those wet pants."

Before Erickson reacted, the clerk approached. "You can go back now. Iris is waiting for you. It's the doorway on the right."

"Thank you." She turned to Erickson. "Get in the van and wait outside in the parking lot. I'll be out in a few minutes... with company."

She moved to the back of the bookstore. The five-minute rest had helped. She pushed the curtain aside and met the gaze of an attractive brunette in her mid-thirties. The woman smiled and pointed to the chair on the opposite side of a card table. "My name is Iris West." She extended a hand and lightly grasped Isabel's fingers.

"Like the Wicked Witch of the West?" Isabel asked with smile.

"It's the Good Witch of the West, I believe."

"Oh, right. I always get that mixed up. My name is Sarah."

"Nice to meet you. Have you ever had a reading before, Sarah?"

"A couple of times at parties." She was older than Isabel had first thought, maybe forty-five or fifty. Her deep brown eyes spoke of an innate gentleness. "I'm familiar with how it works."

"Good. Is this your first time to Cassadaga?"

Get on with it, Isabel thought and nodded.

"I usually find it necessary to explain a couple of things for first-time visitors here. Most people think we're all mediums, that we talk to your deceased grandmother or uncle who tells us all about you."

Isabel really hadn't given it a thought. "You don't do that?"

"It very rarely works that way, in spite of what the people across the street in the camp profess. When I tune in, my higher self or super-conscious mind reaches out to yours. The information I get is usually symbolic so I have to interpret what I receive. Sometimes the symbols do appear in the form of messages from loved ones who have moved on."

"But you're saying it's not really them." Isabel was taking her time, toying with Iris.

She shook her head. "Usually not."

"But don't they get actual names and descriptions of the dead relatives sometimes?"

"Sure. But your higher consciousness is a part of you and knows all about you and your relatives. I'm not saying that it doesn't happen or that it couldn't. Sometimes other entities do come through. I've experienced that myself. It's just not that common."

Iris had an annoying way of qualifying everything, always offering another possibility. It might be a sign of a good psychic, or a slippery one. "Don't you use tarot cards or runes or something?"

"No, I use colors."

"What? Like the colors I'm wearing?" She glanced down at her blue jeans and pink silk blouse.

Iris shook her head and laughed. "Everyone thinks that. Just give me five colors off the top of your head."

"Uh, black, cobalt blue, orange, violet, grey. Is that okay?"

"The colors just get me started. It gives me an overview. It's sort of a crutch, like tarot cards or runes. It warms me up, then I tune in."

Well, you're not tuning into me, dear. You're taking me to Fletcher and the essence. But she smiled pleasantly. "What do my colors tell you?"

"Let's start with black. It tells me there's something hidden around you that's exerting a great influence on your life right now."

"Really?" She was momentarily surprised, but tried not to show any reaction. People always had hidden things around them.

"Cobalt blue is a dark blue, like the color of a Noxzema jar," Iris continued. "It indicates that you're isolated from someone or something. This isolation is blocking you from continuing into your future."

Christ. Isabel was impressed.

"Orange. Before this situation arose, things seemed much brighter. They were in balance for you. But that's no longer true. Now, violet, you're seeking a higher order, a transformation of sorts." Iris's eyes were closed, a crease furrowed her brow and she shook her head. "But it leads to grey. The outcome isn't clear yet. It's fuzzy. Something has to happen yet before the situation is resolved."

"Do I find what is hidden?"

Iris' eyelids fluttered. She seemed to stare right through her. "Man. A man. I… man. No. Man…I."

Isabel shook her head. "What? I don't understand."

"Man…I Man…I."

"Mani?"

"He is saying that…"

Mani! "What is it? What's he saying?"

"He wants to be with you again."

"Stop it!" she hissed. She thrust her hand into her purse, pulled out the Derringer. "You know who I am, don't you?"

Iris looked stunned. "What're you talking about? I don't know you."

"You're going to take me to the Fletchers' place. Right now."

"The Fletchers? What's going on?"

Isabel grabbed her arm, and hustled her out the back door, into the dusk. "Shout and you dead!" Isabel hissed. The van was waiting. She slid open the side door, shoved Iris inside, and crawled in after her. "Which way to the Fletchers?"

"You're not going to hurt anyone, are you?"

Isabel put the gun to her head. "Answer my question."

"Turn left at the post office. It's about half a mile down the road. The old mansion on the hill."

"You heard her, Nigel."

Erickson pulled out of the parking lot and headed back toward the hotel. He turned at the corner. "Is Jack Garity at the house?" Isabel asked.

"I don't know the name," Iris replied.

"Does a middle-aged man live with them?"

"It's possible."

"I thought you were their friend. Don't you know who lives with them?"

"When you see the house, you'll understand."

"How close to them are you?" Isabel persisted.

"I run errands sometimes for Mrs. Fletcher. No one is very close to them. They're very private people. They seldom leave their property."

"Like it or not, they've got visitors on the way."

Pierce hiked up the hill leading from the lake, and paused at the crossroad. He studied the vehicles parked in front of the hotel. No sign of the van. He darted across the street, hurried through the front entrance of the hotel. The lobby was straight out of the '20s—the furniture, photographs, even the wallpaper fit the era.

The aging desk clerk was like a character out of *The Rocky Horror Show*. His long hair was tied in two braids and two more braids grew from the corners of his lips. His Rip Van Winkle beard fell over his chest.

"Can I help you, sir?"

"I hope so. Do you know someone name William Fletcher who lives around here?"

"Fletcher? Sure. I did some work on the Fletcher place last month. I'm a carpenter by trade. I just work here evenings."

No shortage of work around here for carpenters, he thought.

"How do I get to the Fletcher place?"

"Who wants to know?"

"I do. I'm a private investigator." He handed Braids a card and a twenty-dollar bill. "I need to speak with him. It's very important."

"I'll give him a call."

The clerk dialed a number without looking it up. He watched Pierce as he waited for someone to answer. "Jack, is William there?"

Christ, he's talking to Garity.

"When do you expect him back?" Braids asked.

"Let me talk to him," Pierce said.

"Someone here is looking for William. A private investigator. Says it's important. He wants to talk to you."

He passed Pierce the phone. "Hello, Jack."

He heard a click and a dial tone. He handed the receiver back to the clerk. "Guess he didn't want to talk." He set two more twenties on the counter. "I need the directions."

Braids glanced around, snatched the twenties and told him how to find the house.

"Thanks. When you were working there, did you talk much to Jack?"

"I was working in his room, up in the attic. Window frame had rotted away." Braids gave him a suspicious look. "Why do you ask about him? I thought you were interested in William."

"I'm interested in both of them. What's he do in the attic?" He peeled off another twenty.

"He's got some sort of laboratory up there. Hardly ever leaves the place. Talks to himself a lot."

"Didn't that make you wonder about him? You know, a mad scientist hidden away in an attic."

Braids smiled. "Seemed like the fit right in to me. We have our share of eccentrics in town, you know."

"Yeah, I can see that. How do I make a long-distance call?"

"I'll take care of it here. What's the number?"

He pulled out Drucker's card and handed it to Braids.

Drucker closed one of the files Elise had found in the Isabel's desk. "To tell you the truth, Professor Simms, I'm not sure what this proves."

"What do you mean?" Her voice crested. "It shows the link between Jack Garity and Isabel Martin. She's the mysterious missing girlfriend."

"Take it easy, lady. Don't scream at me."

She had to take control of herself. After all, Isabel had only implied that she'd had sex with Pierce. Maybe she was reading too much into her last entry. "I'm sorry. It's just that…"

"Hey, I understand. Of course I'd like to talk to Isabel Martin. But the fact that she has a few files that belonged to Jack Garity doesn't mean shit. She was his girlfriend. She had access to the house."

Drucker was stonewalling, and she wasn't surprised. He had his man, Vance, in jail and Isabel was simply a complication. The journal would convince him, but for some reason she was holding it back.

"You understand, Dr. Simms?"

First professor, then lady, now doctor. "You can call me, Elise, Detective Drucker. I bet your first name isn't detective, is it."

"My name is Paul, but you can call me Buddy. I'm everybody's buddy." He laughed and coughed at the same time.

Paul Buddy Drucker. P.B.D. 20K. 2nd payment. Total 30K. Holy shit! The sonuvabitch was on the take to the tune of thirty grand from Isabel. Good thing she'd concealed the journal. In Drucker's hands, it would disappear, and so might she.

"Okay, I'll remember that." Back off, Buddy, she thought.

"Look, I'll give you a ride home," Drucker said. "We'll contact you as soon as there's any news."

"I've got someone coming to pick me up." She would call Umberto again. She would call a taxi. Hell, she would walk before she got in a car with Drucker.

"Detective Drucker?" One of the uniforms approached. "The dispatcher's on the line. Wants to know if you can take a call from Nicholas Pierce."

"I'll take it," Elise said.

"Put it through," Drucker said, then turned to Elise. "You

can talk to him when I'm done."

A few seconds later the phone rang and Drucker snatched up the handset on Isabel's desk. "Drucker. Go ahead."

He smiled at Elise as he listened to Pierce. "I'm way ahead of you, Pierce. I'm with Elise Simms right now. Where are you?"

"Where is he?" Elise asked.

"Okay, don't do anything. I'll radio the Volusia County Sheriff's Office and we'll send a car out. Stay at the hotel. Here's your girlfriend."

"Nick, are you okay?"

"I'm fine. How about you?"

It was great to hear his voice. "I'm okay. Sort of. I'll tell you about it later." She walked away from Drucker until the cord stretched to its full length. But Drucker was busy yelling orders and not paying any attention her. "What happened? Where's Isabel?"

"Looking for Garity."

"Nick, I know why she wants the drug."

"Oh yeah, why?"

"She's got a deadly sexually transmitted virus. She thinks that the drug will cure her."

"She's got the HIV virus?"

"I think so."

"How do you know anything about it?"

She quickly explained, speaking softly, urgently. The journal. Where she was. What had happened. Then: "Nick, I love you, but did you ...?"

"Did I what? Did I sleep with her? Hell no. Believe me, we didn't exchange any body fluids. I gotta go."

"What are you going to do?" she asked.

"Give my last twenty to the desk clerk here and see if I can get a ride to Garity's hideout."

The phone went dead.

Chapter 24

The Fletcher estate was set back from the road at the crest of a low hill. Even in the dark, Erickson could tell the place was not kept up. The shrubbery was overgrown; weeds flourished. The latch on the gate was broken and creaked when he pushed it open. Iris entered after him, followed by Isabel. The gun that was supposed to have killed Pierce was jammed in his belt, barely concealed under his polo shirt.

Isabel wasn't taking any chances. She didn't want to alert the Fletchers of their arrival, so instead of pulling the van into the driveway they'd parked down the road under some trees.

Four tall columns rose two stories at the front of the mansion, giving the place the flavor of an old Southern plantation house. A tarnished one. Paint peeled from the columns. Two lighting fixtures, statues of black boys holding lanterns, were posted at the base of the stairs. One of the boys was missing an arm and neither of the lanterns worked.

"Get up there, Iris. Knock on the door." Isabel signaled Erickson to stand to the side with her. Iris knocked, but no one answered. "Louder!" Isabel hissed. "Let them know you're here. Nigel, go look for another door."

Iris lifted the knocker and pounded. Still no answer.

Erickson moved away, glad to be out of Isabel's sight. He was no longer her lover. Not even her employee. He was an unwilling accessory to crimes that he didn't want to think about. If there had ever been any love between them, it had ended the night the cat lady was slain.

He found a door at the side of the house that looked as if it might have been a servant's entrance at one time. He opened the screen door, and tried the inner door. Unlocked. He hesitated, then pushed it open and stepped into a kitchen. Listened. The house was quiet, but there was a light on in the next room. The floor squeaked as he moved toward the light. A parlor. No one there.

He heard a noise behind him and jumped. Isabel and Iris had entered the kitchen through the same door he'd used He shrugged as if to say he didn't know where the Fletchers were. "Don't stand there. Go look," she whispered.

Suddenly, Iris broke the silence. "William, Linda. Run! Get out of here!"

Isabel spun around, slapped Iris in the face and shoved her against the wall. "You stupid bitch. Nigel. Upstairs."

He found the staircase, took the steps two at a time, expected at any moment to bump into a surprised and frightened couple. He drew his .38. They might be armed. He slowed down. The second floor was dark with the exception of faint light that filtered under a closed door. He moved toward it, a moth drawn to the only point of illumination.

He stood to the side of the door, reached out, pushed it open. Light flooded the hallway. He cautiously peered around the corner and into the room. A sitting room. Empty.

He moved from room to room, turning on lights. Bedrooms with brass bed-frames, two bathrooms. He checked the closets. He mounted the stairs to the third floor. He flipped on a light switch. The entire floor was a ballroom. Expansive and empty. No place to hide.

He retraced his steps to the second floor, then the first. "Isabel?"

No answer. He stood at the base of the stairs, certain he was being watched. He didn't like being in someone's house uninvited. He walked slowly around. No sign of her. He was getting out of here. He crossed the kitchen, opened the side door, and stepped outside. He heard a door slam to the rear of the house, and headed in that direction.

"Isabel?"

"Over here."

He found her standing outside of an old carriage house that

had been converted to a two-stall garage. "What're you doing out here?" he asked.

"No cars in the garage," she said.

"What's that mean?"

"It means they're out. That's why no one answered the door."

"I thought they didn't go out much. Where's Iris?"

"Taking a nap inside the garage."

"Did you…?"

"She'll be fine."

"I guess there's no reason to search any further," he said.

"Wrong. We're going to go from room to room. I want to find evidence Garity is staying here."

Erickson poked his head in the garage.

"Nigel, I said she'd be fine."

He saw the body lying near the wall, partially covered by a tarp. Blood was caked on her forehead. "You shot her."

"No, I hit her. She was trouble, and I didn't want her around when…"

Isabel stopped in mid-sentence. A noise. "Did you hear something? It sounded like a door closing.

It would be a mistake to knock, Pierce thought, as he approached the side door of the house. He hadn't seen the van on the street or in the driveway, but that didn't mean Isabel wasn't here already. Then again, maybe he'd gotten lucky and found the house ahead of them. It had cost him, but he'd gotten the ride, and now after talking with Elise, he knew a lot more about Isabel.

He tried to door. It opened. He stepped inside, listened. Not a sound. Maybe his call had scared off the Fletchers and Garity. Then again, maybe Garity had hung up because Isabel had just arrived.

He moved through the kitchen and into a dining room, a library, and a living room. No one was on the first floor. He found the stairs. They creaked as he climbed them. No sign of anyone on the second floor, but there were lights on all over. He retreated to the staircase, and continued to the third floor. A ballroom and again the lights were on. He walked into the center of the room and turned in a circle. Where was the attic?

Then he saw a cord hanging from the ceiling in the dimly lit corner farthest from the stairway. As he headed over to it, he saw that the cord was attached to a trap door. He pulled on it, the ladder unfolded.

He climbed up to the attic. He heard a humming noise and felt the cool breeze of a window air conditioner. His gaze was immediately pulled to a long counter in the center of the attic that was illuminated by a florescent light. The counter top was covered with laboratory equipment: test tubes, vials, beakers, burners, flasks, a microscope, a beam balance, and shelves of labeled containers.

He gazed past the laboratory. A single bed heaped with pillows was pushed against the wall below a small window. He moved close, and saw the back of a head.

"Jack?" He didn't move. Pierce stepped closer, called his name again. Slowly, the head turned on the pillow, and with great effort the body rolled over. He looked dead; hollowed cheeks, slack jaw, pale, blotchy skin pulled tight over the skull. And yet, he was breathing.

Pierce saw a telephone on the floor next to the bed. "Jack, I'm the one who called. You're in danger. You have to get out of here."

Blue, watery eyes stared at him. His voice was soft and raspy. "No reason to. "I'm dying and I'll die here."

"What happened to you?" He couldn't think of anything else to say.

Garity didn't respond.

"I'll call an ambulance."

He shook his head, a movement that must have required considerable effort. "No hospital. Too late."

"Why didn't the Fletchers get help for you?"

"Not my way."

Pierce thought he heard a noise from somewhere downstairs. He moved back to the trap door. Listened. He didn't hear anything, but he pulled the ladder back up.

"What about your drug, the Fifth Essence?" Pierce asked. "Isabel thinks it'll save her. Won't it help you?"

"It's more than a drug. It's...a bio...chemical...spiritual

process." He spoke slowly, but his words were barely understandable. "Isabel never understood...never believed...."

"What?"

"That alchemy...is a spiritual practice as well...as a material one. She refused to believe."

"Is that why you ran away?"

Garity seemed to find his voice and spoke forcefully. "Despair. It was despair."

The trap door creaked open. Light from the ballroom filtered into the dimly lit attic. *Shit.* Pierce looked around, then darted over to a metal closet near the wall opposite the lab. He ducked inside, pushing aside hangers and clothing. He pulled on the door, but it wouldn't close. Something was stuck. A belt was wedged between the door and the frame. But it was too late. He heard Isabel's voice and more creaking as she mounted the ladder.

But Garity kept talking as if Pierce was still standing in front of the bed. "Do you know why I was fascinated with Lydia Mullen? Because everything I had learned in my study of alchemy led me to believe that alchemy was a male practice, that there was no such thing as a female alchemist. The reason, of course, is that the primary organic ingredient of the life force, the quintessence, is the male fluid, the semen."

Erickson glanced around. So this is what it's all about, he thought. A crummy lab in an attic and a maniac babbling in bed.

Isabel, a hand in her purse, stared at Garity as if she didn't believe she'd found him. Or maybe it was his condition. He looked like he was about to croak.

"But Lydia was an alchemist, Jack," Isabel said softly.

"Yes, and I puzzled over it for a long time. I knew she could not use a man's semen. It isn't possible. You see, alchemy doesn't work like ordinary science. It's a personal experience as much as science. The alchemist must transmute his own being before he can transmute metal or achieve immortality. He must make use of what is his own in order to create the fifth essence, the life force."

Garity's rheumy eyes stared at Erickson as he moved next to

Isabel. Garity was a madman. But his voice continued to grow in strength. "The transmutation of metals to gold, in fact, is simply the proof that the alchemist has been successful in his personal quest."

But Lydia explained what she was doing in her book," Isabel said.

They were both nuts, Erickson decided.

"*The True Chemistry of Humankind.* There's more to that title than meets the eye." Garity cleared his throat. "When she wrote it, the word humankind was odd, and revealing, much more so than today. But I read the book as a man, and didn't understand that she was explaining the female perspective of the art of alchemy. My own perception of alchemy blinded me for many years to what she was saying."

"But you figured it out, Jack. You made the elixir."

"The female is the regenerative vessel of alchemy," he continued as if he hadn't heard her. "She is passive and the healer, while the male is active, the seeker of immortality."

"And when you discovered the meaning of Lydia's work, you duplicated it with my help, the female touch." Isabel jabbed her index finger at him. "We made it together. It's me, Jack. Isabel. Snap out of it."

Garity just stared ahead.

Isabel tried another approach. "I'm impressed that you found them, or did they find you?"

Erickson had enough. "What the hell are you talking about?"

"The Fletchers, of course. Better known to some as Fulcannelli and Mullen, alchemists extraordinaire."

"I could never duplicate Lydia's work," Garity said. "No man could. But you were my great hope."

"It was working, Jack. Then you abandoned me. Why did you do it?"

His eyes seemed to clear and focus on Isabel. "I wanted so much to believe that you were Lydia. You knew all about her, and her work. Then I thought you were a student of hers, and she had given you the gold coins. Finally, I realized who you were. Mani's successor. And like him, you never accepted the true meaning of alchemy."

"Enough Where is it, Jack? Give it to me."

"You still don't understand. You wanted everyone else to change, but you were never willing to transform yourself, to let go of your old ways. You clung to the prestige and power of Aurum, which hunted the very thing you wanted to become."

"The drug either works or it doesn't, and it was working until you became frightened of me." Isabel's voice was intended to sound commanding, but came off as shrill. "I want the essence, Jack. Now. Just give it to me."

Garity made a gurgling sound that might have been an attempt at laughter. "Look at me. We failed, but you're still blinded."

"You stopped taking it even before you left, but you took the essence with you to spite me," Isabel said. "You hated me for not being Lydia." She walked over to the laboratory counters. "I'll find it, Jack, and I'll live. But tell me, why didn't you let Lydia save you? She could have done it."

"Those two are beyond the laboratory. They are in this world, but no longer of it. Garity's breathing was labored, but he continued talking. "She led me here, and helped me in ways you would not understand."

Isabel opened cabinets, studied bottles. "I know what it is with you, Jack. You feel guilty; you're doing your penance. It was written all over you files."

"Guilty of what?" Erickson asked.

"Well, well," Isabel crowed, ignoring Erickson's question. "So you didn't throw it away. You couldn't do it." She held up a sealed jar. "It's still in the same container with my handwriting on the outside. At this concentration, I have enough to survive decades."

"It won't work," Garity croaked. "But I learned from our failure, and some day a true alchemist will understand my notes and she will succeed in the cure."

"We'll see," Isabel said. "My guess is that it's going to work for me, even if it didn't help you."

"What're you talking about?" Erickson demanded. "What will it cure?"

"Shut up, Nigel."

Pierce had heard enough. Isabel and Erickson were both armed, and he wasn't. But he couldn't let her get away. He stepped out of the closet.

"She's got AIDS, Nigel," Pierce said. "They both do. Mani's brain cancer was related to it, wasn't it, Isabel?" You got it from him, and you passed it on to Jack and now Nigel."

"What?" Erickson's eyes bulged in their sockets.

Isabel glared at Pierce. "So you're still with us, Nick." She turned to Erickson. "That's right, Nigel. I'm a carrier and I guess you are too by now."

Erickson moved a couple of steps toward her. "I don't believe it. How could you...."

"You're a coward, Nigel." She pointed at Pierce. "You couldn't kill him, could you?" She shook her head in disgust.

"Give up, Isabel. You're drug doesn't work," Pierce said. "Look at him."

"He did that to himself. He gave up. He wants to die because he's losing faith. He know AIDS came from an alchemist's laboratory. Fulcannelli's."

"No," Garity said. His voice was a whisper. His brow furrowed and he shook head. "It was created by Mani, the founder of Aurum, her guardian angel and lover."

"That's a lie," Isabel shot back.

"He's like you; he didn't understand," Garity said. "He wanted immortality and wealth, but instead poisoned the life force."

"Shut up!" Isabel barked. "I don't want to hear it."

"Alchemy is a dangerous practice for the uninitiated. That's why so much that is written is encoded." Garity's voice was weakening. "Mani knew too much. But he lacked true understanding and we are living the results."

Isabel pulled her Derringer from her purse, and aimed it at Garity. "I've heard enough. The elixir will cure me."

"No, it won't!" Erickson shouted. He fired his .38 and the jar shattered.

"You sonuvabitch!" Isabel screamed. "Look what you did!" Blood dripped from her hand and mixed with the orange liquid and glass that splattered the floor. She turned the Derringer on Erickson, but he fired again, striking her in the chest. She stumbled backwards and crashed into the counter, knocking over beakers and vials. She hung onto the counter with one arm, refusing to fall.

Erickson dropped the .38 and clamped his hands on the sides of his head and let out a howl of pain.

Slowly, Isabel raised her head, aimed her gun.

"Watch out!" Pierce yelled. He tackled Erickson just as Isabel fired, then fired again. Pierce rolled over and scrambled for Erickson's gun. Too late he realized he was directly in Isabel's line of fire.

He heard the shot. It rang in his ears, but he felt nothing. He looked up as Isabel crashed to the floor into the mix of blood and essence. He saw the ruin of her face, blood, bones, brain; and then he saw Garity's arm dangling over the side of the bed, a .357 in his grip.

Epilogue

A Nor'easter whipped into Virginia Key and the water was dotted with windsurfers. Pierce dashed over the cerulean waves, his custom-designed wave board pointed upwind at a spit of land a couple of miles away. He dropped into a crouch for a moment, then flipped the sail over his head as he executed a smooth duck-jibe. The board arced back toward the beach.

A quarter mile from shore, he eased downwind in the trough between two waves. Seeing the perfect spot, he rose to the lip of the wave and soared eight, ten feet into the air. He landed thirty feet from his point of takeoff, touching down on the lip of another wave. He slid into the trough, and carved an expert jibe and headed out to sea.

A nice fantasy, he thought as he stood on shore and watched one windsurfer after another screaming across the waves. "You ever think you're going to get that good?" Elise asked. She wore a t-shirt and shorts, and a long-billed cap that she was holding to her head. She'd applied an ample amount of sunscreen and her bronzed skin glistened.

"Not by standing here I won't."

"Don't drown out there," she said.

"Thanks for the vote of confidence."

"Don't worry, Elise." Kurt Vance approached them. "It's chest high water at the max. It's a great place to learn how to use your short board."

A few days earlier, Vance had given Pierce a new board and three sails as a bonus for his work on the Garity case. The Astro Rock was nearly three feet shorter than the board that Larry Linder had left him, a board that Vance now called junk.

"Are you sure you're ready for this?" Elise asked.

"Of course." He said it nonchalantly, but his stomach was twitching. At this point, he could hardly back out.

"You can sail this board in anything from twelve to twenty-five knots," Vance said. "It's a good first short board. Then later on you can get a high-wind slalom board or a wave board."

He wasn't sure why he'd need another board, but nodded anyhow.

"What if you just wanted to take a nice, leisurely sail like out to the islands in Florida Bay?" Elise asked.

Vance shrugged. "You can do that with a long board, his old one. But as far as I'm concerned this sport's about speed."

Elise looked out at the array of colorful sails darting across the water. "I guess they'd all agree with you."

"You ready, Nick?"

The wind howled around him, and he felt less and less sure about going out. "I don't know if I can stay up on this board. I've only sailed twice."

"Yeah, if I were you, I'd be scared shitless," Vance said.

"What? Then why am I doing it?"

Vance laughed. "All you should do today is practice water starts. It's a perfect day for learning."

"What's a water start?" Elise asked.

"It's the best way to get back on your board if you fall in the water. You let the wind pull you up, and you sail away," Vance explained.

He made it sound easy, Pierce thought. But after what he'd been through, he was glad to be windsurfingk, and then to his health concerns. He needed a break and he wasn't planning on starting any cases for at least a week. The charges against Vance had been dropped the day after Isabel had been killed. Shortly after Vance's release, Drucker was arrested as an accomplice to murder and was charged with a variety of other infractions as well. Garity had lived less than an hour after Isabel's death. He'd died en route to a hospital.

Erickson and Spenser would be key witnesses in a congressional investigation of Aurum. After the murder of another former Aurum trainee in Washington D.C., both had been placed in protective custody. Neither was expected to be charged, and both had retained lawyers to sue the government. If all went well with the lawsuit, Erickson would start a new career as an investigator for the Pierce Agency, a job that would provide him plenty of time to pursue his windsurfing.

Pierce walked his rig down to the water and followed Vance's instructions for a beach start, the first step to learning a water start. Maybe he'd be lucky and get up on the board and sail away. Disappear like the Fletchers.

Pierce didn't know whether or not the Fletchers were actually Fulcannelli and Lydia Mullen as Isabel had attested. Lydia would be old; Fulcannelli would be ancient. But there'd been no sign of them since the incident in the attic. No one in Cassadaga had really known them. Those who had come into contact with the Fletchers had described them as old, but not elderly. At this point, it didn't matter who they were or where they'd gone. Maybe some day someone would make sense of Garity's alchemical writings, and join the pair in their quest for immortality.

He turned to Elise. "If I don't come back, it means I joined Fulcannelli and Mullen."

"Oh no, you don't. You're staying here with us mortals."

He wouldn't have it any other way.

He stepped up onto his board and the wind filled his sail.

About the Author

Rob MacGregor has written more than a dozen books about mysteries of the unknown and psychic development. He's also a novelist and winner of the Edgar Allan Poe award for his novel, *Prophecy Rock*. *The Fifth Essence* is the sequel to the first Nicholas Pierce novel, *Crystal Skull*.

Rob's non-fiction books

The Jewel in the Lotus: Meditation for Busy Minds
Bump in the Night: Ghosts, Spirits & Alien Encounters
Psychic Power: Develop Your Intuitive Abilities at Any Age
With Trish MacGregor
Beyond Strange: True Tales of Alien Encounters & Paranormal
Mysteries
Sensing the Future: How to Tap into Your Intuition and Read Signs
about What's to Come
Aliens in the Backyard: UFO Encounters, Abductions &
Synchronicity
The Synchronicity Highway: Exploring Coincidence, the Paranormal
& Alien Contact
Synchronicity and the Other Side: Your Guide to Meaningful
Connections with the Afterlife
The 7 Secrets of Synchronicity: Your Guide to Finding Meaning in
Signs Big and Small

Rob's Novels

Time Catcher
Romancing the Raven
Crystal Skull
The Lost Tribe
JUST/IN TIME with Billy Dee Williams
PSI/NET with Billy Dee Williams
Indiana Jones and the Last Crusade
Six original Indiana Jones novels:
The Peril at Delphi
Dance of the Giants
The Seven Veils
The Genesis Deluge
The Unicorn's Legacy
The Interior World
Rob's Young Adult Novels
Double Heart
Hawk Moon
Prophecy Rock
Seventh Born

You can reach Rob at:

www.robmacgregor.buzz
www.synchrosecrets.com
www.synchrosecrets.com/synchrosecrets

Curious about other Crossroad Press books?
Stop by our site:
http://store.crossroadpress.com
We offer quality writing
in digital, audio, and print formats.

Enter the code FIRSTBOOK
to get 20% off your first order from our store!
Stop by today!